Ernest Fallen was born in Montreal, Quebec. He is an emeritus professor in Medicine of McMaster University in Hamilton, Ontario, Canada. As an investigative cardiologist he has published over one hundred scientific articles in peer-reviewed journals. He is the author of an e-Learning interactive textbook of cardiology entitled *Tales from the Heart*. He is co-editor of several textbooks including *Evidence Based Cardiology* published by Wiley-Blackwell. He has taught at McGill University, The John Radcliffe Hospital in Oxford, UK and at McMaster University. In 2008 he was awarded The Distinguished Teaching Award from The Canadian Cardiovascular Society. He now makes his home in Toronto, Canada.

This is a work of fiction. Names, characters, businesses, places, events and incidents are either the products of the author's imagination or used in a fictitious manner. Any resemblance to actual persons, living or dead, or actual events is purely coincidental.

UNIQUELY HUMAN

ERNEST FALLEN

UNIQUELY HUMAN

Vanguard Press

VANGUARD PAPERBACK

© Copyright 2022
Ernest Fallen

The right of Ernest Fallen to be identified as author of
this work has been asserted by him in accordance with the
Copyright, Designs and Patents Act 1988.

All Rights Reserved

No reproduction, copy or transmission of this publication
may be made without written permission.
No paragraph of this publication may be reproduced,
copied or transmitted save with the written permission of the
publisher, or in accordance with the provisions
of the Copyright Act 1956 (as amended).

Any person who commits any unauthorised act in relation to
this publication may be liable to criminal
prosecution and civil claims for damages.

A CIP catalogue record for this title is
available from the British Library.

ISBN 978 1 80016 330 0

*Vanguard Press is an imprint of
Pegasus Elliot MacKenzie Publishers Ltd.*
www.pegasuspublishers.com

First Published in 2022

**Vanguard Press
Sheraton House Castle Park
Cambridge England**

Printed & Bound in Great Britain

Dedication

For Helene.

Imagination is funny
It makes a cloudy day sunny
Makes a bee think of honey
Just as I think of you

Song lyrics by Johnny Burke, 1940

Just a thought...

As humans we are a mess of psychic imperfections. Most of them confer dubious evolutionary benefit. Cognitive gaps, unique to the human species, may be nothing more than our slow decision-making neocortex bumping up against our rapid-fire, emotionally charged reptilian mid-brain. Oh, if it were so simple. The constant struggle between dispassion and fiery sentiment is the price we pay for having acquired that extra bulge hidden behind our forehead. In his book *The Meaning of Human Existence* Edward O Wilson takes pains to declare that whatever humans owe to their uniqueness is based less on purposeful design than on happenstance — quirks driven by the infinite probabilities of mutations.

Picture this.

Two million years ago, one of our ancestors, an ungainly bipedal ape-like creature, was foraging for game when he stepped out from an arboreal forest onto open grassland. He was defenseless. Naked and exposed, he somehow survived. Millennia passed. In due course he evolved into a fully erect straight backed creature with a receding brow, small canine teeth, restless hands, opposable thumbs and an oversized brain. He was easy prey for beasts of the fields with more highly developed chemical sensors, physical strength and cunning. And yet, in an instant of geological time, this defenseless species (*Homo sapiens sapien*), shamefully covered his genitals, exploited the trapped energy contained in his physical world and claimed dominion over his fellow creatures.

How remarkable is it that intelligence, coupled with abstraction, occurred only once in six hundred million years of evolution? While not devoid of instincts, we are mostly at the mercy of our decision-making neocortex as we grope our way through each day. Whereas we are deprived of super sensory pheromones, elaborate antennae, brute strength and physical nimbleness our cranial vault nevertheless swells with goodies. It houses a vast store of memory — both short and long term. It enables us to reason, read faces, communicate in languages, think abstractly, acquire social intelligence, talk in metaphors, be self-aware and even concoct moral codes to protect us from ourselves.

But here is the rub. Substitution of ingenuity for instinct has not triumphed without some glaring 'design' flaws. The reader will note that the word 'design' is herein defined as an evolutionary blueprint as opposed to purposeful intent. As for 'flaws', I do not mean negative emotions such as anger, fear, lust, aggression, suspicion, distrust, guilt or menace — all of which we share with other creatures. I speak of gaps unique to the human condition. Each gap begs a rationale for evolutionary merit in so far as it runs counter to any gain we make in coherent thought and action.

Aristotle defined a virtue as occupying a middle path or 'golden mean' between opposing vices. Courage, for example, is an attribute lying somewhere between cowardice and recklessness. Generosity lies between stinginess and profligacy. And so on. To be virtuous is to seek a middle ground. Is there another way? How do we resolve the continual battle between, let us say, justice and mercy, shame and pride or perception and reality?

Now, before the reader accuses me of being a fusspot, let me say that despite these flaws, we are a species blessed with a powerful tool that may yet sustain us. I refer to that uniquely human attribute — — Imagination. So dare I make the outlandish proposition that the gaps in our psyche can be bridged by compromising neither our self-defense mechanisms nor our self-esteem?

The reader is now asked to suspend belief. For what follows is a book of some fact and much fiction.

The Gap: Ingenuity and Conscience

Behold, a worrisome trend. It is the ever-widening gap between the rapid pace of our ingenuity and our stilted ability to imagine the consequences of its exploitations. Once having made the leap from theory to practice, a workable scientific concept can be unstoppable. There is a time lapse… and suddenly we find ourselves in an ethical quagmire. How do we contain our creative exuberance? How do we slow down this runaway train? Let us consider three instances whereby applied science and human consciousness ran the risk of disengagement.

On December 22, 1938, Otto Hahn and Fritz Strassman, two radio-chemists in Berlin, reported their discovery of a barium precipitate generated by neutron bombardment of uranium. Thanks to a vital insight from their colleague, Lise Meitner, a Jewish radio-physicist, then exiled in Sweden, Hahn and Strassman connected the dots and realised what they had done. The so-called impenetrable atom of Democritus was finally shattered. Dubbed 'nuclear fission', this startling event unleashed frenzy among scientists whose irresistible inventiveness led to the harnessing and exploitation of this new and powerful source of nuclear energy.

Into whose hands would the bounty fall? In Nazi Germany, the secret was now in the hands of the scientists at the Kaiser-Wilhelm-Gesellschaft in Berlin-Dahlem. Meitner's nephew, Otto Frisch, spilled the secret to Neils Bohr in Copenhagen who, in turn, delivered it in person to Albert Einstein in the United States. The race was on. Who will be the first to exploit this new-found energy into an ultimate weapon of destruction?

Nuclear energy enables us to heat our homes, diagnose and treat a host of medical disorders, protect agricultural crops, and — yes, destroy cities and their inhabitants. As the mathematician/philosopher, Norbert Wiener, once said, "...to disseminate information about a weapon (of mass destruction) is to make it practically certain that the weapon will be used." And so it was. After Hiroshima and Nagasaki no nation state need ever be accused of being the first to unleash a nuclear weapon upon a human population.

On February 28, 1953, the double helical structure of DNA (deoxyribonucleic acid) was made known by James Watson and Francis Crick. This long, twisted ladder-like molecule defines our genetic uniqueness. Its discovery laid the foundation for both theoretical and empirical breakthroughs in the nascent field of molecular biology. But it was not enough to simply celebrate this imprint of our extraordinary individuality. Instead, we have tampered, tinkered, scanned, edited and spliced the human genome for both good and ill.

By piercing the very essence of what makes each of us so special, scientists are racing with mind-numbing speed to manipulate our genes. The field is awash with tinkerers. Much of it praiseworthy, vis-à-vis the use of recombinant DNA technology for pharmaceuticals or the application of genetic engineering to improve agricultural output or the use of gene therapy for single gene disorders. But can we stay the hands of those engaged in nefarious enterprises such as breeding designer babies and cloning mirror images of ourselves? Or, worse, creating improved images of ourselves?

In 1959, while fiddling with the innards of semiconductor transistors, Jack Kilby and Robert Noyce, working separately and independently, sought and received patents for their invention of the silicon based integrated circuit. This simple device spawned a digital revolution that has transformed every aspect of our lives. The rapid development of wares — both soft and hard — appears unrestrained. Over a short span of time, we moved rapidly from solid state radio to television to computers. Pausing for a moment we then sped from computers to the Internet, smart phones, cloud computing, nanotechnology, information satellites, rider-less cars, humanoid robotics and Artificial Intelligence. At the time of writing, we have the neuromorphic chip — a computerized version of Frankenstein's monster. It is no less than a simulated neural network composed of over fifty million synapses capable of mimicking the computing power of a rat's brain! It can identify images, read faces, recognize words and understand language. And, oh yes, it has the potential, God forbid, for self-awareness!

Translational research presupposes a meaningful outcome whenever basic science jumps the divide to practical application. But once theory proves adaptable, any technological application is at the mercy of which sector and into whose hands it falls — be it medicine, agronomy, private industry, research, government or the military. Each visualizes different exploitations. In a nutshell, the rapid pace of technology is outgunning our ability to foresee their potential harm. As for ethics — that slow deliberate soul-searching process in our brain — we are barely catching up. This gap between our unconstrained creativity and our slow ability to imagine its consequences may be grist for philosophers and ethicists alike but can we not attempt to narrow the gap?

The Fix: A Paradox of Choice

She sits, primly poised. Her hair is short and neatly bobbed. Her face is pale with lips parted slightly in a beguiling smile. She wears a gray business suit with the skirt's hem resting just below her knees. Her white blouse is collared and crisp. Her eyes are unblinking but engaged. There is a curious lack of scent. A faint monotonic hum is barely detected. The room is a drab enclosure. It is bare save for a square aluminum table and two chairs on opposite sides. A gray light filters in through dusky casement windows. The air in the room is oppressive.

They face each other across the table. She gazes calmly at her interrogator while he is anything but composed. Slick haired with narrow eyes and a receding chin, he shifts uneasily in his chair. He is in charge yet unnerved in her presence. No matter how often he encounters androids or humanoid robots he cannot resist envisioning their electronic innards whirring away as he takes in their lifelike outer shells.

He is told she is different. Not just a synthetic automaton, she is referred to as an AI seed. In other words, she is a technological singularity, furnished with a blend of superintelligence and self-awareness. Most notably, she is said to possess a unique gift for high order ethical behavior. Knowing this, he feels doubly constrained. Not only is her intellect superior to his, she is designed to be assured of her actions. He doesn't quite know how to engage her. She is unflappable while he fidgets and fumbles, mindlessly shuffling a stack of papers before him. He listens. Is that purring coming from her or the light fixture overhead? His head swims.

Unsettled by her penetrating gaze, he focuses on her left ear. "You and Wilcox, your programmer, have been charged with a serious crime." He lets this sink in. She remains impassive. "I am obliged to tell you that at this very moment, Wilcox is being questioned in a room down the hall. Once we have completed our interrogations, each of you will be given an opportunity to make a choice regarding your ultimate disposition. Do you understand?" She nods and smiles demurely.

A different scene, a different mood, unfolds in the room down the hall. Here, the prosecutor is a stocky overbearing man with bushy eyebrows, a slackened jaw and protuberant eyes. He spreads several official-looking documents on the table before him and stares at his prisoner. His assistant, nondescript and half covered in shadows, stands against the far wall. The air is thick with tension. Seated on the other side of the table is the prisoner, Wilcox. He is a lean wiry man in his early fifties. His hair is sparse with a touch of gray. He wears rimless glasses and sits languidly, feigning an air of self-assurance as he peers intently at his interlocutor. The latter cocks his head. His voice is gruff.

"As you may know we are holding your cyborg in a room down the hall."

Wilcox winces. "Excuse me. She is not a cyborg. She has a name. Adriana. Please call her Adriana. She is super-intelligent and, may I remind you, she can out-think and outwit any of you."

The interrogator emits a soft grunt. "Be that as it may, you are both charged with a serious crime." He leans forward. "As a highly acclaimed programmer, surely you are aware of the strict laws governing the creation of new humanoid robotics. In particular, I am referring to the design of Artificial Intelligence seeds with cognitive capacities. The law is very clear. All life-like AI seeds must be programmed to be goal oriented. They must serve specific functions only. Whether as domestic aids, data gatherers, assembly line workers, security enablers, problem solvers or just plain entertainment objects, under no circumstances must they be endowed with any form of consciousness or self-awareness."

The prosecutor hunches his shoulders and looks sternly at Wilcox. "You are also mindful that no artificial induced cognition should ever have the potential for independent action. Think of the catastrophic consequences of such power should your precious Adriana, with all her outward charm, choose to break free and exert her will."

Wilcox shakes his head and smiles. "All of you are sadly mistaken. Allow me to explain. During the past two decades there has evolved a far more frightening deviance in the field of Artificial Intelligence. I refer to the widening gulf between the rapid pace of AI development and the ethical implications or grasp of these technologies. In other words, despite your so-called stringent safeguards, we are heading towards a cataclysm — an Armageddon in the making. I refer to the possibility — nay, probability — that some rogue developer will build a super AI seed that possesses self-awareness but lacks a highly developed moral code to oversee and contain its behavior.

"I can tell you this." It is Wilcox's turn to lean across the table. "To create Adriana, I used whole brain emulation. This machine learning model enabled me to incorporate multilayered neural networks. One of these networks includes a specially designed rapid response reactor embedded with an intuitive code of ethics. In other words, Adriana is designed to make rapid inferential judgments based on a wide variety of moral challenges and circumstances. You need not fear Adriana. She will never act in any way that poses an existential threat to anyone despite the fact she is gifted with an intellect far superior to any human. In short, she is the epitome of God-like benevolence."

The prosecutor snorts contemptuously. "Nevertheless, we are bound by the law. As such, you are now required to submit the encrypted program key containing all your codes and algorithms. Failure to do so will exacerbate your punishment. Remember, you and your treasured Adriana are not on trial here. There is no defense appeal. Both of you have already been found guilty and will be sentenced. I am obliged to tell you that the nature of that sentencing will depend on your compliance in submitting the encrypted key."

Wilcox is silent for a moment. He then shakes his head. "If I complied, how can I be sure my blueprints will not be used to subvert the ethical code while maintaining both the super-intelligence and self-awareness algorithms? You realize that would be a disaster worse than any weapon of mass destruction. Can you imagine the havoc unleashed by an army of super-intelligent, self-aware AI seeds devoid of moral principles? And by the way," Wilcox waves both his hand for emphasis, "Adriana, who also knows the key, will never divulge it. I am sure of that." Wilcox grins assuredly despite a barely perceptible flicker of doubt.

The prosecutor ignores the taunt. He shakes his head and grins. "We have reason to believe the encryption is embedded within your creature. And I need not remind you that she is now in our custody."

Wilcox explodes. "She is not a creature! I refuse to comment on your speculation. All I can tell you is that her computational architecture is firmly based on learning algorithms which give her many degrees of independence. Including, by the way, her ability to constantly improve and update her knowledge.

However, I want to stress that she is human-friendly and thereby a threat to no one — least of all to herself. You must understand. Her cognitive capacities are broad-based. She is not one of your supercharged chess machines, uploaded with an infinite array of factual bits. She is gifted with social skills, intuition, wisdom and a powerful reflexive morality."

Once again, the prosecutor waves his hand dismissively. He then narrows his eyes and stares at Wilcox. "May we at least assume that she is programmed to be goal oriented? And if so, could you at least tell us what those goals are?"

Wilcox hesitates. "I will tell you this much. Adriana is not designed to be goal oriented. In fact, she is deliberately constituted to act otherwise. You see, from an ethical perspective, goal orientation implies that the end, or goal, justifies the means — a model, by the way, responsible for most human initiated catastrophes. As I told you, my aim is to bridge the gap between the runaway pace of our technological expertise and the agonizingly slow ethical responses from deep centers in our human brains. We are forever playing catch-up. With Adriana I have succeeded in closing the loop. She is gifted with algorithms that ensure a rapid-fire moral reflex response to any confrontation." Wilcox is now on a roll.

"Think of her as one blessed with Kantian-like categorical imperatives — forever impartial, just and honorable. In other words, she behaves reflexively with the purest of intentions because, intrinsically, each and every one of her responses is always the correct way to act. Her ethical values are not only beyond reproach they are preordained. Speaking of ordination, she would make the perfect Pythian oracle at a resurrected Delphi; the perfect priestess for a church's confessional; the perfect arbiter for interpersonal disputes — a veritable King Solomon in female garb." With an air of self-satisfaction Wilcox sits back and folds his arms.

With equal smugness the prosecutor sighs. "Have it your way. In any event I am obliged to inform you that you will remain in this room until sentencing is conferred. A team of magistrates will soon arrive to pass judgement on both you and your creation. Pray they will be merciful." With that the prosecutor collects his documents and, together with his shadowy accomplice, retires from the room.

Wilcox is left to sulk. He always knew the risk of granting an AI seed the power of consciousness — that all too hazardous gift of self-awareness. But he is equally confident the risk was minimized in so far as Adriana was configured to respond to any circumstance with flawless judgement bolstered by moral purity. He is convinced she will act accordingly when interrogated. On the other hand, he is fearful they will harm her in some way. Will they attempt to forcefully extract the embedded key? If so, it is superfluous. Surely, they know he carries the key in his head. Hence, nothing could prevent him from creating Adriana's duplicate —

unless, of course, he is rendered powerless in some way. Wilcox shivers.

An hour passes. Wilcox is restless. The longer he waits the more his anxieties mount. It is curious how unsubstantiated worries, having no basis in fact, are among those energy consuming inefficiencies peculiar to humans. Alternatively, down the hall, Adriana sits and waits oblivious of time, oblivious of worry. She is unable to feel the discomfort of morbid anticipation.

Another hour passes. Wilcox, clearly distraught, is now seen pacing the room. The high windows reveal a darkened sky. The gray walls hint of incarceration. Finally, the door opens and a trio of somber looking judges, each resplendent in black robes, enters the room. There is no formal greeting. They sit stone-faced along one side of the table and motion Wilcox to sit opposite. Save for the occasional rustle of their robes, the silence is deafening. They whisper to each other briefly before turning to Wilcox, staring at him as if trying to read his thoughts. The judge in the middle is gaunt and slightly stooped. He is grim faced with hollowed cheeks, a long bony nose and thin compressed lips. His eyes are grey and lifeless. The heavyset woman on his left sits stiffly and wears an expressionless mask. She gazes steadily at Wilcox. The third judge, a beefy man with an air of self-importance, slouches in his chair as he regards Wilcox suspiciously. There is to be no introduction.

The gaunt one folds his arms and addresses Wilcox. "As you have been told, we are here to pass judgement on what can only be described as a malicious act on your part. Needless to say, we are appalled not only by the impudence with which you conceived your spiteful invention but the conceit in actually carrying it out. And so we have no option but to render a verdict. However, in the light of your past contributions to machine learning algorithms and Artificial Intelligence we offer you and your AI seed three options from which to choose your individual fates. Please do not interpret these choices as a scurrilous prank but are you aware of the philosophical thought experiment known as 'The Prisoner's Dilemma'?"

Wilcox shakes his head.

"Well, never mind." The judge fixes Wilcox with a baleful stare. "We have chosen a unique variation that we feel is commensurate with your crime. Both you and your AI seed will be required to divulge the key set of codes containing all the algorithms and computational details of your illicit brainchild. On the basis of your individual replies, each of you will then be offered three choices concerning your ultimate fate." There is a pause. The light in the room flickers briefly. All three judges sit, specter-like. Wilcox feels a slight chill.

The judge continues. "Here are the three choices. If either one of you confesses by revealing the secret code while the other remains silent, the confessor will go free. The other, however, will spend the rest of his or its life in captivity. For you, captivity means a life sentence behind bars, stripped of access to all means of technology. She/it will be dismantled." The judge lets this sink in for a brief moment. He then went on. "Should both of you choose to remain silent you will each be incarcerated for five years with no access to electronic resources of any kind." There is a hushed pause. The judge leans forward. He locks eyes with Wilcox. There is a hint of a devious smile on his face. "Now, if both of you confess by divulging the code you will each serve ten years in captivity with no chance for parole." There is tittering from the other magistrates. "That is our final verdict. You will not have an opportunity to contact or communicate with your AI seed. We will give each of you one hour to consider your response. Good luck." With that, the judges rise and leave the room.

The identical choices are presented to Adriana. She sits and stares, her eyes soft, unblinking and all-knowing. The same smile plays about her parted lips. Here, in surreal surroundings, the three judges sit awkwardly, each exhibiting an unmistakable aura of unease. After all, they are facing an automaton who just happens to possess intelligence and moral chasteness loftier than their own. There is an uneasy silence and then the three options are delivered quickly in a metallic monotone. Having completed their task quickly the judges are only too eager to leave the room.

Up to now Adriana had no occasion to speak. Neither was she prompted to do so. It is as if both the interrogator and the judges deliberately avoided any exchange that smacked of social interaction. In human terms she may not understand the nature of her dilemma but the translational bits of her neuronal wiring, renders her fully 'cognizant' of her vulnerability. Because confidence and self-awareness are critical components of her make-up, she is designed to react rapidly at decision points such as these. Hence, the one-hour allowance is meaningless, since her response to any challenge is immediate and impeccable. But what will her decision be? How can we know since we are mere humans? Well, to put it bluntly, her decision is irrelevant. Judging from the elliptical nature of the three choices her only coherent response surely depends on how Wilcox interprets what her decision will be.

In stark contrast, the one-hour reprieve is all too brief for Wilcox. He has already been moved to a smaller enclosure. We enter his thoughts and wait as he paces back and forth in his cell. He starts by reviewing and then weighing the relative fates for each of the three options. He thinks. If I confess and Adriana remains silent, I will go free and she will be destroyed. But not before she realizes I betrayed her. He shudders.

He scratches his head. If she confesses and I remain silent, I am doomed, whereas she is free to wander the earth as a detached yet formidable entity. If we both confess, I will be incarcerated for ten long years during which time the authorities will have in their possession a priceless set of codes to do with what they please. If we both remain silent, Adriana and I will enjoy the lighter sentence of five years — except of course if one of us should rat on the other!

Wilcox stops and faces a blank wall. He thinks. How extraordinary is it that my mushy human brain, with its myriad neuronal couplings of reason and emotion, is so ill equipped to solve this merciless dilemma. And yet I created a singular lifelike AI seed who, assuredly, will unravel this enigma in a snap. He frets. He recognizes that it is not his choice that matters. The solution lies in anticipating what Adriana will do. Or, realizing that Adriana already knows the choice he will make. He is trapped unless he can puzzle his way out of this conundrum.

He begins pacing again. He suddenly recalls a worrisome glitch in his creation. While he equipped Adriana with a perfect set of moral codes, he also awarded her a powerful sense of survival. Until now he had not anticipated that this combination could pose an intriguing dilemma should her life be threatened. He never foresaw a confrontation in which she was forced to choose between self-preservation and sacrificial altruism. Wilcox throws up his arms in despair. He can only speculate. Knowing he would not relinquish the key, would she turn him in and thus go free? Did she need him any more? After all, she is designed to be fully capable of self-learning and self-improvement. If she confesses and goes free while he languishes in prison what is to stop her from replicating into an entire species of cloned super-intelligent automatons? No match for humans.

But surely her beneficence would override such a selfish act. Or would it?

He considers an alternate tact. Even if both of us either confess or remain silent does she have the same sense of time as he? To her, mortality is a concept with little meaning. Nor is time a traceable continuum. Besides, while I pine away in captivity, I will be deprived of access to all electronic resources whereas Adriana's neural networks are designed for continued self-improvement and correctional feedback. She will be humming while I decay. Impervious to time, she may intuitively choose confession as her most viable option. Go free or a meaningless ten-year entrapment during which time she will likely devise a clever way to break free. Think of it. As long as they don't dismantle her, she will continue to develop, learn and improve herself. Is there a prison wall that can contain her? Only I can destroy her by simply confessing. That is if she were to remain silent. But will she? Wilcox groans and pounds his head

He suddenly stops pacing. A new thought emerges. What does Adriana think I will do! Does she feel — yes feel — an obligation or closeness to me? If so, will she assume I will not betray her and thereby remain silent? She may mistakenly think no one knows the encrypted key is embedded within her. It is her lifeline. On the other hand, what would prevent her from blurting out the code and going free, especially if she is so sure I will not confess? What is exasperating is the fact that she knows exactly what to do. She is not programmed to hesitate — a distinctly human trait.

Wilcox looks up at the barred window and catches a glimpse of an overcast sky. Somewhere through these walls he visualizes Adriana, his child, sitting unperturbed. He wants to kick himself for failing to implant a telepathic device to monitor her very 'thoughts'! He chuckles at this absurdity.

Another thought comes to his mind. Having endowed Adriana with Christ-like moral principles, is she prepared to sacrifice herself as a martyr? Especially if she is convinced, I will surrender the code. Does either he or she have an inkling of how self-sacrificial she is? Has she already concluded that I will choose the cowardly option of confessing and thus leave her with no other option but to remain silent and perish? A supreme and noble surrender!

Wilcox is beside himself. The clock ticks away. A half hour has gone by and he is obsessed with conjectures. His lips move as he mumbles to himself. The most egregious ambiguity lies in the fact I created her and yet cannot fathom what her choice will be. A choice, by the way, more consequential than his own!

Once again, he stops pacing. I need a clear head. He grimaces in mental anguish and wonders. Is she capable of predicting evil intent on the part of her prosecutors? Am I? What if my tormentors acquire the algorithms for self-awareness but ignore or discard the ethical codes? Who can guarantee they will apply the algorithms judiciously? In the history of mankind, no great discovery was ever unleashed without someone exploiting it for nefarious purposes. He sweats and wrings his hands in frustration, cursing his inability to be as assertive as his own creation.

As for Adriana, we find her in a similar cell, no less confining. She is standing before a wall, staring at the brickwork as if codifying some hidden secret within. The enigmatic smile never leaves her lips. What is she thinking — or is thinking the right word? What is she conjuring? As her author I confess I do not know. After all, she is so much smarter than me. How can I judge the machinations of a superior intellect? Better to get back to Wilcox where I can at least fathom how his human brain is wrestling with this exasperating dilemma.

Wilcox has resumed his pacing once again. Is he trying to outrun time? He stops and rubs his chin. It suddenly dawns on him. Maybe I am too focused on what Adriana will choose. Instead, shouldn't I decipher why the judges chose this particular set of bizarre options as a sentencing strategy? They probably figured it would be the cleverest way to extract a confession from at least one of us. Let's face it. Rather than forcibly pry the key from us through torture why not make confession the most palatable option? Assuring themselves that a humanoid robot is incapable of making a confession there is every chance she will be dismantled and the codes revealed. What a clever ruse. Ah, but what they did not bargain for is the fact I have the entire code locked within me. Short of frying my brain they cannot prevent me from resurrecting it over time. Adriana must surely be aware of this. But at the expense of her own destruction?

Wilcox quickens his pace as if this would somehow prolong the time remaining. Another thought emerges. Who exactly is Adriana? Why did I make her a woman? Did I somehow believe that beneficence and purity of action are attributes best exemplified in the form of a feminine exterior? Or, did I think she would have a better chance to interact with humans? My colleagues often expressed a sense of ease in her presence. Regrettably, I don't expect the judges to treat her with anything but objective scorn. Indeed, despite her femininity and charm, she may appear to them as duplicitous, only to be disposed of as another mechanical irritant.

Time is the enemy. Wilcox stops pacing. He stands perfectly still and considers another option. What if I simply refuse to make a choice? He lowers his head and sighs. Surely, they will equate my muteness with a refusal to divulge the secret codes. Or, on the contrary, they may invoke *qui tacet consentire videtur* — he who is silent is seen to consent. Consent to what? Wilcox is beside himself. He wipes his brow and starts to shiver. OK, be calm he says to himself. Let me consider the worst-case scenario. I remain silent while Adriana relinquishes the codes. That may net me only five years in captivity but she will be let loose, severed from any control I may have on her. Besides, do I possess even a trace of martyrdom? By refusing to divulge the code am I capable of sacrificing for the greater good? The major justification for my enterprise is the notion that in the absence of a powerful ethical framework, super-intelligence plus self-awareness is a toxic blend. Surely, Adriana understands this. Or does she?

For the first time, Wilcox sits down. He is bent over with his head lowered and cradled in both hands. He thinks. I must try and get into her 'head'. For God's sakes, I created her. I should know what she will say. Did I not take great pains to circumvent all goal oriented ethical principles for her? Is she not designed to be other-directed, devoid of inhibiting sensations such as pleasure and empathy? Is she not dependent on reason as the sole guide for her actions?

He calls to mind the foundational principles that govern Adriana's ethics. I was careful to eliminate any hint of ulterior motives as justification for her actions. Did I not purposefully avoid religious or self-serving doctrines of morality? Did I not dismiss, out of hand, principles guided by utilitarianism, Aristotle's golden mean, the Bible's golden rule or Abelard's emphasis on intent? I rejected the ethical concepts of Locke and Hobbes wherein morality ought to be driven by enlightened self-interest. As for the relativist positions of William James and John Dewey, they required an unrealistic equilibrium among too many circumstances.

Instead, I turned to Plato, Spinoza and Kant — all of whom perceived a morality based on pure reason. In particular, was it not Immanuel Kant who preached, that consequences should determine neither the rightness nor wrongness of an action? Accordingly, Adriana's moral judgements and actions are predicated on pure unadorned unemotional rational thought. She is blessed with a set of categorical imperatives in which each response to a challenge is justified as an end in itself. Unlike the human brain, her neural circuitry has a built-in rapid-fire crosstalk between the rational and whatever serves as the emotional centers of her 'brain'. I purposefully avoided implanting any circuitry that awarded pleasure. She always knows what is right. She is the living embodiment of wise King Solomon without the heart.

Wilcox glances at his watch. Ten minutes to go. He shakes his head. Alas, I am at the mercy of my all too sluggish neocortex. The pain/pleasure and anxiety centers of my brain are too hyperactive for me to think clearly. Why are humans cursed with decision making powers? Despite my conviction that Adriana will act according to those imperatives, I simply cannot predict what her choice will be. Wilcox gets up and walks to one end of the cell. Oh Adriana, speak to me through these walls! He starts pacing again. He tears at his sparse hairs and moans. He goes over all the options again and again. He curses whoever devised this trickery.

But wait. He turns and leans back against the wall. He contemplates an alternate strategy. If I choose to divulge the code, I will at least have an opportunity to pursue my mission. Granted, I may be incommunicado for ten years but at least I will have the key codes in my head and I could start over again. Besides, Adrianna will not be destroyed. What are the drawbacks? He squeezes his eyes shut. What is extraordinary is the fact that she knows exactly what I will do and act accordingly. How? Her only survival choice is to confess. But if I also confess, she will know I betrayed her. This is monstrous.

He stumbles and rights himself. He is visibly shaken. How powerful are her moral checks and balances? If her every action is 'the right thing to do' according to a priori reasoning, do they automatically apply when challenged by deceptive options such as these? Having a muddled set of moral principles himself he wonders whether he may have imbued Adriana with a self-referential touch of that all too human trait of cognitive dissonance. If so, I am at a loss to predict what her option will be. If, on the other hand, her ethics are of the purest sort she will surely remain silent and be prepared to sacrifice herself. But that presupposes a utilitarian choice — one that is goal oriented. Good God, I created her and now find myself at her mercy!

Wilcox decides he needs to approach this problem from a different angle. He paces furiously around the cell, trying desperately to clear his head. Another thought emerges when suddenly he hears a click.

The door opens and the judges enter.

The Gap: Memory and Experience

Experience is fleeting. Memory is a cheat. In Daniel Kahneman's book *Thinking Fast and Slow*, he draws attention to a number of cognitive illusions among which is our failure to re-experience an event by way of recall. The two processes, memory and experience, are sometimes garbled — or at least asynchronous. We take a snapshot to capture an incident, or an experience, but this freeze frame of history fails to arouse the sensations we actually felt at that very moment. Reminiscence is a remembered as opposed to a reproduced experience. For example, whenever we attempt to describe a recent vacation to others, we end up editing the experience rather than reproducing either the pleasurable sensations felt or the frustrating discomforts of travel. We offer only a vicarious narrative as our reward. In other words, recall is nothing but a watered-down version of a transitory reality. It is as if memories bereft of emotions are all we have left from our experiences.

As memory recedes so vanishes our imprint of a happening. For instance, when attempting to recall the experience of an event one is at the mercy of the so-called 'peak-end rule'. In a classic experiment by Kahneman et al., subjects were asked to submerge one of their hands in 14 °C water for sixty seconds. Following a prescribed interval, they were then asked to submerge the other hand in 14 °C water for sixty seconds, but this time they were to keep their hand submerged for an additional thirty seconds, during which the temperature was raised to 15 °C. When offered the option of which trial to repeat they were more willing to repeat the second trial, despite the more prolonged exposure. Many similar experiments have confirmed this odd selectivity. When asked to re-experience an event through recall it is uncanny how often this 'tail end of an event' colors one's memory of the whole.

From a neurophysiologic perspective the cerebral wiring responsible for experiential processes is assumed to operate on a space-time continuum distinct from those that store sensations in the hippocampus or memory bank. Is this a protective mechanism — sparing us from emotional buzzes both good and bad? Can you imagine withstanding repetitive shocks each time you recall an unpleasant sensation? And yet how embracing it would be to call forth and actually relive a pleasant episode without dampening the effect through overuse.

Experience is sensory and continual. Memory is fragmentary and anecdotal. Consider the memoir as a literary genre. It is designed to express the essence of moments in time. It is safe to say that most memoirs suffer the dilemma of having to force one's memory to recapture past experiences. In Annie Dillard's classic meditation *Pilgrim at Tinker Creek*, she writes:

I stand by the creek over rock under trees. I never merited this grace, but when I face upstream, I scent the virgin breath of mountains, I feel a spray of mist on my cheeks and lips, I hear a ceaseless splash and susurrus...

Here we are greeted with no fewer than four senses — sight, smell, touch and hearing. Dillard recalls these sensations for our benefit but at the time of writing did she actually feel them? Instead, it is her extraordinary creativity rather than her evocation of sensations that enables her to share those delights with us.

Recall is highly selective whereas the 'experiencing' self feels sensations continuously. How to bridge the gap? In his book *Mathematical Psychics*, the late nineteenth century economist, Francis Edgeworth fantasized a 'hedonometer' — a device that could measure and record experience as it happens.

...imagine an ideally perfect instrument, a psychophysical machine, continually registering the height of pleasure experienced by an individual ... the delicate index now flickering with the flutter of the passions.

Indeed, we can at least imagine.

The Fix: In the Cold Light of Day

Someone, I don't know who, once paraphrased, 'Nothing in life is important as you *feel* it should be than when you are *feeling* it.' It brings to mind a mysterious set of incidents after I saw the movie *Heart of a Dog*. A masterpiece of sensual imagery, the film was spun from the inventive mind of the multimedia artist, Laurie Anderson. As I watched it in the darkened theatre, I was captivated by the mix of emotions it evoked. And no wonder. The film is a kaleidoscope of animation, music, lyric fantasies, meditations on love, death, ghosts — all sprinkled with dustings of Buddhist philosophy.

While watching it I felt an array of sensations not the least of which were enchantment, wonder, allure, exhilaration, awe, terror and a quaint sense of bereavement. But now I can only describe them as mere words. What was once sensate is now descriptive. As I walked home from the theatre, I tried but failed to recapture those feelings. It was as if the cold light of day conspired to expunge those sensations as forbidden lusts. If my memory of the film's impact was so evanescent were my sensations real?

I tried but failed to reproduce those feelings whenever I described the movie to others. "You have to see it," was all I could muster. I wondered if others were equally frustrated by the same inability to recapture emotions of the recent past. I rummaged through film reviews from various critics to see if their written accounts of the film could reignite what I experienced in the theatre. *Heart of a Dog* received critical acclaim by most reviewers. Some chose to dissect the collage into component parts while others expressed the imagery in fanciful prose. All failed to restore any semblance of the sensations I felt.

From *Variety* there was this:

Heart of a Dog becomes both a demonstration and a critique of the art of storytelling, which is to say the art of making meaning from the random effluvia of daily life, in ways that can both deceive and enlighten.

Here, a review from *Toronto's Globe and Mail*:

Shot largely (and beautifully) by Anderson herself, its collage of animation, paintings and drawing, found footage, home movies, text and video becomes the instrument for, variously, a lyrical essay, ghost story, meditation, Buddhist teaching and confessional that becomes more knitted together and deeper with each sweep of the net.

A.O. Scott of *The New York Times* came closest to admitting that *Heart of a Dog ... both invites and defies interpretation.*

I tried parsing the reviews to determine if critics were working from memory — as I was. I learned that many, if not most, critics view new films at private screenings. Depending on their idiosyncrasies, some jot down their impressions during the screening — perhaps with the aid of a small spotlight in the dark. Some, guided by a cookbook list of qualifiers, organise their reviews in terms of genre, setting, lighting, direction, acting and so on. Style may be anecdotal, flowery, analytic or just plain descriptive. None are evocative in so far as they appear to be distractions from sensory input. Whatever the technique, it is hard to imagine how any critic can bridge that gap between a post hoc impression of the movie, no matter how poetic, and the sensual experience actually felt during the viewing.

I was about to abandon my search when I stumbled on a cryptic description of the film that gave me a jolt of sudden recall. It appeared in an obscure small-town newspaper. I stared in disbelief. There before me was a rather pedestrian description of the movie and yet a clear exposé of familiar thrills:

Seen through the prism of a wide window streaked with gently falling raindrops I feel a slight shiver, a prickly sensation spreads across my skin and my heart slows to fifty beats a minute. In another sequence I am the eyes of Laurie's rat terrier, Lolabelle. Suddenly I see a hawk hovering just above me — ready to strike! I feel a paralyzing grip. My heart is now racing and thumping at a hundred and twenty beats per minute, my blood pressure surges to one hundred and seventy, a trickle of cold perspiration spreads across my back. My fingertips feel numb. I am tingling!

It was déjà-vu! Here were lifelike descriptions of the same sensations I felt when watching the movie. It was as if this reviewer had miraculously reconstructed his vital signs and inner feelings while viewing the film — a feat hard to fathom. And yet, he fused memory with experience. How did he do it? I had to find out.

After several fruitless attempts, I finally reached the critic by phone. He introduced himself as Jason B and agreed to meet me the following day at a cafe on the main street of his small town. The trip took just under two hours. It was one of those exurban centers whose main street, lined with low-lying red brick buildings, served as its commercial thoroughfare. The cafe was easy to spot. As I pulled up, I became aware of how quiet and languid the surroundings. The street was lined with threadbare saplings and the storefronts, reflecting the glint of the sun, appeared empty of commercial bustle.

Inside the cafe I was greeted by my affable host who led me to a corner booth. Jason B was a short stocky man in his late forties. He had a flat roundish face with a tuft of yellow beard jutting from his chin. His eyes were pale blue and squinting. His light brown hair was closely cropped and he exhibited an unnerving perpetual smile. He wore a T-shirt emblazoned with a Superman logo, cargo shorts and bright yellow sneakers. He was most ingratiating and expressed an eagerness to help in any way. He was astonished that I would travel all this way to inquire about his craft as an itinerant film critic, which he was quick to explain, was a mere sideline of his. There was an air of caution about as if he sensed I was to be handled furtively.

"I'm a digital junkie," he said after we settled ourselves and ordered coffee. "I run an advertising mall on the Internet which I operate from home. I get my kicks fiddling with bits and pieces of wireless circuitry to make weird programs. As an aside I write reviews of movies for the county newspaper. I gather one of my reviews caught your fancy?" He said this with a hint of wariness.

I nodded and went straight to the point. I asked him how he was able to capture, so vividly, the sensations induced by the movies he saw. Jason shrugged. "It's simple. I snap on my sensors and away I go." He sat back and grinned. He was a plain-spoken man.

When he saw my puzzled stare, he laughed. "Sorry, let me explain." He drummed on the table distractedly and then leaned forward. "Whenever I review a film, I have to see both the forest and the trees. I refuse to be bound by arbitrary rules of film criticism. I just want the reader to experience whatever I happen to feel at the time of viewing. Not some interpretation I dream up from memory. The only way I could express my feelings is to record them during the actual viewing. So I've put together a contraption that monitors and stores whatever I feel. You know what I am talking about?" Jason squinted.

I hesitated. "Do you mean to say you record your actual bodily sensations while watching the movie?"

"Yes, I register the precise changes in my vital signs during selective sequences of the film." Jason sat back and stared at me. I didn't flinch but nodded as if I understood. Encouraged, he continued.

"As you know, some movies generate all kinds of emotions — sadness, disgust, happiness, fear — you name it. Unfortunately, those feelings pass too quickly. To grab them in real time it is important to match them with the event during the running of the film. And yet, at the same time, they must not interfere with the viewing. So, as I write the review, the recording must be spot on with the exact time I feel the sensation. In other words, my memory of the film should be connected with the experience simultaneously. There can be no gap!"

He took a sip of coffee and gazed at me. For the first time his smile vanished and he spoke in a steady tone. "I made a study of this. As you may know our bodies contain a vast network of independent neuronal activity called the autonomic nervous system. It is not under voluntary control. It has a mind of its own. It expresses our emotions in various ways, through changes in our skin temperature, heartbeat, blood pressure, gut reaction and breathing. Although we cannot control it, it is nevertheless a truthful expression of our feelings.

"Now, to tap into this truth I use an electronic monitoring system that records my heart rate and rhythm, skin temperature, blood pressure, oxygen saturation, breathing rate, brainwaves and muscle tension. The apparatus is light, compact and easily attachable. I don't even know it's there. And presto! I now have the means to get a permanent record of all that I feel while watching a movie." He paused for emphasis and stared at me giddily. He was pumped. He had lost his defenses and was eager to let me in on his secrets — up to a point it seemed.

"Now, here is the trick" he resumed. "In order to connect the different frames of the movie with my actual sensations, I installed a voice activation system. Picture this. As I am watching the film, any part that moves me I quickly identify by voicing a code name into my device. And there you have it." He cocked his head with an air of self-satisfaction.

"But hold on," I objected. "I fail to understand how your technique bridges the gap between memory and experience. When it comes to writing your review, in the cold light of day, are you not dependent on memory when you play back the recordings? Unless of course, the recording itself magically reignites your biological sensations. Surely, one cannot command a recorded display of a heart rate or blood pressure sequence to suddenly be felt as such. Don't you see? You are still operating from memory. Are you not?"

I could see Jason was visibly shattered by my outburst. He probably feared I had travelled all this way only to encounter a fraud. I quickly regained my composure. "Look, I appreciate your candor. You have satisfied my curiosity and I must say I do marvel at your efforts to inform your readers what you actually experienced. You see, I had the same sensations as you reported. And so, it was gratifying to have them vindicated by someone able to communicate those very same feelings." I hesitated for a moment and then said, almost accusingly, "Even if it was by way of reference to electronic recordings."

Jason sat silent for a moment. He was no longer grinning. His brow furrowed as if wrestling with something he wanted to say. He looked at me curiously as if weighing my trustworthiness. He then looked around, lowered his voice and said quietly, "Look, I am sorry if I misled you. It turns out, that like you, I have also struggled over the frustrating disconnect between memory and experience. What I told you so far was a half-truth. Come, I want to show you something."

I accompanied him as we left the coffee shop and got into his car. It was a short drive to his home, a modest white clapboard cottage with bevel siding. It was shaded and set back on a quiet side street. Jason introduced me to his wife, Sally, a pleasant shy woman who did not appear ruffled by our sudden intrusion.

After a few pleasantries Jason took me downstairs to his inner sanctum. There, a mystical world unfolded. The room was a curious blend of space age gadgetry amidst an eerie ambience of the supernatural. A ghost-like den, it was soundproofed, windowless and bathed in a vaporous pale blue light. In the center of the room, facing a wide screen, was a black Naugahyde recliner festooned with an array of wire attachments, a padded headset with wide angled goggles and leather straps. Embedded within a side wall was an aquarium of brightly colored fish, warmly lit with a luminescent green glow. Softly, in the background, were heard pleasant intermittent sounds of crickets, bird warbles and the rush of a distant waterfall.

Jason was silent, allowing me to take in this preternatural mood-altering atmosphere. He then strapped himself into the recliner, turned to me and, without a hint of irony, said, "Here is where I truly close the gap between memory and experience. How is it done? Well, instead of relying on our memory to recover past sensations why not get rid of memory altogether." His grin grew wider. "Here, in this sanctum sanctorum, I have no need to recall past sensations, I can actually re-experience them at will. To do this I must be in the — how do you say it — experiential state of mind. As I am recording my review, in the cold light of day as you put it, I have to create a so-called déjà vu experience."

He laughed when he saw my jaw drop. He leaned toward me and whispered. "You are right by the way. The fanciest technical gizmos, no matter how ingenious they may be in capturing and displaying physiologic sensations, cannot do it alone. Somehow, I had to trespass into my inner autonomic world. Only then could I hope to resurrect, in real time, all the feelings I experienced when viewing different scenes in a movie. How was I able to do this?" Jason waved his hand to take in the sweep of the room.

"At first I tried biofeedback. Our bodies are chock-full of electromagnetic frequencies many of which are detectable by special sensors. As you may know, these sensors enable subjects to mind-control certain parts of their autonomic nervous function including blood pressure and heart rate — at least to some extent. The problem is calling them up in real time. This requires memory which is what I want to avoid. I insisted on a vivid re-enactment of my feelings and sensations." Jason stared at me to see if I was following his line of thought. My demeanor assured him I was more captivated than dubious. Satisfied, he went on.

"I then focused my attention on that mysterious cerebral phenomenon known as déjà-vu. Here is the perfect psychic state that doesn't depend on forcibly recalling an incident. It is spontaneous! Have you ever experienced it? It is spooky. I can only describe it as an unprovoked spine tingling yet miraculous sensation of living through an event from the past. Unlike recall, déjà-vu comes out of the blue with all the emotions and sensations intact. The problem is how to trigger it."

Jason paused for a moment. He knitted his eyebrows as if trying to choose the most convincing explanation. "I needed a mechanism which would transform an ethereal representation into corporeality. First, I had to rig a reliable system of virtual reality. This was easy given the availability of modern technology. But I also needed to sink myself into a state of altered consciousness — a trance so to speak." Jason smiled as if harboring a forbidden secret. He watched me to see if I was evincing any doubt. I held my tongue although I confess, I felt a sense of intrigue and incredulity. Seeing once again that I was engrossed, he continued.

"Yes, it was critical for me to be in a fugue-like state so as to shut out the external world. Simply put, I had to learn to hypnotize myself. For this I needed someone to teach me, someone with expertise — a professional guru. Unfortunately, in this neck of the woods, there is a paucity of swamis or yogis. I searched every corner. I even had a go at online instruction. Alas, no luck.

"I was about to give up when one day I happened to stumble across a strange old codger named Tom S. An indigenous man with a strange dignified aura about him, he occasionally was seen at one of the local shops in town. In spite of his poor appearance and shabby clothes, he was blessed with an unmistakable mystique. He told me he was a shaman — a prophet and a diviner. As a former member of the Midewiwin group of the Ojibwa, he served as both a healing practitioner and ceremonialist. For a small fee he agreed to teach me a special form of spiritual meditation. After many attempts he finally succeeded in having me self-induce an extraordinary trance-like state — one in which I was able to not only relive past events but actually feel them. He helped me design this room so as to create a suitable ambiance. And so, after about eight months, I became quite good at triggering a déjà vu state of mind — at will, no less."

I was about to interject when he waved me off.

"Now, all that remained was to choose and record an emotionally charged event such as a scene from a movie. I then return here to my lair, strap myself in this chair, put on my headgear, set the sensors, prepare the voice activation code button and drift into a trance. Sure enough, in these ethereal surroundings I discovered I could re-experience, at will, all the sensations I felt when viewing the film. It is then I write my review right here while experiencing the sensations by way of déjà vu." Jason B broke out in a wide grin. "And there you have it. I have successfully fused memory with experience." Jason fell silent for a moment. He saw I was both stunned and dubious.

"Unfortunately, I cannot reconstruct this reality for you. You realize you would have to literally join me in my trance-like reverie which is impossible. But let me assure you the system works."

Jason then shrugged his shoulders in a gesture of vulnerability. "It does need some tinkering though. Sometimes, I may not hit the spot and other déjà vu experiences appear. Some of these, like grainy double exposures, can be upsetting. No matter. I am sure with a bit of fiddling I can fix the problem."

As Jason extricated himself from the recliner, I shook my head in amazement. Unable to come up with any intelligent rejoinder, I simply congratulated and thanked him for the mind-boggling exposition. We went upstairs where Sally had already set out tea and cakes. We were back in a familiar domestic world. Following a pleasant interlude I expressed my gratitude for their hospitality, thanked Jason once again for his remarkable demonstration and quietly took my leave.

On the trip home I puzzled over Jason's astonishing concoction. Was it nothing but a flight of fancy fabricated by an overwrought computer nerd? Had his powers of invention run away from him? Or, did Jason actually succeed in fusing memory and experience through some bewildering form of self-imposed déjà-vu? The mystery occupied my thoughts for several days until I finally discarded the whole episode as a figment of a zealous imagination.

Three months went by. One day I happened to see the taut movie thriller, *Eye in the Sky*, starring Helen Mirren. Here again was another film that evoked palpable sensations. One disturbing sequence showed an innocent young Arab girl, selling loaves at a sidewalk stand. Suddenly she was in the cross hairs of a lethal drone attack. I swallowed in fright. But once again, after emerging from the cinema in the cold light of day, I could neither reproduce my sensations nor feel the dread.

And yet I was curious to know if Jason B had resurrected the same, pulse throbbing shivers I felt, during tense scenes of that movie. I searched and finally came across a copy of that county newspaper. But instead of Jason's piece there was a review by a different critic. One that was rather bland and devoid of any arousal. I wondered what happened to Jason B. Out of curiosity, I phoned his home.

Sally answered with a quavering voice. She remembered me and instantly broke into a distressing moan. "Oh, forgive me," she cried with a catch in her voice. "I am so upset. Jason had a stroke and is in hospital. The doctors are having a difficult time trying to make any sense of what he is saying."

I was shocked. "What happened?" I asked.

Sally muttered through choked sobs. "He was in his chair reviewing a movie when suddenly he let out a shriek. I quickly ran to him. He was shaking and trembling badly. His eyes just stared wide like a mad man. I am sure he could not see me. And suddenly he went limp."

"Has he made any progress?"

"Not really. The doctors seem helpless. Oh, it is awful. He is so young." I could feel Sally's distress and did not want to prolong the conversation. But I had to find out if he was showing any signs of coherence.

"Has he said anything?" I asked.

Sally tried to collect herself. She stuttered briefly and then replied. "The only sound he makes, is a mumbling which I can barely make out. He repeats it over and over. It sounds like '…Cold light of day'."

The GAP: Faith and Reason

The heart has its reasons that reason does not know
Blaise Pascal

One glaring incongruity of human contemplation is the scuffle between faith and reason. It can be especially disquieting when incontrovertible evidence emerges to shatter entrenched beliefs. Will the chipping away at superstitions by scientific evidence do away with orthodox faith eventually? Some say this is no less than a rationalist's conceit, for it may leave us shorn of a basic human need. As Blaise Pascal intimated, it would be wiser to live as if God existed if for no other reason than it offers not only a more fulsome life but hedges one's bets, just in case there is an afterlife.

But what if faith is blurring our conception of right and wrong? During the testy United States Senate hearings for the appointment of a new Supreme Court Justice in 2018, the candidate, Judge Brett Kavanaugh, was seen to bristle as he was subjected to intense questioning regarding an alleged sexual assault accusation. Following one particular stinging attack from a Democratic senator, the chairman turned to

Senator John Kennedy, a Lousiana Republican, who had only one question for the candidate.

"Judge Kavanaugh, do you believe in God?"

Without a second's hesitation, Kavanaugh replied that he did. It was as if that question — and its reflex response — sealed any doubt as to the qualification of an individual to be the ultimate arbiter of justice on the nation's highest court.

The struggle to find common ground between faith and reason is a never-ending quest. How does a literal translation of purposeful dogma coincide with the randomness of exploding alpha particles? In other words, how can the laws of nature be deterministic when there is so much uncertainty in the nanosphere? If God doesn't play dice, as Einstein said, he or she has some explaining to do. And on and on the argument goes.

Can we learn anything from that rare breed of jugglers — the cleric/scientist? How have they reconciled their faith with disclosures of elemental truth and the acceptance of a universe open to exploration? Let us consider the arguments of four prominent theologians, each of whom it so happened, chose to dabble in scientific exploration.

In the late seventeenth century, John Wilkins, the Anglican Bishop of Chester, England, was an outspoken promoter of science and experimentation. He was a co-founder of the Royal Society of London, that venerable group of clandestine scientists, struggling to endure in a tumultuous era of religious upheaval. Despite the swirl of fanatical orthodoxy about him, Wilkins served as both a practicing bishop and a natural philosopher. He did his best to promote an age of experiential reason. He tweaked his fellow clergymen by claiming science as an ordained privilege. He even went so far as placing experimentation above religion and the law. As a microscopist he could often be seen peering through his eye glass, never failing to marvel at, "The symmetry of God's small creatures".

Blaise Pascal was a seventeenth century polymath, equally at home as inventor, physicist, mathematician and Catholic theologian. An authority on probability theory he used his gifts to promulgate a belief that God's existence is worth a wager. In his major philosophical work, *Pensées*, he offers salvation in the form of hedge betting. If man is so convinced that God does not exist, he is consigned to a life of emptiness — forever consumed in his own vanity and hollowness. Salvation can only be assured if one accepts the statistical probability of a divine presence. He felt that imagination is illusory, deceptive, a distortion of reality. The heart is the soul of man. It has its reasons which by its intuitive actions reveal the nature of God.

Moses ben Maimon, better known as Maimonides, was blessed with an extraordinary gifted mind. He was a twelfth century logician, physician and theologian who served as principal physician to the Grand Vizier of Saladin's court in ancient Cairo. For his magnum opus, *The Mishneh Torah*, he codified all the laws of the Torah in addition to deciphering many ancient Hebrew texts. He wrote treatises on logic, astronomy and mathematics. He translated learned manuscripts from Greek into Arabic, authored no fewer than ten medical textbooks (some of which became universal practice guides) and delivered theological epistles, in both Hebrew and Arabic, to his followers throughout medieval Europe and the Levant. Affectionately known as *The Rambam*, his works grace the walls of Yeshivas throughout the world.

But in a curious, gut-wrenching turn of mind, Maimonides wrote, *A Guide of the Perplexed.* A convoluted text, it was written in the form of personal letters addressed to an errant pupil named Joseph ben Judah of Ceuta. This acolyte was a young physician and poet who left Alexandria to study with Maimonides in Fustat (a district of ancient Cairo). The year was 1190 CE. Joseph was bright, eager to learn and in awe of his master. Maimonides steered him through a predefined sequence of studies that progressed from logic and mathematics to astronomy and the natural sciences. And then, after two years of instruction, Maimonides abruptly switched course and introduced his favorite disciple to metaphysics and biblical prophecy. For reasons undisclosed, Joseph ben Judah, quit his studies in mid-term and eventually set up a medical practice in Aleppo.

It is said that Maimonides took the departure personally. So much so that one school of thought believes the master felt a burning need to reach out to his prized student by writing *The Guide*. But who was perplexed? Hidden within the pages of *The Guide* is the voice of a self-doubting mind seeking to resolve the conflict between his spiritual and rationalist sense — a heroic attempt to reconcile divine essence with rational thought. Maimonides has always taught us to believe nothing that is not supported by evidence. Nevertheless, he writes in *The Guide* that the key source of knowledge, besides observation through the senses and logical deduction, is the divine gift of prophecy. Did the impressionable young Joseph detect a conflict between Maimonides' fierce belief in divine prophecy and his rationalism? I suppose we will never know. But it does not mean we cannot imagine.

The Fix: Reading Between the Lines

"Again, he writes!"

The thick packet of Egyptian paper had just arrived from Fustat. Joseph ben Judah removes the wax seal. The epistle, written in elegant Arabic script, is not dated but the year is 1192 CE. Joseph thumbs through the pages, sighs helplessly and turns to his wife, Rebekah.

"I am sure it is yet another long and incomprehensible letter from Moses ben Maimon. They are tentacles made to strangle me." Joseph is of short stature, pale and gaunt as a rake. His eyes sparkle with intelligence and fervor as he pulls at his beard in frustration. In an exasperating gesture he waves the sheaf of letters giddily above his head, exclaiming, "He calls the collection *A Guide for the Perplexed*. And perplexed it most certainly is."

Rebekah stares at Joseph and blanches slightly. Like her husband she is also slight of stature but with expressive eyes and delicate features. Her brow is perpetually knitted as she listens to her husband's diatribe. "But Yousef, is he not a most revered man?"

Joseph nods. "Ah my dear Rebekah most assuredly he is. There is no one more erudite, more brilliant while at the same time, mysterious. Just imagine his extraordinary accomplishments. He compiled and then codified all the laws of the Torah, including many ancient texts. It was a monumental feat. Even today he continues to explicate and, yes reinterpret, the vast teachings of the Gaonim and other arbiters of Jewish law. Think of his insightful treatises on logic, astronomy and mathematics. His translations of learned manuscripts from Greek into Arabic are standard source material for seminaries everywhere. If this wasn't enough, he continues to write practical medical guides based on his interpretations of Hippocratic and Galenic teachings.

"But this," Joseph slaps his hand on the packet, "I do not understand. Yes, he has circulated many theological response to devoted followers throughout the Mediterranean region and Arabic lands. But don't you see Rebekah, these letters are specifically addressed to me personally. Why is he baiting me? What is he trying to tell me?"

"But Yousef, did you not suddenly leave him before completing your studies? He probably feels your education is incomplete."

"I had no choice," Joseph exclaims. "I believe he accepted me as a student because he recognised something in my poems. Perhaps he sensed my restlessness for inquiry or my longing for speculative matters. Do not think I was not privileged. I was elated to be chosen by such an eminent teacher. But what did he do? From the start he insisted on a strict order of instruction." Joseph places the letters on the kitchen table and sits beside Rebekah. There is a pause while he collects his thoughts. His composure regained, Joseph begins quietly.

"At first, he introduced me to the basic elements of science, including astronomy, mathematics and logic. I was hopelessly entranced. Just when he had me imbued with a rationalist and objectivist view of the world, he suddenly changed course and insisted I was now primed to learn the metaphysics of biblical prophecies. It was a depressing jolt. I was suddenly confronted with a choice between reason and faith. I kept wondering. Why must there be a choice?"

Joseph suddenly throws up his arms. He gets up and paces about the room. He points at the packet and shouts, "And now he fears I lost my way. These letters or 'guides' as he calls them, contain nothing but convoluted indecipherable passages. I can't make any sense of them. Listen to this." Joseph pulls a sample page from another bundle and reads:

To understand the totality of a subject you must grasp each word that occurs even if that word does not belong to the intention of the subject at hand.

"Or this:

Prophecy is a certain perfection in the nature of man. For the existence of that perfection in its extreme and ultimate form in every individual in that species is not possible. It must however exist necessarily in at least one particular individual if in order to be achieved this perfection requires something that actualizes it, that something necessarily exists.

Joseph rolls his eyes, heavenward. He groans and shakes his head. "My saintly teacher will not let me go. He once insisted that having acquired knowledge of science and logic I will be prepared to feel the power of divine prophecy. What did he mean? In these letters he refers to eleven degrees of prophecy, each one more abstruse than the other. He maintains that one can only know the negative attributes of God because there is no possibility of a positive knowledge of Him." Joseph stands rigid, gaping blankly at the pages in his hands.

Rebekah stares at her husband in dismay. "Dear Yousef, you are taking this much too hard. Please calm yourself. You have a contented life here in Aleppo, two young healthy daughters, a steady medical practice and an ambitious plan to open a school for young boys. You still enjoy writing your poems. Why are you letting this upset you so much?"

Joseph looks at Rebekah and shakes his head. "Don't you see? It is because of my reverence for him. I believe he is trying to tell me something but I cannot seem to break the code? By the way, his thinking is not dissimilar to that of Ibn Rushd, the great Muslim jurist who ben Maimon venerates. The similarities are uncanny. Both men were born in Cordoba. Both became philosophers and physicians. Both served as the personal physician to prominent caliphs — Ibn Rushd to the caliph Abu Yusuf of Cordoba and ben Maimon to the grand vizier of Saladin in Cairo. However, the critical distinction is this. Ibn Rushd was a jurist, a grand Cadi — sworn to the dictates of Shari'a law. And so I understand his conciliation between spiritual and rational thought. For instance, in his recent work, *The Decisive Treatise*, Ibn Rushd writes:

Acting in accordance with the law men behave according to reason even though it is not reason that inspires them.

"Ibn Rushd goes on to claim that while faith may not imply knowledge or reason it does not exclude it. In other words, he has no trouble reconciling reason and faith. He does it by way of juridical interpretations — a blind faith in the law."

Joseph pulls at his beard again and moans. "And yet here is my master, imploring me to believe in the prophets. But why do it with such ambiguity, such obfuscation? What is he trying to say?" Joseph stomps around the room beating his head with his fists. Rebekah looks on aghast.

"Yousef, please get a hold of yourself." She rises and holds his hand. "By the way, have you shared these letters with anyone? Perhaps someone could help you decipher the script. What about your friend, Joseph ben Aknin? Wasn't he also a disciple of Moses ben Maimon?"

Joseph shakes his head. "Dear Rebekah, please understand. My master addressed these letters to me. He is trying to tell me something. Perhaps there is a kernel of truth within these pages somewhere."

Joseph resumes his pacing. He stops and turns to Rebekah with a sheepish grin. "I do have a confession to make. The other day I happened to be in a tavern, sharing a mug with my trusted friend, Judah. You remember Judah. He is the son of the *dayyan*, Barukh ben Isaac? Well, I did quote a few passages of *The Guide* just to get his reaction. My good friend, Judah, is most learned but even he could not fathom what ben Maimon is saying." Joseph stamps his feet and lets out another groan. "And so you see. It is hopeless."

Later that night, Rebekah wakes from sleep and feels a chill in the room. She peers through the shadows and notices Joseph, sitting at his study table, poring over ben Maimon's letters. His face is twisted with puzzlement. Is he weeping? She is frightened and fears her husband is becoming ill over his obsession with *The Guide*. She decides she must do something. But what? Her mind is feverish with dubious options.

The next morning, while Joseph is away attending to his patients, Rebekah quietly and deliberately makes preparations. She stuffs a batch of ben Maimon's letters in a small satchel and quietly heads out in the direction of the Kanisat Mutakal synagogue in the Parafara quarter of the city. As an unaccompanied woman on the streets of ancient Aleppo, Rebekah takes precautions. With her head covered in a dark cowl, she walks furtively through the narrow streets, keeping to the shadows of the walls and skirting the covered souks. At the synagogue she is shown into a narrow antechamber where she sits and waits.

A half hour later she is met by the rabbi, a short, corpulent man with a gray streaked beard and narrow eyes. He greets her politely. In a soft, hesitant voice Rebekah explains her mission and asks the rabbi if he would be good enough to read and decipher the letters for her. The rabbi sighs and nods his head. He takes one of the letters, settles himself in a chair and begins reading.

"Ay, ay" he exclaims. "Are these words really written by the notorious Moses ben Maimon!" He looks at Rebekah. "He may be saintly to some but he is known to spout blasphemy. Without doubt, he is a most erudite scholar and teacher. His *Mishneh Torah* and that extraordinary compendium of blessings, the *Sefer ha-Mitzvot*, serve as the foundation for most of the teachings in our prayer houses. And yet, forgive me for saying this, but his writings have created much dissent in certain rabbinical circles." The rabbi winks. "I refer, in particular, to a group of spiritual leaders such as the Gaonim of Baghdad."

The rabbi's gaze is steady. "Did you know that ben Maimon's stubborn rationalism refuses to acknowledge an anthropomorphic God, let alone the act of creation? He also denies the afterlife and dismisses the very existence or possibilities of miracles. His aim, some believe, is to advance a philosophic interpretation of ancient Hebrew texts based on Aristotelian rationalism — a heroic attempt to reconcile divine essence with rational thought. Such perversity!" The rabbi snorts and then reads silently, occasionally furrowing his brow and shaking his head.

Rebekah sits and waits. She watches the rabbi and flinches whenever he clucks his tongue and tugs at his beard. Every now and then he emits a soft groan. After twenty minutes or so, he turns to her and shouts, "This is impossible to understand. You say ben Maimon specifically addressed this tortuous epistle to your husband? But why?"

Rebekah recoils. "I don't know. Perhaps the teacher is attempting to finish what he began as a course of studies for my husband. You see, for almost two years my husband studied with ben Maimon in Fustat. But he left prematurely. I believe the teacher sends these letters with the hope that my husband will comprehend some ultimate truth." Rebekah is now teary eyed. "And now my husband is beside himself with frustration. He is desperate to know what ben Maimon is trying to tell him. He still reveres the old man."

The rabbi scratches his beard. "Tell me, my child. Has your husband written to his master to ask for clarification?"

Rebekah's face reddens. "Yes, he has. But you must understand. My Yousef writes in poetic metaphors, almost as a prank. I believe he was too embarrassed to admit ignorance or perplexity. You see, Rabbi, my husband thinks the great ben Maimon may be losing his faith and is attempting to reconcile his dilemma by writing this so-called *Guide*. Could that be it?"

The rabbi waves off the insinuation. He hands the letters back to Rebekah and says, "I am afraid I am at a loss to help you. I can neither interpret nor make any sense of these writings. I am sorry."

Rebekah is crestfallen. She makes one more plea. "Do you have any suggestions as to how my poor Yousef can interpret any of this?"

The rabbi shakes his head. "I can only suggest your husband try to read between the lines." With that, the rabbi smiles and wishes Rebekah a safe journey. With tears in her eyes, Rebecca pulls the cowl over her head and retraces her steps home.

Joseph ben Judah, pale and distraught, is waiting impatiently. When Rebekah arrives, he takes her hands gently and asks where she had gone. Rebekah, shaken and despondent, sits down at the table. With quivering fingers, she extracts the letters and lays them before Joseph. In an unsteady voice she says, "Oh, Yousef, please forgive me. I was so upset by your fixation with ben Maimon's letters I felt I had to do something. And so I went to the rabbi to see if he could explain the content of these letters to me. I thought perhaps he would have some insight or interpretation which could relieve your own bafflement." Rebekah bursts into tears.

Joseph lays a tender hand on her arm. "Please don't be upset. It is true, I am greatly mystified by my master's writings but I doubt any rabbi could decipher them better than I can. After all I am considered a prize scholar and ben Maimon addressed them to me exclusively and not to any ignoramus." Joseph sits down next to his wife. He then cocks his head and says, "By the way, what did the rabbi say?"

Rebekah looks at him and replies innocently, "He said you should read between the lines."

Joseph laughs. "Oh, my dear Rebekah, that is just a phrase. It means nothing. It simply shows the rabbi is as perplexed as I am." With that, Joseph gets up and prepares to wash his hands for the noon day meal.

Later that night, Joseph quietly arises from bed and sits at his study table in the corner of the room. He is lost in thought as he stares blankly at the wall. He sits a long time in the dark, brooding. The moon offers a faint eerie reflection on the ceiling and walls. Suddenly Joseph stirs. He reaches for a taper and lights it. He then spreads the pages of *The Guide* across the table and picks up one sheet at a time. Holding it close to the flame, he tilts it aslant and scrutinizes it. He then picks up another page and examines it carefully. He shakes his head, sits back and gazes at the pile of pages on the table. Slowly, he chooses another page at random and again peers at the spaces between the lines. Nothing.

An hour goes by and Joseph is about to give up when he suddenly notices, on one sheet only, a smudge-like hieroglyphic squeezed between the lines. He looks closely and sees what appears to be faint lettering. His eyes are tired but he persists. He then realises the script is in Aramaic, not Arabic. Moreover, the lettering reads from left to right rather than the usual right to left. Joseph feels his heart pounding. Adjusting the light just so, he becomes thoroughly engrossed. By tilting the page at just the right angle he is able to read and decode the brief message. Here is what it says:

Joseph, I beseech you. Hear these words. To know God is to know his works. The emphasis is on the phrase 'to know'. Unlike the beasts of the field, God has endowed us with the capacity to reason and, in so doing, He grants us permission to inquire into the mysteries of the universe. There is no disconnect between faith and reason. God offers reconciliation between our spiritual and rationalist senses by exposing the wonders of the universe for our enjoyment and especially for our discovery. As a student of mathematics, astronomy and logic you must have had doubts about the contradictions between new discoveries of natural phenomena and the static dictates of religious law. But even the Talmud is a moving document as shown by its proclivity to reinterpret, refute and revise.

When you completed your studies of the natural sciences, I introduced you to metaphysics and biblical prophecies. I believe you misinterpreted my abrupt change as a declaration of the fixed boundaries of human reason. There are no boundaries, Joseph. If reason fails it should not be replaced by irrefutable dogma. Unfortunately, I am not at liberty to declare this aloud. It would be interpreted as blasphemy by the rigid Goanim. The so-called inelastic boundaries must be stretched — outward through a process of unrestrained reasoning as opposed to blind obedience to 'revealed truth'. Our sage, Aristotle, taught us no less. Neither did our father of medicine, the venerable Hippocrates, who rescued medicine from superstition. So must we free our minds from unsubstantiated edicts and conspiracies.

I still believe that the purpose of the universe is the existence of man so that he can serve God. And you serve God by recognising that nothing is so sacred in his vast universe that is inaccessible to human understanding and to human consciousness. I caution against laziness of thought lest it led to a blind adherence to doctrine. God's wonders and works are explicable. There is a confluence of God and nature. Knowingness comes from coherent reasoning. The human mind, being part of God's substance, is gifted the potential to unlock nature's mysteries. And when all of nature's secrets are revealed then and only then can there be a fusion between reason and faith. Go, Joseph, and impart these words to your young pupils. Open their minds.

And remember my son. God's secrets are penetrable after all and therefore we need not fear Him.

Joseph looks up and sees the morning light. He leans back in his chair and smiles. Before he knows it, the curriculum for his new school is already taking shape.

Pierre Teilhard de Chardin (1881–1955) is the fourth member of our august group who struggled with the wrenching divide between faith and reason. He was a Jesuit priest who hopped between science and religion as if walking on hot coals. An *enfant terrible* of the Catholic Church he was banished to China in 1929 where, as a paleontologist, he worked on the archaeological digs that unearthed Peking Man. It was there he experience a spiritual awakening.

By sinking my hands into the earth I could feel its history.

Teilhard was a sworn evolutionist. And yet he rejected the notion that the ascent of man is purposeless.

Contretemps
Dr Norman Bethune meets Fr Pierre Teilhard de Chardin

"Bloody hell!"

The scalpel slipped, nicking his left middle finger. As usual he was operating expeditiously. If it wasn't for the sharp pain, he could not have distinguished his own blood from that of the soldier's gaping leg wound. Maskless, gloveless and bent in a perpetual crouch he was immersed in his eighteenth surgical procedure that day. Needless to say, he was exhausted. A nurse mopped his brow. He looked around at the impassive faces of his surgical assistants. He then raised his head and gazed at the scorched hillside. The mobile operating suite, such as it was, had been hastily assembled inside a peasant's hut. On this occasion they were in Hei-su at the base of the Mo-t'ien-Ling mountains in north-east China. It was late October, 1939. Less than five hundred meters away, Mao Tse Tung's eighth Route Army was engaged in a pitched battle with a fierce Japanese battalion.

Dr Norman Bethune, the Canadian battlefield surgeon, was martyring himself in a frantic effort to repair, restore and redeploy as many wounded Chinese soldiers as possible. The air was rank with carbolic acid and the nauseating stench of open flesh. Bethune listened to the rumble of gunfire in the near distance. He stood rigid — his jaw set, lips moving silently as he cursed his inability to keep abreast of his mission. His long-suffering Chinese aides watched and waited patiently, in awe of this enigmatic and impetuous foreigner who once more bent to the task at hand. Bethune sutured the wound, washed his hands and then hastily dressed his cut finger. After gathering his instruments, he slowly made his way back to his hut.

He was less than halfway when suddenly he saw his trusted servant, Ho T'zu-hsin, running towards him. "Pai-ch'iu-en," Ho shouted. "There is a stranger in your house waiting for you. He is a round-eyed stranger. I have come to warn you." Bethune nodded wearily. I'm not expecting anyone, he wondered. Who would risk traveling to this godforsaken outpost just to see him? As he entered the hut, Bethune was greeted by a tall distinguished looking gentleman wearing a beret and a coat with a fleeced collar. There was an aura of composed eminence about the stranger. He had a prominent brow and a thin face that exaggerated a bony nose. His most distinctive features were his eyes — soft, intelligent and penetrating. His thin lips were pursed in an engaging smile. His relaxed bearing somehow put Bethune at ease.

"Please forgive this intrusion," the visitor said. "Allow me to introduce myself. My name is Pierre

Teilhard de Chardin. You may have heard of me. I am a humble Jesuit priest who happens to be an itinerant paleontologist. For many years I travelled throughout China mapping the geology of this ancient land as well as unearthing its human fossils. Because of the war I am confined, or rather quarantined, in Tientsin and Beiping. There is talk of your remarkable exploits in this perilous border region and so I was determined to meet you, face to face." Teilhard cocked his head and added, "Unannounced, I confess."

Bethune stared at his illustrious guest — not sure whether to play the congenial host or beg for release. Many months had elapsed since he last conversed face to face with a Westerner, let alone one of such eminence. Warily, he extended a welcoming hand and motioned Teilhard to sit on the only chair in the room. He ordered Ho to make some tea and then sat on the edge of his cot.

Bethune looked at his guest and muttered, "I regret to say I have had a long day and so you will forgive me if I am less than an ideal host." Fatigue clearly visible on his grey lined face and stooped shoulders. "But I am curious. What do I owe the privilege of such a distinguished visitor?"

Teilhard removed his beret and jacket, paused and looked around. The hut, a single room, was constructed of mud and stone with a brick oven in one corner. The narrow cot and one small table made up the sparse furniture. There was a tin stove for burning of either wood or coal. A single window was papered over and the floor was packed mud. Teilhard sat down and began.

"I do not easily indulge in flattery and so what I am about to say should not be construed as unctuous on my part. I learned that as a battlefield surgeon you have performed over three hundred operations on the shattered bodies of Chinese soldiers. Mostly, by the way, under extraordinary hazardous conditions at the very front lines of battle. You have single-handedly trained many Chinese peasants as paramedics and set up two medical mobile units at Ch'i Hui."

When Bethune tried to intervene, Teilhard held up his hand and continued, "You may not be aware of this but your selfless sacrifice in providing on site surgical restitution to soldiers and civilians alike — all trapped in a ghastly war — is already the stuff of legend. I realise you are probably very tired but I beg your indulgence to hear me out. I have not travelled this long journey for simple cajolery but to express to you some deep-seated thoughts of mine. May we talk a while?" Bethune simply shrugged and waited. What did this iconic theologian want of him? Teilhard leaned forward and continued.

"As you may know, I am an ordained priest who made a choice to forsake the trappings of an ethereal divinity for a more earthbound spiritual force. One I believe underlies God's purpose. I want you to know that I stand in awe and reverence of your achievements because I have always believed in the intrinsic divination of human endeavour. Your actions are testimony to God's grace. Despite all the squabbles you have had in interpersonal affairs, especially with those in authority, let me assure you that your actions have more than compensated for your irascible temperament. In 1937, in Spain, you achieved an historical breakthrough in military medicine when you set up and operated the first mobile blood transfusion service — directly on the front lines of that devastating civil war.

"I know for a fact that here in China, when you were appointed Mao's medical advisor, you refused to be confined to central headquarters in Yenan. Instead, you insisted on hauling your makeshift mobile unit to where the battles were waged — first in the Chin-Ch'a-Chi border region of Shansi province and then to Ho-Chin Chang. I learned that at the battle in Hei-ssu you and your team of bedraggled Chinese assistants, operated non-stop in the field. Miraculously, you succeeded in returning one-third of the wounded to active duty.

"You lived and operated in caves, abandoned houses and mud huts all within earshot of mortar shells. In addition to setting up these mobile units you even had time to teach surgical techniques to untrained Chinese recruits. Moreover, I understand, you have built a medical school and a thirty-six-bed hospital along the way. Whether you realise it or not, you are ordained a selfless hero of the Chinese people, an honour not easily bestowed on a Westerner."

Sensing his host's quizzical stare and apparent discomfort, Teilhard hastened to add, "Forgive me for rambling on. I am not on a missionary's quest. My objectives are, in a way, self-serving. You see I have always believed that human action is valueless without the intention that drives it. And that intention is the force of divine will." Bethune winced but did not interrupt. Teilhard ignored the slight and went on.

"I am convinced that your actions in this remote outpost, far from the spotlight, are nothing less than the manifestations of a sanctified life. What else can anyone construe from your work here? You labour ceaselessly in a remote and dangerous corner of the world, surrounded by foreign tongues, without recompense or need for adulation from your peers. I see it as the gospel of human effort. By that I mean you have a sense that your work here has a purpose. As such your talents and skills are gifts — consecrated because they contribute to a common endeavour." Bethune sat, mostly in awe of the sheer force of Teilhard's intensity.

"As a paleontologist, I experience a spiritual awakening whenever I sink my hands into the earth in search of its history. I suspect you sense a similar epiphany whenever you sink your surgical hands into the flesh of wounded soldiers. I reject the classic Christian view of suffering as a passive acceptance of divine will. On the contrary, the more we are engaged in actions to overcome suffering the more we are collectively participating in a common venture — one that is no less than an evolutionary path guided by increasing complexity and shepherded by God's grace. To put it bluntly, deeds not only speak louder than rhetoric they convey a moral injunction — one that contributes to humanity's advancement. Do you not agree?"

Bethune fumbled at first. He then sighed and shook his head, a head whose profile bore an uncanny resemblance to Lenin's godless visage. "My dear Teilhard," rejoined Bethune. "I am less driven by so-called divine will than by a fury levelled against those who exiled both of us to this wretched corner of the earth. I am not ill informed of your curious pronouncements. And from what I have learned I can say, with no disrespect, that we stand at opposite poles when it comes to our respective outlooks on religion and politics. But despite our differences, or perhaps because of them, we share dubious commonalities." Bethune smiled knowingly before proceeding.

"For starters, there is roiling Gaullist blood in both our veins. I believe your saintly mother descended from the unsaintly Voltaire of all people while my ancestors, the 'Baytunes', hailed, I believe, from Normandy. We each survived a household of unabashed religious orthodoxy. My father was an austere Presbyterian minister whereas your devout Catholic mother exercised a powerful, some might say overbearing, influence on you. We were both stretcher bearers in the Great War — you with the Eighth Moroccan Rifles in

North Africa and I in the trenches of France. For your efforts you were awarded a *Chevalier* of the *Légion d'honneur* while I was bequeathed shrapnel in both my legs."

Teilhard took all this in with restrained bemusement. Rather than object, he seemed to encourage Bethune to continue. There was now fire in Bethune's eyes as he straightened and retorted boldly, "There is, however, a major difference between us, one that may be judged unforgiven. It is simply this. I detest war and decry man's innate cruelty to his fellow man whereas, judging from your writings, you see war as a perverse justification for cleansing humankind of unwanted detritus — all in keeping with a so-called divine convergence towards some undefined cosmic consciousness, whatever that means.

"To put it simply, I have no lofty divine purpose here. I am self-exiled because I have experienced the bitterness and hopelessness of man's vindictiveness and brutality. You, on the other hand, were not only banished by your own church but denied the right to publish your theological writings. As for my so-called celestial inspired actions, let me assure you that the communist ethos that I embrace is, for better or worse, directed at the real plight of the suffering compared to all the sanctimonious claptrap offered by organised religion."

Teilhard remained unmoved by the sudden tirade. He smiled beneficently as he took a sip of his tea. He then sat back, looked up at the ceiling and then at Bethune who was silently fuming. "My dear doctor, you misinterpret my meaning. You see, there is another similarity that binds us. We are both suffused with the sufferings of man. Action is purchased at the price of human agony and so we both believe there is a meaning to human distress regardless of our different ethos. I do not subscribe to the notion that human suffering is engrafted in the concept of original sin. It is rather a necessary albeit unexplained burden humans bear as we evolve towards a more perfect species — what I call an inevitable convergence to a higher consciousness. Sufferance by such definition is a noble condition.

"Despite our opposing views we are both inextricably implicated in the human condition — you in the flesh and I in the spirit. You as a man of action and deeds and I as a commentator and interpreter of the phenomenon that is man. We differ not so much in our views but in our temperament. Impatient, irascible and short tempered, you do not suffer fools gladly. And yet you are known to exhibit infinite kindness to the sick and dying. I have my shortcomings as well but, like you, I am ill prepared to surrender what I believe in."

Bethune shook his head. He wasn't quite sure what Teilhard wanted of him. The more he hungered for compromise, the more Teilhard's asceticism sparked an emboldened attack. I will provoke him. "My dear sir, while I am here trying to heal the shattered bodies of brave soldiers, you are safe in the embrace of the

Koumintang authorities in Beiping — sheltered from all the bloodshed. I suspect that as a good Catholic, you fear the takeover by a Godless communism more than the subjugation by an imperialist enemy." Surprisingly, Teilhard continued to show no visible signs of offense. The same calm expression spoke of an untroubled soul. This made Bethune all the more irritated.

"Many years ago, back in my native Canada, I foolishly strutted about as an antiestablishment conservative — right of center and anti-labour. But as a surgeon, I witnessed the devastating consequences of preventable diseases such as tuberculosis. A disease by the way whose outcome depended less on the virulence of the bacterium than on whether the patient was rich or poor. I became appalled by the recalcitrance of public health policies in Canada and, as a consequence, the widening disparity in the provision of health care. In 1935 I went to the Soviet Union to attend an international conference in physiology. For the first time, I saw the benefits of socialized medicine in action. I swore then and there I would do everything in my power to correct the inequities of privatized health care. And so, in 1936, I initiated a movement called The Montreal Group for the Security of the People's Health. It included free public health clinics for the unemployed and underprivileged. It required all of my efforts to keep it afloat, and when it met overwhelming intransigence from those in authority, I hastily packed my bags and went to war-torn Spain to get my surgical hands moving again.

"Alas, in the midst of that heart wrenching civil war I was once again the victim of insufferable bureaucratic resistance. Believe it or not I found more solace caring for the wounded on the front lines of combat. The more I saw of the devastation, the more I came to reject fascism, imperialism and organised religion. They are all interconnected to subjugate and oppress the masses. What are you fleeing from if it isn't the suffocating orthodoxy of your own church — the same church that opposes your views in favour of an outdated and tiresome dogma?"

Teilhard listened attentively, his expression temperate and relaxed. He then raised his eyebrows and said, "My good friend, I hear the voices of the earth more than the singing of celestial angels. Someone once asked, 'How do you contemplate the sphinx without succumbing to its spell?' It is by asking questions and working out the answers yourself. As for my so-called banishment, I was invited years ago by my good friend and fellow Jesuit, Pére Emile Licent. As paleontologists we began our excavations in Tientsin not far from here. In 1929 I then went to Chou-Kou-Tien to work on the archaeological digs that unearthed Peking Man. I am a sworn evolutionist but I reject the notion that the ascent of man is purposeless — a random process that somehow evolves in fits and starts. The fossil record is not inert. Neither is the earth that harbours them. All matter is possessed of energy — a universal spirit — a faith if you will. I cannot grasp the concept of a directionless evolution. Neither can I accept the pessimistic claim that man's sporadic cruelty is innate or permanent. Surely, your own actions are testimony to the existence of a loftier human spirit.

"You see, my good man, I believe in orthogenesis. It is an evolutionary process driven in part by human endeavour such as yours. The trajectory of all that is contained in the universe forms an arced convergence towards an ultimate state of shared consciousness. Matter is not inanimate. It is, I believe, an externalization of a universal spirit. This convergence, or centrism, indicates that all of nature, be it material or psychic, is driven by a complex force — a spiritual energy if you will. How else can one explain the increasing complexity of biological forms throughout the millennia?"

Bethune shrugged and waved his hand as if shooing away an invisible fly. "I do not pretend to understand the nature of evolution," he replied. "But how do you, as a scientist, reconcile Darwin's theory of evolution to your idea of a future state of spiritual purification. Don't you need to taint Darwinism with a dollop of Lamarckism?"

Teilhard tittered and cocked his head in a manner of scholarly tolerance. "Ah, but it depends on how you interpret Lamarckism. I do not accept the facile self-serving interpretation by your Soviet poster boy,

Lysenko. He who justifies the revolt and future prospects of the proletariat in terms of Lamarck's theory of acquired inheritance. No, my interpretation of Lamarckism is based on sound observations of the fossil record. In short, from many Hominids there came one. Why? We are the sole surviving hominid species because evolution is a process of ever-increasing complexity. The fossil record does not lie. I accept there are antagonistic forces of speciation which account for the emergence of human sub-types through, yes, natural selection. But I contend there are equally convergent forces of so-called *sapientisation* which, through interbreeding and socialization, have led to cerebralization and with it a spirit of immutable purpose or predestination. I see it as a psychic wave culminating ultimately at the omega point — the divine fulfilment in Christ."

Bethune scowled and rolled his eyes. "To me, it smacks of metaphysics masquerading as science." He was strangely torn between the comforting presence of Teilhard and a wish to be petulant. "I cannot believe that your anthropocentric view of evolution has shown any indication so far that man is becoming less malevolent. You are not the first to propose such an absurd notion. Have you heard of Dr Richard Maurice Bucke? Like me, he was not only a Canadian physician — an alienist actually — but he also grew up in Southern Ontario, the son of a lapsed minister. He was a prolific writer who, at the turn of the century, postulated that man was acquiring a sixth sense. Like you, he referred to it as a form of cosmic consciousness. Bucke foresaw a gradual human evolutionary process whereby man acquired a sixth sense — one that conferred a behavioral change which, in time, would enable him to become more humane towards his fellow human beings."

Bethune paused, emitted a contemptuous 'Hah!' and then declared "Bucke died in 1902 having been spared the ignominy of witnessing man's atrocities during the twentieth century. Collectively, the savage forces of fascism and imperialism during this century so far are responsible for more blood spilled than by all the tyrants of the past put together. How does this square with your theory of convergence towards a Christ-like omega point — a messianic vision if ever I heard one. I do not wish to be unkind but can a rational unbiased person accept your prophetic utterances knowing your prior claims of authenticity included that of Piltdown man — a hoax if ever there was one?"

Teilhard was well aware of Bethune's history of spontaneous vitriol. He remained unprovoked, calmly stood his ground and replied, "I say to you once again that despite our different viewpoints we are both imbued with humanitarianism. Yours is expressed in action and mine is driven by a faith in the unity of the world and the existence of an immortal spirit. The difference between your bitter pessimism and my sanguinity is explained as a time-space analogy. Allow me to clarify. From an evolutionary perspective this war, this unfortunate tragic blip in human history, is but an incidental stumbling block if you will. And for every stumbling block there is a correction that elevates man and nature to a higher level. My vision is one of a synthesis — a coming together of science, metaphysics and Christian belief. There is a spiritual energy contained in matter of which we are a part.

"I believe, based on scientific evidence, there exists a 'transformism' involving both physical and psychic energy, a predestination of a convergent evolutionary process — an ascent towards a common enlightenment. You are demonstrating, by your actions, that you are very much part of it. Isn't predestination a cornerstone of Presbyterianism?" Here Teilhard winked mischievously and then continued in a somber tone. "You are embittered because you feel entrapped in this tragic freeze frame of human history. You cannot see the cosmic whole."

Teilhard leaned back and looked at Bethune with an expression of paternalistic concern. "Norman, you are an old sybarite at heart. You are always wanting to be in charge. And so you have found your métier here in China among a people that shuns vanity and ambition. Your repulsion of authority ought not be directed at me. I come hat in hand to pay my respects and honor what I consider a superhuman contribution by a selfless surgeon in this broken war-torn land."

"Forgive me, Pierre," Bethune interrupted. "I am tired, weary and frustrated. My eyesight is failing and I am deaf in one ear. Speaking of deaf ears, all my requests for financial assistance from the West have met with silence. I have limited support and I operate every day with no time for my former pursuits of painting, writing and poetry. The work, come to think of it, is a blessing in that it substitutes for my loneliness and despair. Speaking of poetry may I interest you in some humble jottings I wrote during my aborted stint in Spain." Bethune rummaged under his cot and came up with a frayed sheet of paper.

"It is called 'Red Moon'." Bethune handed it to Teilhard who read aloud:

And the same pallid moon tonight,
Which rides so quietly, clear and high,
The mirror of our pale and troubled gaze
Raised to a cool Canadian sky.

Above the shattered Spanish troops
Last night rose low and wild and red,
Reflecting back from her illumined shield
The blood bespattered faces of the dead.

To that pale disc we raise our clenched fists,
And to those nameless dead our vows renew,
"Comrades, who fought for freedom and the future world,
Who died for us, we will remember you."

In the hut the light was fading. Teilhard slowly got up, turned to Bethune and said, "My dear friend, I do not wish to tire you any further. I am sincere when I say how much I treasure this opportunity to see and speak with you. Given the circumstances, you have been a most amiable host. I want you to know that I shall cherish this moment forever. Please forgive me if I have burdened you in any way."

Bethune rose, smiled warmly and shook Teilhard's hand. "Thank you for coming. Were I to blame my brash insults on mere physical exhaustion, it would serve little purpose? Therefore, I apologise most sincerely."

As Teilhard prepared to leave he looked at Bethune's bandaged finger and noticed some oozing. "Please look after that wound, Norman. I recall the unfortunate consequences of neglected care when I served in North Africa."

Bethune smiled wearily. "I appreciate your concern but it is just a minor scratch. I am more upset by my clumsiness than by the wound itself. As to our meeting, I can only say, that despite any harsh exchanges, I actually enjoyed our contretemps and I wish you safe passage."

EPILOG

In the week following the surgical mishap, Bethune became aware of persistent swelling and discomfort in his injured finger. Seven days later, on November 5, 1939, he experienced fever, chills and general malaise. In just a few days, an abscess appeared in his left armpit and he began suffering from high fever, vomiting and progressive weakness. The blood poisoning (septicemia) persisted. It finally claimed his life on November 12. He died a lonely hero in a remote peasant hut in Huang-shi K'ou.

Teilhard de Chardin remained in China for another seven years. Back in Paris he suffered a heart attack in 1947. The following year, he was called to Rome by the superior general of the Jesuits. In Teilhard's mind this represented hope that the ban on his writings would be rescinded. However, the prohibition, including the publication of his most important work, *The Phenomenon of Man,* was once again renewed. He was also denied a teaching post at the College de France. In 1951 he became a permanent resident in the United States and died in New York City in 1955.

The Gap: Curiosity and Suspicion

Linus Pauling, a double recipient of a Nobel Prize, once said, "Satisfaction of one's curiosity is one of the greatest sources of happiness in life." But what if the curiosity is not satisfied? What if it leaves a yearning, a foreshadowing — a knot behind the breastbone? What if it is replaced by suspicion? It is said, that despite its nine lives, a cat's curiosity can be lethal, if its quest is unfulfilled.

As a fundamental basis of learning, exploratory behavior is a critical trait of all living organisms. Nevertheless, as a human motivational drive, curiosity can also be either needlessly transient or all consuming. Its appetite is strident but the object of its pursuit is often trivial. How often have you found yourself lured by a distraction only to be disillusioned by the outcome? Our interest in external phenomena can be both fleeting and mesmerizing. As an innate drive, curiosity compels us to acquire new knowledge. It accounts for our wanderlust. It helps us disengage from a revolving rut. It spurs our desire for self-improvement. It enriches our store of factual bits. It leads us into temptation.

Take the case of a scientific discovery. As is often the case, it is spurred by a curiosity that while frequently sidetracked refuses to be dismissed. The thread of this stubborn pursuit is unwound but rarely abandoned. For personal advancement, the very act of learning is fueled by our inquisitiveness. Unlike other traits, curiosity's tenacity for learning does not diminish with age. Even the folks who dabble in Artificial Intelligence recognize the importance of incorporating learning algorithms into their AI designs. Humans and robots alike are spared the indignities of pointless repetition.

On the flip side, curiosity, once satisfied, often leaves little enticement to continue exploring. You are reading a plot driven whodunit novel. There are many suspects. You think you have identified the perpetrator based on motive, weapon and opportunity. You turn the page and voila! — the murderer is revealed. What could possibly compel you to continue reading once you learn the identity of the culprit? How many scientific pursuits were abandoned because of premature confirmation of an errant hypothesis? How often were you persuaded to stick to a mission once an objective was met? How often has a conspiracy theory substituted for an unresolved event so as to appease a nagging curiosity?

Since the 1970s, much has been written about the science of curiosity. Erudite theories abound but cross-validation of experimental data is hampered by statistical quirks. One tenuous theory holds that curiosity, as a human trait, motivates people to fill gaps in knowledge. In other words, the drive to explore stems from a feeling of deprivation that cries out for closure.

According to this theory we are compelled to expunge this deprivation. Get rid of it. Fill in the blanks. Our mind abhors a vacuum. Someone once said, 'Curiosity is akin to scratching a mental itch'. And you know what it feels like when the itch is inaccessible to your probing fingers.

But what if the quest for information confers no benefit? In today's age of instant access to information — much of which is devoid of evidence — we are inveterate browsers. Glued to our devices we are distracted as we stumble over mindless trivia. Astonishing are the occasions when our demand for what turns out to be useless trivia is unmet. Or, the occasions when our demand for information is not resolved by the information itself, simply because it is incapable of conferring any benefit.

Take the case of patient autonomy — a patient's right to know. Here is a not atypical scenario: On the basis of a careful medical assessment a doctor recommends a specific course of treatment. The patient hesitates. The patient is curious. Are there alternative treatments less intrusive or distressful? Whether the patient consults the Internet for a more agreeable option or seeks a second opinion, he or she is now in the tenuous position of having to make an inexpert choice between two or more alternatives. In other words, spurred by curiosity, the demand for more information is not always met with an ability to make the right decision.

In a curious sense, *curiosity* is one of the shallower and more inconsequential of human traits. What is bewildering is the discomfort one often feels when the curiosity is unresolved. This can occur even if the distraction is self-induced. That is to say, nobody twisted your arm to pursue the object of interest. This brings us to an interesting dilemma. While there is an extensive literature on the science of curiosity there is precious little on the failure to bring closure to an exploratory action.

Watch a dog suddenly aroused by a noise or the flicker of a moving object. More often than not the animal is easily distracted without seeming to agonize over its failure to satisfy its curiosity. On the contrary, most humans expect a resolution to any intrigue that happens to engage them. We are suckers for closure. Take the final scene of a typical Hollywood movie. How was it imagined? It is not unlikely that in the executive producers' boardroom, a meeting took place between the director, the writer and the producers. The script was massaged, manipulated and reworked so that the final scene would satisfy an audience's expectation of a fitting resolution. We are natural gossips and yet our story telling is incomplete without a punchline or satisfactory denouement. There is a nagging emptiness without an upshot. Is it conceivable that the detritus of unresolved conflicts comes back to haunt us in the form of disturbing dreams?

So here is a question. If much of our curiosity is a distraction in pursuit of the trivial? Why do we get so upset if the search is unfulfilled? How can we prevent an unfulfilled curiosity from slipping into morbid suspicion?

The Fix: A Need to Know

Larry awoke one morning in a cold sweat. He lay trembling as he recalled his frenetic dream. In it he discovered his wife, Carol, and a shadowy figure brazenly exposed *in flagrante delicto.* Although it was only a dream, he couldn't shake the notion that she was having an affair. There was no particular reason for his apprehension. In this their fifth year of marriage they seemed happily settled in a snug domesticity. True, they were childless but they shared many interests, traveled abroad and enjoyed good times with friends and relations. And yet he couldn't stop shaking. He thought hard but was unable to recollect any change in her habits or routines. Nor were there any signs of distancing herself. Simply put, there was nary a hint of infidelity. And yet he remained unconvinced. Surely the dream meant something.

As the days went by Larry became more obsessed with the irresolution. It preyed on his mind constantly. At first, he was gripped more by curiosity than suspicion. Something was amiss. Could he have overlooked some vulnerability in their relationship? Perhaps something illicit is afoot during the days of separation when his business requires him to be out of town. To make matters worse there is the undeniable fact that Carol is a beautiful and desirable woman. This only intensified his doubt. But has not their love matured, if not grown stronger? As the days went by, his curiosity would not abate. It nagged and gnawed. It planted itself as a seed — an irritant in his brain which rapidly evolved into a stubborn kernel of morbid wariness. He couldn't sleep. He became restless and short-tempered. As time went on it was the unresolved curiosity, rather than distrust, that begged for relief. In short, Larry was consumed with a need to know.

His first step was to purchase a mynah bird. Larry was drawn to the bird's alleged reputation for human mockery and verbal impersonation. And so, one day he visited a pet shop, where he was shown a cage housing a rather austere looking bird. Its glossy black feathers, bright yellow beak and beady eyes gave the bird an inscrutable, albeit surly appearance. Larry was assured by the pet shop owner that this particular bird was gifted with full throated mimicry. It was reputed, according to the owner, to repeat phrases in a clear, albeit somewhat cackled voice. Larry inquired whether the bird was fixated on only one human voice. Oh no, the owner was adamant. This bird, in particular, is adept at repeating, verbatim, conversations from multiple sources. Moreover, it was guaranteed to be especially voluble when mimicking new and unfamiliar utterances. With a glint in his eye the owner took Larry aside and whispered, "Would you believe that one of this mynah's siblings, hatched from the same clutch of eggs, once testified at a court hearing on a house break-in. The bird identified the burglar by voicing the culprit's exact intonations during the heist!" Larry was awestruck. He couldn't wait to get home and begin testing the bird's skills.

At first, Larry set to work learning the bird's current vocabulary. He then taught the bird to repeat certain phrases on command — purposefully avoiding words of endearment. Larry felt that such utterances from the bird's newly acquired repertoire would confirm that an illicit conversation was taking place. Carol, oblivious of Larry's intentions, looked on with amusement while Larry spent hours bantering with the bird. Little did she realize the bird was being trained to spy on her. She not only adjusted to the bird's peculiar behavior and mimetic cackles, but welcomed its companionship during Larry's absences.

Several weeks went by but Larry could elicit no suspicious utterances from the bird. Other than nonsensical verse the mynah simply repeated a litany of familiar domestic phrases. "One cup of cornstarch," squawked the bird over and over again as it echoed a telephone conversation Carol had with one of her friends. To make matters worse the bird was creating havoc. When out of its cage, its ravenous appetite had it pecking at any food morsel in sight. Its droppings were everywhere. Carol was beside herself, begging for relief. Finally, Larry had no choice but to give in and return the bird. And yet the more obstinate the mynah bird's behavior the more Larry's curiosity was piqued. An alternate strategy was called for.

Larry's next gambit was to consult a clairvoyant. One who could peer into the veiled souls of duplicitous people and — just maybe — uncover sordid affairs. He was convinced, or at least talked himself into believing, that such a telepathist existed. After much discrete inquiry he was referred to a Madame Radanski, an eccentric crystal ball gazer, who when told the purpose of her collusion, insisted that Carol be present during the seances. A deal was struck whereby Madame Radanski would convey to Larry, behind closed doors, the nature of any illicit triste. Again, amused by her husband's eccentric distractions, Carol was only too happy to indulge his fantasies.

Madame Radanski's 'emporium', as she called it, was a windowless room bathed in a garish purple haze and festooned with kitschy wall hangings and beaded curtains. Madame Radanski wore a mauve turban and a billowing black gown laden with multicolored sequins. All three sat around a small ornamental table covered with a crimson silk cloth. In the center of the table was perched a black onyx statue of a gnome-like figure bearing a fierce grin. In this eerie bubble the readings began. Each session opened with ten minutes of deep breathing exercises and meditation. Madame Radanski then proceeded to invoke the spirits while gazing intently at Carol. One could barely hear a low-grade moan from deep within the clairvoyant's throat. There was the occasional fluttering of hands alternating with head bowing and eyes clenched shut. This went on for about an hour following which Madame Radanski declared a successful seance and scheduled the next meeting.

If the purpose of this fiction was to induce a trance-like state, the sessions were unsuccessful. Oh yes, there were the occasional titterings from Carol but all Madame Radanski could relay to Larry were mundane references to Carol's impregnable soul and glimpses of superfluous banter. Nothing came of the seances, and once again, Larry was left consumed with that persistent burning curiosity which, by now had morphed into an unsettling suspicion.

What now?

Coincidently, Larry's business happened to be in cyberware. Although he was in sales, his position offered an opportunity to chat with members of the creative team. One day Larry was sharing a coffee break with Omar, a skittish digital junkie with expressive eyes and an overwrought imagination. Omar just happened to be working on a special hush-hush application. "It's in the works." Omar confided to Larry. "We now have a prototype of a special heat sensitive sensor that could detect, identify and code the presence of a human body in any moderate sized room".

Larry inquired whether the device was capable of differentiating the heat of a familiar body from that of, let us say, an intruder. Omar's eyes popped. Oh yes, indeed. That is precisely what it is designed for. In fact, it contains a display item which reproduces, in dazzling colors, distinct spectral arrays of no less than six human bodies in any room of average size. Mind you, it is in its preliminary stages but already has proven to be effective with small samples of individuals. Larry could not contain his excitement. At last, a perfect bug to chafe out an interloper.

Omar was only too happy to indulge Larry's eagerness to test the device in a real-life setting, off campus as it were. And so, despite cautionary mumblings about the sensor's primitive state of development, Larry took the device home and secretly installed it behind the ceiling light fixture immediately above the connubial bed. As a critical precaution Larry had to be assured the sensor really worked. To verify its efficacy Larry feigned illness one day and stayed home for three days in succession. He then brought the device to Omar for testing.

Sure enough, there in glorious color, two distinct spectra were displayed. The luminous blue band was presumed to be that of Larry's while Carol's heat emanations were represented as a shimmering violet tint. Having convinced himself that the device was genuine, Larry prepared for the entrapment. Unable to constrain his suspicion any further he reinstalled the sensor and went off on a business trip. On his return two days later, he quietly retrieved the sensor and had Omar display the recorded images in a private room.

To his horror, Larry was shown an unfamiliar spectral band. There was the familiar violet hue of Carol's, albeit slightly faded. But close beside it was a gut-wrenching hideous ochre, signifying an unfamiliar body! Omar stared at Larry's pale face. "What is it?"

Larry hesitated at first but then lied. "I tested the device with three people in the same room including myself. But why is my color not there?"

Omar just shrugged. And then his eyes lit up. "By the way, were you absent from that room for any extended period?" he asked.

"Why yes. I was away on a trip for a few days. Why?"

"That must be it." Omar brightened. "I guess I should have told you. The device has a limited memory. And so, I presume it failed to re-register your color pattern or in your absence simply changed your color pattern. Furthermore, it has a habit of reproducing the spectrum of a previous body even though the color may have faded. I need to work on those glitches. But hey, look." Omar smiled. "At least it is workable during a short run."

Larry was now in a quandary. Each contrivance, each attempt to satisfy his morbid curiosity had so far failed. Furthermore, his schemes only exacerbated his suspicion. Carol, meanwhile, had indulged her husband through each of these bizarre forays with no suspicion as to what Larry was up to. On the other hand, she became increasingly concerned that he was losing his grip. He was often distracted, curt and fidgety. She believed he was becoming obsessed with something related to his work. As for Larry he was no longer curious. He was smitten with an unbridled suspicion so intense he was displaying erratic behavior. He couldn't sleep at nights. He lost his appetite and couldn't concentrate on his business affairs. If he wasn't moaning in his sleep he would often get up in the middle of the night and pace the room. Carol pleaded with him to seek professional counselling. Finally, in desperation, he agreed to see a clinical psychologist.

Marta possessed an uncanny ability to filter the detritus of a patient's neurosis. Her office was patterned as a comfortable living room with unobtrusive paintings on the wall, soft lighting from table lamps and a sofa and chairs intimately arranged. She listened carefully as Larry, slowly but surely, confessed all. He described his tormenting suspicion of his wife's alleged infidelity. Granted, it was based on a disturbing dream. He detailed all the steps he had taken to confirm his hunch including the mynah bird, the visit to the clairvoyant and the heat sensor. The more the words poured out, the more agitated he became until he threw up his arms and fell back on the couch in a deep funk. It was clear to Marta that his initial curiosity, based on nothing but a nightmare had wormed its way into morbid mistrust and suspicion.

After a long silence Larry recovered himself. Marta then leaned forward and murmured gently, "You realize that with one simple act on your part you can easily allay both your anxiety concerning your wife's presumed disloyalty and, at the same time, satisfy your curiosity without feeling any mental anguish whatsoever."

Larry stared at her in disbelief. "Really? Please tell me how."

Marta smiled. "Well, let us first review your actions so far. In retrospect, do you honestly believe that any of them had a serious chance of success? Think of it. Each of your attempts was nothing more than an exercise in futility. In other words, you had, consciously or unconsciously, chosen methods that were doomed to failure. Take the mynah bird. Did you really believe the bird could somehow be trained to spy? Why not simply enlist the professional services of a private detective? As for the fortune teller, did you truly imagine she could miraculously penetrate and read the inner thoughts and fantasies of your wife, let alone make her confess? And did you actually believe an untested heat sensor, as opposed to a standard reliable camera, could be so discriminatory that it would confirm, beyond a shadow of doubt, a secret tryst?

"Don't you see?" Marta tilted her head and gazed knowingly at Larry. "You chose these methods because, deep in your gut, you really did not want to know. Your premise, based on a nightmare, was shaky to begin with. What you hadn't bargained for was the excruciating discomfort of a curiosity unfulfilled. A curiosity that could not be contained grew into a suspicion which became the driving force that has so unnerved you. It created an irksome discomfort worse than the curiosity itself. After all, there is neither reason nor hint to suspect your wife of duplicity other than a dream gone viral."

Marta sat back and gazed at Larry whose face had an uncomprehending look. He shook his head and asked, "So what do I do now?"

"There is only one sure way to bring closure to your anguish. It's simple. You have a desperate need to know. So go home and ask her directly. And I promise. You will have your answer." Larry somehow felt a weight lifted but he didn't know why.

That evening, Larry and Carol were having a post prandial port in the living room. The lighting was dimmed. They were sitting on a divan when he turned to her, and said, "Dear, I have something to ask you."

"What is it?" she asked

"Are you having an affair?" There was a combination of tension and fear in his eyes.

"Why, no darling. Whatever made you think I was?"

The Gap: Forethought and Intuition

Experimental psychologists get their jollies by showcasing the rich trove of our behavioral inconsistencies. Take, for example, the infamous 'Conformity' experiment. In 1951 Solomon Asch demonstrated the extent to which social pressure within a peer group of fifty male college students could persuade a subject to act against his better judgement. Or the notorious Milgram experiment in 1963. Here, Stanley Milgram, a psychology professor at Yale, demonstrated how far the average person will go to obey authority even if it meant harming another individual. But are these so-called psychic aberrations unique to humans? Neither conformity to peer pressure nor subservience to authority are traits distinguishable from that of other creatures.

Let us, however, consider this question — If our decision-making neocortex is critical to our survival as the sole hominid species, why is it so often out of joint with our rapid-fire instinct-laden mid brain? Making a decision, any decision, is a deliberate act. There is nothing reflexive about it. Forethought, or the very act of planned thinking, is energy consuming. Contrast this to the thrift of snap decisions that supposedly sprout from our primitive brain centers. In Malcolm Gladwell's book, *Blink*, he states that spur-of-the-moment impulses often serve us well — under some circumstances. The luck of the draw as it were? Be that as it may, we are sadly at the mercy of uninformed reflexive judgements among which are all too hasty opinions of strangers, events, beliefs and pronouncements. Rather than pause and parse our impressions we are likely to take counsel from our emotions — our 'gut reactions'. Deliberate unbiased rationalized thought is just too labor intensive, too time consuming.

The philosopher, John Stuart Mill, once said, "Truth gains more from the errors of those who think for themselves than from those who do not suffer themselves to think." To think is to suffer? Well, partially since it is demanding of extra energy. Try imagining it in neurobiological terms. In the knee jerk reflex the arc of neural transmission is along a path of least resistance — to the spinal cord and back — avoiding the long trek to the upper reaches of the central nervous system. Likewise, the reaction time between a stimulus, "What is your opinion of those people who…" and the quick (mindless) response, "I detest them…" is abbreviated by short circuiting through a black box somewhere in our lower brain centers. The response does not pause long enough for a thoughtful vetting by those entangled wires in our neocortex. This neuroanatomical depiction is admittedly facile but it provides a conceptual framework for the lack of engagement between rational thought and intuition.

When faced with a difficult question we not infrequently answer a simpler one — a favorite ploy of politicians. George Carlin, the renowned stand-up comedian, recalls posing this question to his Jesuit teacher. "Can God create a boulder so heavy that even He cannot lift it?" According to Carlin this was met with the flippant reply, "It's a mystery." Scientists are not immune. For instance, they occasionally invoke Occam's Razor by opting for the simplest explanation to a problem rather than suffer the stress of heavy thinking. As a protective mechanism we often decide issues in a risk-averse manner — choosing a safe instinctual response rather than gamble on strenuous deliberation. It seems that the more we puzzle over an issue the more we are at the mercy of making a wrong choice. Alternatively, we tend to jump to conclusions based on little evidence. Decision making is tough.

And yet, as one becomes skilled in a task, the effort required to make a decision related to that task becomes less onerous. It almost looks *intuitive*. I recall a rather brazen intensive care unit nurse whose limited intellect and offhand mannerisms afforded her little opportunity for advancement. She was a heavyset, somewhat awkward person with a hoarse voice attributed to heavy smoking. Her seemingly blasé attitude brought mild rebukes from her colleagues and superiors. However, should a patient under her charge suddenly experience a precipitous drop in blood pressure or worse, a cardiac arrest, she would instantly spring into action. With remarkable intuition she would size up the situation in a flash, leap to the patient's bedside and, more often than not, have the crisis under control. Meanwhile, frozen in awe, others on the team could be seen standing by as if they, like Shakespeare's Cassius, were 'thinking too much'.

Was she gifted with an uncanny intuition or was it learned through experience? If asked, she would likely shrug her shoulders and emit a hoarse guffaw. This 'knowing without knowing' is characteristic of instinctual behavior. Or as Malcolm Gladwell says "There can be as much value in the blink of an eye as in months of rational analysis."

But is instinctive action, always bereft of logic? There are many who contend that baseball is a slow game. It is if you are waiting for the pitcher to stop fidgeting and throw the ball. But once the ball is in play — a sharp grounder to the shortstop with a runner on first base — it can be the fastest sport with split second timing. I remember one day watching the Hall of Famer, Robbie Alomar, play second base for the Toronto Blue Jays. The visiting team had a runner on second base with no one out. The next batter hit a sizzling grounder towards Alomar. Now let us stop-frame the action and enter Alomar's mindset. Here is what he may have been thinking before the ball was even hit. 'If I scoop up any ball hit to me, I have a sure out at first base. After all, the batter has to run ninety feet to reach first base while his mate at second, already leading off the base, has less than eighty feet to reach third base. But this would put a runner at third, in scoring position for a sacrifice fly ball to the outfield. Let me mull this scenario in my mind. I have to consider the speed of any ground ball coming in my direction, my coordinates in space, the baserunner's known reputation as a slow runner, the pitcher's ability to throw a wicked slider down and inside to a left-handed batter forcing him to hit a ground ball pulled to the right side towards me and the confirmation of that pitch from the catcher's hand signal.'

So what did Alomar do? He fielded the sharply hit ground ball, pivoted, fired a bullet to the third baseman and nailed the runner from second. It was poetry in motion. But was his action reflexive? I think not. Alomar was using logic to plan for contingencies. He primed himself with alternative strategies using his decision-making neocortex based on a vast store of memorable patterns. Intuition, as opposed to mindless snap judgements, often relies on pattern recognition. From an evolutionary viewpoint it is a defense mechanism, sharpened by experience. The stimulus that made Alomar appear to react reflexively was logic since he did have choices. Give experience its due.

Let us contrast this 'acquired or adaptive' intuition with snap judgements based on innate biases, unconfirmed impressions and human cognitive illusions. The advertising industry, retail establishments and populist politics are particularly exploitative when they feast on our cognitive vulnerabilities. We are putty in their hands. Consider, for instance, the 'mark down' ploy that many retailers use whenever they reset an artificially high 'original' price on a sales item. Customers are prone to be lured more by the percent discount figure than the 'bloated' sticker price of the goods.

Or consider this trick of the trade. You are dining with acquaintances in an upscale restaurant when the waiter hands you the wine list. You are not only penurious, you are illiterate when it comes to wine selection. To avoid embarrassment, you choose the second least expensive wine on the list. Savvy restaurant owners are only too familiar with such human fragilities. And so they raise the price of their 'second least expensive wine'. We are inundated by advertisements. Successful copywriters, besides being clever wordsmiths, are amateur psychologists as they prey on our base instincts and desires.

As for distortions in decision making, we are awash in cognitive biases. In their eye-popping experiments, the psychologists, Daniel Kahneman and Amos Twersky, could barely keep abreast of the numerous ways in which their subjects became jumbled when faced with decision making choices. One such illusion is the so-called 'anchoring effect' — the tendency to be influenced by the latest piece of information when making a choice between comparable items. The amount one is prepared to pay for a house or a new car is not infrequently primed by the sticker (or asking) price. Speaking of a 'priming effect' there is the tendency to make a decision influenced less by rationality than by a contrived set up of sorts. For example, donations for homeless shelters are more successful if the campaign is held in a makeshift tent situated in a depressed area than in an ornate ballroom. The advertising industry exploits these tendencies with clever images that sensitize the soul.

Which brings us to the emperor who, while fully clothed, wishes to bare his innermost thoughts.

The Fix: The Emperor's Dilemma

The emperor summoned his spiritualist. There in his private chambers, the emperor received Hakim, his trusted confidante and ersatz mind reader. Resplendent in his royal silk robes the emperor stood tall and austere. His hawk-like gaze held a brooding glint as he motioned Hakim to take a seat. There followed a prolonged silence while the emperor slowly paced back and forth. Hakim could feel something sinister afoot. The emperor then settled his bulky frame astride an ornate chair and stared at Hakim. Did the emperor suspect malfeasance on Hakim's part? But no, the emperor was seeking a confidentiality — a special hush-hush piece of advice he could not trust with any of his most loyal courtiers.

"I am troubled, Hakim," his voice boomed. "As you are well aware, my imperial duties oblige me to consult with my most dependable advisors on matters critical to the realm. These matters include such vital issues as international disputes, internecine intrigues, fiscal policies, selection of magistrates and declarations of war. I am fully aware that my counselors faithfully consult among themselves on these momentous issues before submitting their advice to me. As a consequence, they never fail to produce clear and insightful recommendations to help me in my decision making. I need not remind you that whatever they advise, it is my final word that must be obeyed."

The emperor paused and wrinkled his brow. "Now here is my dilemma, Hakim. Despite their expert opinions I always overrule them and choose an alternate path. I cannot help it. It is not because I am stubborn. It is certainly not out of spite. Nor do I have a sinister craving to assert my authority. In fact, I readily acknowledge the merit of their suggestions." The emperor suddenly stood up and with a helpless shrug of his shoulders exclaimed, "It is just an instinctual feeling I have. It seems to come from here." He pointed to his well-proportioned midriff. "Instead of here," he roared loudly as he pointed to his head. "It is one thing if my contrary decisions happen once or twice but these antagonistic pronouncements of mine occur all the time. I can only guess that my faithful counselors are beginning to question my sanity. Not that it matters."

The emperor was exasperated. He squinted at Hakim as if trying to read his mind. "Come, Hakim. If there is anyone who knows my inner secrets it is you. What do you make of this? Why would I ignore the advice from the best minds of the empire? Have I lost my sense of proportionality? Why these gut reactions? And most important, how can I be assured that when it comes to a crucial decision affecting the future of the empire my gut can be relied upon to make the right choice?"

Hakim sat panic-stricken. A shiver spiked though his body. His previous encounters with the emperor dealt with paltry matters such as prescribing tinctures for insomnia, herbal concoctions for constipation or simply serving as a sounding board for the emperor's diatribes. But suddenly he was asked to diagnose and possibly restore a proper alignment between rational thought and instinct.

"May I be so bold, sire," Hakim inquired with a shaky voice. "Has not all your pronouncements and final decrees met with success?"

The emperor looked at Hakim and snorted. "If I do say so, most outcomes are favorable. There are instances, however, when my judgement results in unpleasant circumstances which I am forced to set right. But that does not worry me. Who cares whether my decisions are of any consequence to my subordinates, or to the masses? Am I not considered infallible? Why should I care what my advisors think? Don't you see? My primary concern is this uncontrollable urge to render judgement by instinct as opposed to deliberate thought. It seems I have no desire to weigh alternatives. It is as if I have become intellectually lazy. Or worse, that I have sacrificed rational decision making to uncontrollable inner demons."

The emperor grabbed Hakim's shoulders in a taut grip. "Hakim, I rely on you to put my mind at ease. You must unburden me from this nightmare."

Hakim tried to exude a professional calm but, inwardly, he was quaking with fear. He was being asked to solve what appeared to be an impossible task. He felt utterly helpless. Indeed, fearful for his life. The emperor was notorious for his callous disregard for any subject who either challenged his authority or failed to follow his edicts. Depending on his mood, even the slightest act of disrespect had been met with grisly torture — a favorite being a toss into a vat of boiling oil. Hakim had to think fast.

"Sire, forgive me, but if most of your decisions bear positive results, does that not indicate you possess extraordinary skill in passing judgement regardless of wherefrom you think your decisions originate?"

The emperor shook his head and sighed. For the first time Hakim detected a rare streak of vulnerability in his master. The emperor leaned forward and spoke in a low conspiratorial tone. "Although the consequences of most of my decisions are of little import, I am afraid I have a confession to make. There is one decision I must make whose outcome is absolutely critical for the future of the empire. I cannot afford to be wrong on this one." The emperor paused to let this sink in.

"As you can imagine, Hakim, there are many suitors after my daughter's hand. Mariya is my only heir and, accordingly, she will succeed me as empress over our vast empire. Alas, she is shy, unattractive and weak. She has never been able to assert herself let alone capable of making any decisions no matter how mundane. And so, whoever she marries, will certainly be master of all."

With a frustrating gesture, the emperor swept his hand about the room. He then turned, fixed his gaze on Hakim and through clenched teeth said, "It is, therefore, vital that I make the right decision this time. I cannot help but feel that my choice of her betrothed will spring unthinking from my gut rather than from cold hard rational thought. Don't you see, Hakim? In this particular case I have to be certain. I have to choose the right husband for her. And so, I beseech you. You must do whatever is necessary to ensure that my brain is in control when the time comes to make that fateful choice. The future of our empire is at stake. You have one week to come up with a solution. I am counting on you." Before Hakim could respond, the emperor stood up and dismissed him. Trembling with fear Hakim barely made it out of the emperor's quarters on wobbly legs.

That night Hakim couldn't sleep. Tossing fitfully in his bed, he wracked his brain and tore at his hair. How could he possibly penetrate the very soul of the emperor? It was clearly a hopeless task. Imagine being asked to somehow bring clarity to a person's impulsivity. To miraculously recalibrate the emperor's decision making ability from reflexive blink to deliberate thought. Hakim could not conceive of any hypnotic potion, herbal brew or enchantment which could unravel the emperor's triggered judgements. Poor Hakim, he was doomed.

Suddenly it hit him. He sprang out of bed and raced around his room. Yes of course — the sorceress! What is her name? Hakim pounded his head with his fist. "Esmerelda!" he shouted. A reclusive enchantress, she is alleged to have cultivated an infamous herbarium containing numerous varieties of exotic plants. It is said that some of her herbs, when properly decocted, induce powerful hallucinatory auras. Rumor has it that one of her special potions can extract the truth from any duplicitous suspect. Hakim clapped his hands. I will see her first thing tomorrow. I must be discreet in my approach.

Following several inquiries, Hakim located the elusive crone in a remote mountainside. Esmerelda was not your typical witch. Although elderly and somewhat frail she was alert of mind and possessed an uncanny knowledge of each plant in her vast and diverse herbarium. She listened carefully as Hakim explained his need for a special potion that would ensure lucidity of thought, unblemished by external interference. He was careful not to divulge any sources. "In my capacity as the court's special prosecutor," Hakim lied. "I require a herbal concoction that guarantees critical judgement on matters of the utmost importance. I cannot afford to be swayed by false prejudices or unsubstantiated hunches. Moreover, this special brew of yours must open one's mind to the truth. I emphasize this most strongly — the truth, my good woman. For this I am prepared to pay you handsomely."

Esmerelda smiled and nodded. "Good sir, you need not be concerned. I have the perfect potion for you. Come, let me show you."

She led Hakim along a narrow dirt path. On either side were rows of variable sized shrubs, patches of low-lying herbs and fresh seedlings. A blend of pungent odors made Hakim feel he was walking on air. Esmerelda finally stopped before a small plot and pointed at a display of delicate green leafy sprigs peppered with succulent dark purple berries. She turned to Hakim and whispered. "Behold the genus *Solanum,* better known as the deadly nightshade. When ingested or inhaled it can induce a powerful reaction. But have no fear. I will show you how to prepare a decoction that will be safe and yet effective."

Hakim hesitated. "Tell me, my good woman. I have to be sure. Do you guarantee it will enhance a person's decision-making skills?"

"Well, sir, it will produce a pleasing aura that blocks out unwanted sensations. The feeling is so inspirational the person can do little but concentrate on their innermost thoughts. In so doing, the potion frees the mind of all negative emotions and pesky sentiments. Indeed, as you so desire, it will compel the subject to focus on the truth — devoid of nagging distractions. As a bonus, your subject need not be discomfited. You see, this magical herb induces all this in a state of euphoria. Besides," Esmerelda winked at Hakim, "if it is a woman to whom you are administering the potion, her pupils will dilate, making her suddenly appear beautiful — a *bella dona* — with wide expressive eyes."

Hakim could not afford to be ingenuous. His life depended on it. Neither could he afford to be distrustful. Perhaps it was the sensuous miasma of the surroundings that made him seal the agreement. He watched as Esmerelda mashed six berries into a pulp. She then ground both the root and a handful of leaves into a dry powder. She wrapped and stored the mixture in an airtight sachet of vine leaves. After handing the packet to Hakim, she instructed him on how to dissolve the dried extract in a solution of *spiritus* ammonia. Waggling a bony finger at Hakim she cautioned. "For best results and a more jolting effect, this dried mixture must be evaporated over a flame and then quickly inhaled. Be sure this is done in a darkened room."

Later that day, Hakim sent word to the emperor indicating that he had in his possession a powerful potion which would ensure a judgement driven by untainted logic. Hakim then waited for the summons. A week went by without a word from the palace. Hakim fretted. Had his message gone unheeded? Worse, had his message gone astray, misappropriated or intercepted? He sweated and wrung his hands as he waited impatiently for any sign from the emperor. He imagined himself the target of a conspiracy orchestrated by one or more courtiers, most of whom were embroiled in machinations of one sort or another. Another week passed without a word from his master. Hakim was beside himself. Finally, a third week had hardly elapsed when Hakim was beckoned to appear before the emperor.

It was midday and the emperor appeared restless. They spoke in hushed tones in a side chamber. The emperor informed Hakim that he was now prepared to render his most decisive judgement. Hakim stood shivering as the emperor strode around the room in a vexed state. He then turned to Hakim and indicated that no fewer than seven different suitors had made a formal request to marry the princess. "In my opinion they are a sniveling bunch of guttersnipes and opportunists," roared the emperor. "But I have to make a decision. My choice will be all the more difficult since my daughter has indicated no preferences one way or the other."

Curiously, the emperor showed no interest in the nature of the secret concoction. "I have faith in you, Hakim" he beamed proudly, laying a heavy hand on Hakim's shoulder. "Since I am anxious to get this out of the way we will meet in my private chambers tomorrow evening after sunset. There we will conduct the ritual. It should not escape you, my trusted friend, that this will be the most important decision of my life. And yours!" Hakim's knees almost buckled. He flashed a weak smile and bowed out.

The stage was set.

On the following evening, the fateful scene was surreal. There in the emperor's private quarters the light was dimmed. A pale moonlight filtered through narrow windows. In the center of the room stood a small circular table covered with an embroidered cloth. The furniture, baroque and sumptuous, could barely be seen in the shadows but their weight was felt. From ghostly portraits on the surrounding walls, pairs of eyes looked down accusingly on the proceedings.

The emperor and Hakim sat hunched over the table facing each other. No one spoke. Hakim placed a silver trivet at the center of the table. Upon this he lit a taper. He then gently lowered a small bowl over the flame and slowly filled it with a mixture of *spiritus* ammonia. The emperor remained silent, absorbed in the proceedings but never once questioning Hakim's moves. His eyes were fixed on Hakim who, in turn, did his best to control his nerves as he prepared the decoction. He opened the airtight packet and sprinkled the dry powder of nightshade into the heated solution. The emperor and Hakim now leaned over the bowl, their foreheads lightly touching. Within seconds, there arose a sweet pungent aroma which both the emperor and Hakim inhaled deeply. What happened next could only be described as ethereal.

Within seconds their hearts began beating loudly, their faces became flushed and an eerie sensation of euphoria enveloped them. The emperor was suddenly mesmerized with an uncanny focused attention. What was most intriguing, and here the reader will bear with me, was the extraordinary effect on the emperor's eyes. His pupils, like those of Hakim, had become so dilated he was able to peer into the vast inner sanctum of Hakim's skull where among the tangled neurons he read

Hakim's mind. Together, the all-powerful emperor and his lowly spiritualist found themselves locked in a state of mutual trans-illumination, seeing and absorbing the other's innermost thoughts and feelings.

The emperor suddenly gave a shout. "I have it!"

He leaped up from his chair and grabbed Hakim's hands in a fierce grip. There were tears in the emperor's eyes. Joyfully, he broke into a wide grin. "I have chosen my heir at last," he exclaimed as he embraced Hakim in a paternal bear hug. "Bless you my dear Hakim. Your magical potion enabled me to see the truth. I need not beat it out of anyone any more. Hakim, with my own eyes I have seen your true essence, your strength, decency, intelligence and total lack of guile. My heart is brimming with joy. I have never been more convinced about making the right decision. This time, at last, it originates from the deep recesses of my brain, not from my gut. I shall announce the betrothal to my counselors and then to my people. You have made me very happy." And with that he dismissed his heir apparent.

Hakim walked out of the emperor's chambers in a daze. He could only wonder at the sudden events that catapulted him into becoming the most powerful and richest man in the empire. All because a lowly herb helped bridge the gap between fast instinct and slow rational thought. He glanced down at the remaining bits of dried nightshade powder in his hand. He wondered. The emperor's daughter may not be attractive but with a whiff of this she can be a *bella donna*.

The Gap: Shame and Pride

"Humans are the only species on earth who blush — or need to." — Mark Twain

Notwithstanding its whimsy, this quote is a half-truth at best. More likely is the notion that shame and its inverse, pride, are traits acquired during the battle of selective dominance that characterizes the social order of most primates. Picture yourself astride the bars of a chimpanzee cage at the local zoo. Observing the antics on both sides are you not struck by similar displays of dominance and submission between the chimps and the human gawkers? As they peer at each other the simians exchange open mouthed grins with clenched teeth, downcast gazes, jutting jaws, averted faces, straightened shoulders, slouched posture, puffed and sunken chests. All while trying to outstare each other.

A keen observer, you notice a pecking order among the chimps, not too dissimilar from the makings of one among the *sapien* children. You think about it and perhaps come to realize that the effort to establish a position within the human pecking order determines whether an individual feels pride or shame — driven by a powerful urge to preserve one's self-image. And so, a price is paid for reaping the benefits of group interaction.

What is uniquely human is our denial that a pecking order exists. According to the psychologist, Glenn Weisfeld, we are the unwitting victims in a 'dominance hierarchy'. An individual's place in the queue accounts for his or her feelings of shame or pride. In any social order the outward appearance of peace and harmony is often a smokescreen. To maintain such apparent order there is an unwritten law of rank selection in which each individual does not infringe on the prerogatives of those above. One who wishes to jump the queue does so at one's peril.

Kicking and screaming, you are hauled into a game of musical chairs. Before a gallery of onlookers you are racing around a circle of empty chairs, hoping to secure a seat the instant the music stops. But one chair is missing. Round and round you run. Suddenly there is silence and a mad scramble for an available seat takes place. So eager are you to establish your rightful place — anything to avoid humiliation — you are prepared for a shoving match, a clash of backsides. But, you are the one left standing — exposed for all to see! Fortunately, under these arbitrary gaming rules, your mortification is short lived. Nevertheless, for that brief moment, there was a pang of exclusion — a raw empty feeling of shame.

The pull and push of shame and pride is said to begin early in life. The sandbox at the local park serves as a useful laboratory. There you may witness a fundamental motivation at play. One in which each child attempts to avoid feelings of inadequacy by declaring their own territory. Children need a sense of pride. Even the young feel shame as an instinctive response to public humiliation, bullying, rejection and segregation. To gain self-esteem and develop a sense of self-worth, a child seeks praise, approval and acceptance from adults. The tot in the sandbox suddenly turns to her adult guardian and, brandishing aloft a small pail half-filled with sand, shouts, "See what I have." Years later she may feel shame when as the butt of social exclusion she is taunted, bullied and constantly criticized. Or her shame may be expressed as anxiety in anticipation of being undermined.

Pride, on the other hand, is not infrequently manifested as aggressive behavior. You can see it play out in that very same sandbox. A toy is snatched. Sand is kicked in the direction of others. There is nothing subtle about the display of pride in toddlers. As the child matures into adulthood, pride is more subdued. It need not be manifested as aggressive behavior. He or she learns to disguise pride in acceptable behavior such as humility, feigned or not. In fact, according to the concept of reciprocal altruism, good deeds such as philanthropy serve as coveted rewards flaunted by dominant individuals. As one grows up, society's norms and prejudices dictate one's social position in the hierarchy.

There are different shades of shame and pride. For example, embarrassment is a temperate form of shame whereas self-hatred and humiliation are severe forms. You are relaxing on a nude beach where modesty is an extraneous factor — swept away by the gentle breeze. Your fellow sunbathers are engaged in a collective behavior, congratulating themselves on their right to be natural, free, naked, exposed and uninhibited. That is, as long as you remain within your enclave. However, you decide to get up and wander aimlessly along the beach. Deep in thought you inadvertently climb over a hillock and suddenly find yourself on a different section of the beach. One in which you are suddenly surrounded by naturally clad sunbathers. Who feels embarrassed? Is the uncontrollable reddened blush of your skin seen in all parts?

Speaking of how one is clad, it is intriguing how the fashion industry exploits this all too human trait. Whether it is catering to the orthodox fringes of religion wherein female garments, as guardians of modesty, are designed to leave little flesh exposed or, conversely, designing outfits that all but strip the female form of cover. No matter how widely divergent the fashion, the individual is miraculously spared from shame.

Does shame or pride have a purpose? Unlike guilt, shame enables one to cope with social threats within a group. Guilt, on the other hand, evokes a sentiment that contravenes one's moral standards. Shame and pride are human traits — each requiring a symbolic sense of self. Think of it this way. Shame is a self-conscious feeling projected in the eyes of others. Charles Horton Cooley, an early American sociologist, advanced this interesting concept:

The degree of personal insecurity you display in social situations is determined by what you believe other people think of you.

There is interplay between how we see ourselves and our sense of how others see us. In other words, our self-image is a projection from other people's eyes. Cooley describes this phenomenon as the 'Looking glass self'. How often have you made a spontaneous outburst in company and then kicked yourself later for not having phrased your remarks differently? Too late, the damage is irrevocable. You reproach yourself. Can you imagine the humility if you sought out each member of that company and said, "What I meant to say…" Either way, you feel shame as a result of what you think other people thought of you.

What is extraordinary about this reflective 'looking glass' is that its impact on our sense of shame or pride is determined by the presumption — not the evidence — of how others see us. In other words, many of us acquire our self-image based on a falsehood. As a result, we are likely to project this image outward, thus reinforcing the false impression others have of us. And so on… Amazingly, we have self-selected our own spot in the pecking order.

Is there a way out?

The Fix: Mirror, Mirror on the Wall

"Why so sad?" The two teenagers were sipping smoothies at a local juice bar. Sophie gazed with concern at her friend, Emma, who sat hunched over the table, eyes averted, shoulders slumped. The two rarely hid intimacies from each other.

Emma sighed. "Oh, Soph, I feel terrible. In just a few weeks I'll be moving to an entirely new neighborhood in an entirely new city. I'll be going to an entirely new high school where I know absolutely no one. I can't help feeling I'll be humiliated and looked down on as an outsider. They don't know me and so they will decide where I fit into their special pyramid. I'll be treated like a foreigner. It will be so shameful." Emma shivered. Her friend had never seen her look so forlorn.

"Emma, you are being silly." Sophie exclaimed. "Look at you. You are bright, attractive, friendly and so much fun. You have so many wonderful qualities not to mention a great personality. I'm sure you will fit in perfectly."

"You don't understand, Soph. Here I have a niche. And yet it took some time before I felt I was accepted. It wasn't easy. It didn't come naturally. Can't you see? In any new environment you can't decide where you want to fit in. It takes time and depends who you fall in with, who to trust and who will be your enemies. Just think. I could easily be looked down upon and assigned to a lower position in their social order. How do I present myself? I don't even know who they are, let alone their standards." Emma drooped further in her chair and appeared as if she were about to cry. Such was her anguish. Sophie could only shake her head and flash an encouraging smile. With nothing more to say the two finished their drinks in silence.

That night, instead of the customary text messages, Emma received a phone call from Sophie. Her friend's voice was animated. "Hey, Emma, I have the perfect solution for your problem. Listen to this. My sister, Louise, just happens to know a senior classmate at that new school of yours. They are forever sharing Facebook and Instagram messages. So here is our suggestion. We use the power of social media to introduce you. It will say you are a special person — popular, attractive and full of charisma. Just imagine. The text messages and your best photos will go viral. Like an upcoming attraction the news will spread quickly. In just a few weeks everyone at that school will have an advanced portrait of this wonderful person who is coming. Don't you see? By splattering your positive qualities all over Facebook, Instagram and Twitter you will be welcomed as a special someone they will want to know personally. You can even write your own bio and choose your best head shots. You don't need to feel shame any more. What do you say?"

At first, Emma felt a weight lifted. Sure, why not. With a properly embellished self-portrayal she need not fear suspicious whispers or sidelong glances. Why, she could even redefine herself. Blot out the smudges. Through the portals of social media, she would be gained a perfect entrée into her new milieu. "It sounds great," Emma purred into the phone. "Thanks, Soph. Let me think about the portrait and I'll get back to you."

Her sprits buoyed, Emma prepared to retire for the night. Humming to herself she sat at her makeshift boudoir and looked in her mirror. It was an odd oval shaped looking glass with a wood frame filigreed in pseudo-gold leaf. She recalled selecting it on a whim when attending an outdoor antiques' show a few months ago. She was taken with its ornate appearance and slightly tarnished sheen.

Emma stared. At first, she didn't recognize her reflection. "Is that me?" she winced. She looked closer. There was something unnerving about the pair of eyes glaring back at her. They appeared what? Accusatory! It was as if a voice behind the reflection was chanting, 'If you are worried about how others see you, how do you see yourself?' The eyes were not only reproachful they were emitting a powerful signal. 'You are the last person to author your own biopic.' Emma sat stunned. Was the mirror talking or had she herself come to realize she was not meant to be a mock icon for display. I will tell Sophie the plan is off.

Several days went by and, once again, Emma felt the unnerving dread of having to face a hostile peer group. It was getting close to that fateful moving day and she was feeling anxious and vulnerable. How should she present herself? Who was she? Why the shame? One Saturday morning she happened to be cooped up in her room. The enclosure was stifling. It only enhanced her vulnerability. She stole a peek at her mirror but it registered a non-judgmental stare. She put on a light jacket and decided to get some fresh air. She had no particular destination in mind and so she went outdoors and began walking aimlessly, deep in thought. Without realizing where she was going, she entered a park and took a stroll along an embankment.

The day was calm save for a light breeze. At first, there didn't seem to be anyone about. Emma sat on a bench and tried to relax. She even resisted the urge to thumb through her smartphone but her sense of shame overwhelmed her. Poor Emma. Mulling over her obsession she couldn't suppress her angst. Suddenly she turned and noticed a tall gangly youth. He was standing alone in an open area below, quietly but skillfully juggling four balls in the air. Four balls, not three! There he was, oblivious of his surroundings. With practiced ease, he expertly lofted the multicolored balls through a perfect sequence of arcs. A solitary figure, he was thin and loose jointed, seemingly unaware that he was being observed. Emma was transfixed. The colorful balls defied gravity as they floated weightlessly in the air, spinning and tumbling in a dream-like array.

Emma was incredulous. How was such a feat possible? She sat in awe of the performance, convinced she would be incapable of juggling three, let alone four balls. And yet, here was this awkward, spindly-looking lad executing what could only be described as an improbable stunt. Emma reflected. Well, he is human isn't he? I suppose if you blend the laws of motion, the restraints imposed by gravity, the deftness of hand-eye coordination, some basic biological principles governing manual dexterity and sheer single-mindedness, what appears impossible is actually do-able. Emma was reminded of the musical *A Chorus Line* which her parents took her to see several years ago. She never forgot that number when an equally lanky member of the dance ensemble stepped forward on the stage and reminisced on how he was motivated to dance. When he was but four years old, he watched his sister perform dance steps in preparation for her class. 'I can do that,' he shouted, whereupon, he abruptly spun around like a top and danced, or rather glided swiftly across the stage, combining tap, pirouette and grand jeté with remarkable agility. Emma mused on this as she stared at the juggler.

"I can do that."

Emma walked over to the youth. "Sorry to interrupt," she said as she approached. The young man stopped and gazed at her.

"Forgive me. My name is Emma," she smiled. "I was watching you from that bench up there. You really are good. I am curious. How long did it take you to juggle like that? With four balls no less."

The boy shrugged. He was about fifteen years old, graceless, shy and self-conscious. He had a thin bony face with a protuberant Adam's apple. His light brown hair was tousled and his pale freckled skin was spotted with pimples. He averted his eyes as he responded, "Oh, not too long, once you put your mind to it."

Emma detected a hint of pride beneath the shyness. She tried to put him at ease. "You know, I was thinking, anything that looks impossible to do can really be accomplished once you are determined to see it through. Do you believe that?"

"I guess so. I never thought about it like that."

"It must make you feel proud," she said. He shrugged and reddened slightly. Emma pressed on. "Forgive me again for prying but are there other extraordinary feats you are known for?"

The youth laughed, more like a honk. "I'm afraid not. I just had an urge to do this. That is all." He stood awkwardly, his angular body slightly tilted.

Emma smiled again, waved her hand and thanked him. As she walked away, she felt a strange rush of exhilaration. She couldn't put her finger on it but it bore the uncanny sensation of what can only be described as an epiphany. And yet, there it was — an unmistakable shudder of self-revelation. Just think she mused. One need not go through the effort of learning to juggle four balls. It is sufficient to believe that it is possible. By daring to overcome the effect of gravity, as in this case, anyone can overcome the presumptions of other people's opinions.

As soon as she returned home, Emma quickly went to her mirror. She needn't have been surprised. There, staring back at her was an expression of eerie beatitude. Her face glowed, her mouth pursed in a knowing smile and as for her eyes — they gleamed with an odd mix of self-understanding and assurance. 'You can do that!' it silently cheered. The affirmation spoke to her, 'It is enough that I am here to remind you of your capabilities, your sense of self-worth and pride'. Surely, she need not feel shame any more as long as those reflected eyes — her eyes — keep reminding her of her unlimited potential.

As she stared at her reflection, Emma wondered whether her mirror was possessed. Or worse, was it non-selective? Had it the same magical power on everyone? She needed confirmation. She quickly texted Sophie and asked her to come over. When Sophie arrived, Emma playfully sat her down before the mirror.

"What do you see, Soph?"

Sophie glanced at her reflection and murmured offhandedly "Nothing out of the ordinary. I suppose I could have my hair cut."

"Be serious, Soph. Look closely. Does your reflection tell you anything about yourself?"

Sophie glanced at Emma with a quizzical look. Thinking this was some kind of joke she decided to indulge her friend. Leaning close to the mirror and staring intently, Sophie shouted, "Oh my God!"

"What is it?" Emma felt a sinking feeling.

"I put on the wrong lipstick," Sophie giggled. She then swung around and looked at Emma. "What are you expecting me to see? Is something not right? Tell me."

Emma sighed. "It's nothing. I was just wondering if this old mirror was causing any image distortion. You see, my parents are deciding which furniture to take along and which to sell or give away. This old thing could very well be tossed in the trash heap except I have a sentimental attachment to it. That is all."

After Sophie left, Emma remained unconvinced. Was the special intimacy with her reflection a property captured only by this mirror? She quickly slipped into her parent's en suite bathroom and gazed at her reflection in their mirror. All that greeted her was an expressionless mask. Gone was the special glint in her eyes that spoke of poise and self-assurance. What a relief. Emma was now convinced her unique, slightly tarnished mirror bore a mystical imprint of her own consciousness. It not only evoked a magical transcendent bond, it unmasked a deeper conscience. Claiming a particular nostalgia for her mirror, Emma persuaded her parents to include it among the furniture to be delivered to their new home.

Moving day was chaotic. Three burly men with oversized biceps worked swiftly as they pounced upon, dragged, lifted and tossed items into their moving van. The entire changeover proceeded smoothly, or so it seemed. When all was done Emma found herself in her new home, a modest brick and limestone dwelling set in a leafy suburb of a university town. She cautiously entered her new bedroom and began rummaging through the unpacked parcels and crates on the floor. When she tore open the wrappings on her mirror, she emitted a sharp cry. A deep jagged crack was seen running diagonally through the glass from top to bottom.

With quavering hands, she propped the mirror against the wall and stared in horror. Instead of the crack distorting her reflection it revealed two distinct images, side by side. To the left of the fissure her image shone with an angelic affirmation of self-esteem and pride. The reflection on the right could only be described as accusatory — suffused with a mix of consternation, self-doubt and shame. Pride and shame — side by side. Which to believe? In a state of numbness, and without thinking, she reached for some loose opaque wrapping on the floor and quickly patched over the 'shameful' right side of the mirror. To her relief, the left-sided image continued to smile back at her with that effervescent glow of encouragement.

At that moment her mother entered the room and emitted a gasp when she saw the damaged mirror. "Oh dear, I'm so sorry, Emma," she cried and then quickly began sorting through the remaining unpacked items in search of further mayhem. "Please don't fret, Emma, we have insurance. We will replace that mirror of yours." Before Emma could object, her mother stalked out of the room.

At dinner that evening Emma remained in a funk. She sat shoulders drooped as she listlessly poked at her food. Her father tried to cheer her up by waxing philosophically about the loss or damage to mere inanimate objects.

"What is a mirror anyway?" he began. "I am reminded of a morality tale that goes something like this. There was once a very rich self-centered man who had amassed a considerable fortune, mostly at the expense of others. He had a habit of constantly looking at himself in his mirror. He was consumed with pathetic narcissism. Despite his considerable wealth he was miserable. Something was missing in his life and so he consulted a venerable sage. After listening to the rich man's frustrations and fears of being shunned by others the wise man said, 'My good man, your mirror is nothing but a reflection of your solitary self. In essence it is only a sheet of glass layered with polished silver. Remove the silver and you would be able to see through the looking glass and into the eyes of all those who wish to know you better. In other words, the silver, symbolizing your money, has forced you to look only at yourself. And so you see, Emma, mirrors have limited utility."

Emma scoffed. "But doesn't a mirror reflect the truth about you? It doesn't lie." Without waiting for a reply, she quickly got up and ran to her room.

That night, Emma was in ferment. True, tomorrow was to be her first day at her new school and there was the prospect of encountering hostile forces. But something else was making her restless, edgy. What was it? Tossing and churning in bed she was in proper angst. It wasn't only the disfigurement of her mirror. Something else was gnawing at her. She suddenly sat up and stared blankly through the dark. Why did her cracked mirror reveal two opposing personalities? More to the point, which one was projecting the truth?

She jumped out of bed, turned on the lights and propped the mirror against the wall. Gingerly, she removed the opaque patch from the right-sided frame. She gazed once again at both reflections. There on the right was the same puzzled self-conscious stare, tainted with a hint of indictment. She looked closely. There was indeed something accusatory, a warning perhaps. What was it trying to say? She gave a start. The image moved. Her lips were seen to part slightly, her eyebrows arched. Emma suddenly realized the image was imitating her own movements. She grimaced and stuck out her tongue. Her reflection followed suit.

She turned to the left-sided image and stared in disbelief. Grinning back at her was a fixed copy. It stubbornly expressed the same wondrous look of cheeriness, encouragement and adoration. But no matter how much Emma grimaced or contorted her facial expressions, the beneficent expression remained fixed. She then shut the lights in the room and, in pitch blackness, shone her smartphone's torch onto the mirror. All she saw on the right side of the crack was the reflected light beam. However, embedded in the left glass was a freeze frame of her self-satisfied smirk. There was no reflection of the light beam. Emma gave a whoop. She had patched the wrong half of the mirror!

Emma returned to bed and quickly slipped into an exotic yet exhilarating dream. Floating and weightless she felt herself carried aloft — somersaulting through a magnificent starry expanse of outer space. Buoyantly, she soared amidst dazzling moonbeams and bursts of solar flare. Through a chorus of clouds, she became enveloped by silent explosions of tiny nebulae. Light-headed and carefree, she scooped up fistfuls of angel dust as she whirled through an enchanted blue firmament. Suddenly, she turned her head and saw, hovering above her, the dancing spinning figure of the teenage juggler. He was also gliding ever so majestically through the misty stratosphere while juggling chromatic balls of celestial debris. As he drifted past, he flashed a radiant smile and tilted his head towards her beckoning her to join him.

Together they flipped, wheeled and swung weightlessly though a looping arc, tossing not three but four luminescent balls of shivering stars back and forth. They danced and juggled together through rapturous rays of sunbeams, impervious of gravitational forces. Despite the emptiness of space, they felt fullness in their hearts. Whirling side by side through the fathomless ether, Emma, a Peter Pan in glorious flight, and he, a soaring figure bestride a comet's tail.

When she awoke Emma felt purged of anguish and shame — a curious weightlessness. Her mirror confirmed her singular state of unabashed tranquility.

That afternoon, Emma's mother was busy preparing food in the kitchen when she heard the front door open.

"Is that you, Emma?"

"Yes, Mom."

"How was your first day at school?"

"It was great. I met some wonderful classmates. They all greeted me warmly."

"That's nice, dear."

The Gap: Justice and Mercy

The blindfolded lady of justice stands forthright. In her left hand she holds aloft a pair of balanced scales — a symbol of impartiality and fairness. She is immune to passion, prejudice or corruption. Not only sightless, she is deaf to pleas of mercy. Indeed, the double-edged sword in her right hand warns of swift uncompromising justice. Where, pray tell, is the symbol for leniency? The scales are equipoised, a signal that the laws governing our everyday behavior are anchored against any drift towards clemency. Any tipping by human forgiveness will, assuredly, inflict injustice on someone else.

Here lies a philosophical conundrum. If justice and mercy are equally acclaimed as meritorious virtues, why are they so often juxtaposed? After all, each is distinguished as positive attributes — fairness, equality and evenhandedness as components of justice versus compassion, empathy and benevolence as attributes of mercy. These are not adverse traits. And yet, as is so often the case, our brains (and hearts) struggle to find common ground when passing judgement on transgressions — intentional or otherwise.

There is this presumption. Any society which administers its laws fairly, incorruptibly and without compromise is often considered more just and harmonious than one that bends its rules in favor of judicial leniency. When a criminal shows remorse and asks for mercy, is it not a request for justice to be denied to some other? On the whole, people expect justice to prevail in every dispute. Fairness implies that perpetrators get exactly what they deserve — no more, no less. In other words, justice ought to ensure strict adherence to established laws so that no one is accorded an advantage at the expense of another's loss.

And yet our tolerance for bending certain laws has matured over time. For instance, our former adherence to laws against homosexuality or possession of marijuana has softened, come undone through painstaking enlightenment. The best we can hope for is a judicial system that evolves *pari passu* with our slow agonising growth as an open-minded species. An unbendable law can become a straitjacket. Surely, there is room for compassion and clemency.

One example of the ever-changing views on what constitutes fairness in the judicial system is the emergence of truth and reconciliation commissions. These collective mea culpas are attempts, by nations or large groups of people, to acknowledge and, hopefully, bring closure to past judicial failures, albeit after the fact. Forgiveness, a key tenet of Christian theology, reaches into the soft underbelly of our otherwise hard-edged nature. The problem with pardons, reconciliations and post hoc clemencies is their deferred or overdue application. On the other hand, can you imagine a setting where absolution is granted in anticipation of a collective wrong yet to be perpetrated? We seem to be forever catching up. In most democratic jurisdictions, a Charter of Rights and Freedoms is a late addition (an afterthought) to that nation's judicial statutes. The sad reality is this. Our collective remorse over past injustices is a learned behavior — not bred in our bones.

Historically, the effort to balance justice and mercy was never static. It advanced in fits and starts over many years. In contradistinction to cosmic (or celestial) adjudications, justice on earth is devised by humans and, accordingly, is inconsistent and contradictory. Take the case of the United States Supreme Court — the ultimate arbiter of that nation's laws. Despite being guided by such watchtowers as the constitution, legal precedence and a wealth of learned decisions, the appointed justices are human. Each member is a prey to ingrained socio-political biases. They cannot help themselves. Witness the frequency with which so many Supreme Court rulings are decided by a predictable vote — be it five to four or whatever the political tilt is at the time. Justice and mercy are human contrivances, quirks of our selective preconceptions and partialities.

Does religion offer an answer to this knotty divide?

In most universal belief systems there is promise of an afterlife wherein the good are rewarded and the wicked are punished in ways commensurate with their mortal deeds. But who decides? Notice how such ominous verdicts are taken out of human hands. However, when it comes to any reconciliation between justice and mercy on earth, the sacred texts offer nothing but contradictions. This does not deter theologians from splitting hairs when justifying God's resolution of this thorny dilemma. A case in point is the Old Testament Book of Jonah.

Here, an infallible supreme being is seen to reverse judgement on the heathens of Nineveh. As a result, poor Jonah, believing in the consistency of God's notion of justice and mercy, becomes the victim of God's wrath — not once but twice. The book opens with Jonah repudiating God's command for him to go and proclaim to the pagan citizenry of Nineveh the imminent destruction of their city. A justice so harsh compels Jonah to flee on a ship heading in the opposite direction. God is not amused. He unleashes a tempest that eventually forces the ship's crew to toss Jonah overboard. Through God's good grace Jonah is saved from drowning by being swallowed by a giant fish. There, in the belly of the fish, Jonah swears his allegiance to God and so agrees to pursue the mission to Nineveh. But a curious incident takes place and it is here that theological interpretations clash.

In accordance with God's original proclamation, we find Jonah lying in the hot sun outside the walls of the city. Awaiting its demise? For it is presumed that Jonah would never question God's form of justice.

Neither would he doubt any inconsistency in God's original intent. But God has changed his mind!

...and God repented of the evil, that he had said he would do unto them; and he did not.

The sacred text clearly states that Jonah, is displeased. Why? Some, if not most, biblical scholars argue that Jonah is disappointed that an adversarial enemy of Israel is not vanquished — as God intended. Then why did Jonah refuse to carry out his mission in the first place? One inference from the text has Jonah firmly convinced of God's resolute stance on justice and mercy. Hence, a plausible interpretation for Jonah's displeasure is his realisation that even almighty God cannot make up his mind — particularly when deliberating between justice and mercy.

Perhaps Aristotle had the answer.

In his classic treatise, *Nicomachean Ethics*, Aristotle advanced the concept of the 'golden mean' based on his abstraction of virtues. According to his theory, a virtue is defined not by what it is but what it cannot attain. That is to say, a virtue is any human trait that occupies an intermediate position, or golden mean, between two opposing vices. The vices are absolutes. The virtues are malleable. For instance, courage lies somewhere on a continuum between cowardice and recklessness. A composed temperament lies between anger and indifference. To be virtuous is to be constrained against both excesses and deficiencies.

Think of it as composure, balance, harmony and/or equilibrium. It is the 'Aequinimitas' of Sir William Osler, the famous physician-teacher, who exhorted his medical students to drape themselves in the cloak of imperturbability. It is Daedalus warning his son Icarus not to fly too high or too low as they escaped from the tower — wings akimbo. It is the Delphic Oracle advocating a neutral course in political and military matters.

But how does one perceive a mean between the virtues of justice and mercy? You are either culpable or not. Aha, but according to Aristotle, the mean need not be fixed. And herein may be a resolution to the justice-mercy conundrum. Historically, the golden mean between justice and mercy has shifted over time. Our forebears, more often than not, adhered to an uncompromising application of justice at the expense of mercy while our current generation seems willing to tolerate a more conciliatory interpretation of its laws. In general, we seem to be more flexible with justice's strict codes now compared to a century ago.

From a legal perspective, one of those conciliatory challenges to judicial decisions is determining the state of mind of the defendant at the time of the crime — the so-called 'insanity defense'. Here, mercy is granted some leeway despite the difficulty in assessing psychological motivations at a distance in time. The onus is on the prosecution to prove that a defendant not only committed a lawless act but had intent at the time of the crime.

Ah yes, intent!

In Albert Camus' existential novel *L'Étranger*, the defendant, Meursault, is accused of willfully shooting an Arab on a beach in Algiers. Was it an act of indifference triggered by no other precipitant than the glare and heat of the sun? To the prosecuting attorney it was a deliberate act perpetrated by a callous criminal who couldn't even shed a tear at his mother's funeral. In other words, the ultimate verdict was based on nothing more than the exploit of a perverted soul.

So, here is a question. To reconcile justice and mercy how does one allocate blameworthiness on a suspect who commits a grievous offense, not from malice aforethought, but out of sheer detachment?

The Fix: The Retrial of Meursault

The view over the parapet takes in the blue sheen of the Bay of Algiers. The modest *pension* is perched on a sandy embankment overlooking a long snake-like stretch of beach. On the terrace sit two figures sharing a late morning *petit déjeuner*. Monsieur Julian, a French forensic psychologist from Toulon, stares eastward, shading his eyes from the glaring sun.

"I believe it could very well have occurred on that beach there." He waves his hand in the direction of the shoreline.

His host, Kamel Djaballah, a local magistrate, grunts and shakes his head. "I suppose so. Although I doubt Camus cared one way or another for geographical precision. After all, it was a work of fiction. Mind you, that beach scene did play into Camus' peculiar brand of existential cant."

Kamel studies his guest closely. Despite the heat, the Frenchman is wearing a dark blazer, a white shirt with starched collar and grey ankle length trousers. His slick black hair is brushed back off his temple. His facial expression is pinched and brooding. As for his eyes they appear fish-like, hidden behind thick glasses. The Frenchman keeps glancing down at a bulky satchel nestled by his feet, nervously nudging it as if to ensure it is there. Kamel's willingness to meet with his guest was aroused by the fact that M Julian, a forensic neuroscientist, claims to have a new slant on the circumstances of Meursault's murder trial as described in Albert Camus' novel, *L'Étranger* (The Outsider).

"On the face of it the story is simple and straightforward," Kamel remarks. "Meursault is an ordinary man whose outlook on life happens to be that of a spectator — a voyeur if you will. He is detached, impassive, apathetic and occasionally amused by the absurdity of life around him. I recall that in the opening pages of the novel, Meursault's mother has just died, and while he attends the funeral he feels neither grief nor remorse. Likewise, his relationship with his girlfriend, Marie, is one of sensual pleasure without a trace of affection despite his willingness to marry her. He readily succumbs to whatever life offers him and wherever it takes him. He is portrayed as a bystander, one who stands above the fray — a victim of happenstance. He is perfectly content to be distracted or even involved by whatever amuses him or catches his attention at the moment. As a consequence, he is easily drawn into perverse schemes including those of his neighbor, Raymond, a gangster and a pimp who happens to beat his kept women."

M Julian nods his head, encouraging Kamel to continue.

"One day, Meursault finds himself a guest at a beach house of one of Raymond's friends. When out on the beach one morning there is a brief altercation between Raymond and some Arabs, one of whom happens to be the brother of Raymond's current prostitute. Nothing comes of it. Later that day, in the sweltering heat, Meursault takes a leisurely stroll along the beach. He is alone. He suddenly comes across Raymond's Arab who is reclining in the shade of a boulder on a bare stretch of sand. The Arab is holding a knife, the glint of which sends a sharp flash to Meursault's eyes. The sun is blazing hot. Meursault just happens to have Raymond's revolver with him. He stops, aims the gun and shoots the Arab five times."

Kamel pauses and stares at his guest as if expecting a response. M Julian says nothing but again nods to his host to continue. "The second half of the novel is taken up with the trial. One in which Meursault is ultimately sentenced to death, not so much for the crime as for his irrepressible insensitivity. Much is made of his lack of emotion at his mother's funeral, his indifference to God and his failure to show any remorse for his crime."

Kamel sits back and slowly shakes his head. "As a magistrate I hold to the belief that a civilized society can only exist when its citizens are accountable for their actions. Granted, Meursault was judged less by the commission of the murder than by his exasperating apathy. But he did take a life and regardless of his motive he had to pay accordingly."

Kamel notices his guest flinching. He leans toward the Frenchman. "I am sure you are aware that this fictional work of Camus has been the subject of innumerable analyses by philosophers, literary critics, jurists and the like. It has been dissected, shredded, scrutinized and probed to death from every conceivable angle. Nothing has been left unexplored. And so, I ask you, my friend. What possible interest do you have in dredging it any further?"

M Julien hesitates. "I must confess I have no interest in the philosophical or metaphysical aspects of the story. Rather, I see it through a different lens. As a forensic psychologist I am not infrequently asked to ascertain the intent of the accused and/or the circumstances of a given crime at the time it occurred. Under considerable constraints I am obliged to render a professional opinion within a prescribed judicial framework. To judge the competence of someone to stand trial is one thing. To determine the state of mind at the time of the offense is nothing but a guessing game. Unless!"

M Julian taps his forehead and squints at Kamel. "As a neuroscientist I am intrigued by the challenge such a seemingly impossible task presents. Can one actually get inside the head of a defendant and recreate not only the scene of the crime but the thought processes, emotions and intent of the alleged perpetrator at a specific moment in time? Allow me to propose that such conditions are critical for justice and mercy to be truly reconciled. For instance, what if a person commits an unlawful act but the circumstances at the time — and only at that time — prevented that individual from appreciating the act as morally indefensible? Surely, there is room for clemency if one can recreate the scene of the crime and thus demonstrate the plausibility of mitigating circumstances."

Kamel stares at his guest in disbelief. "Are you suggesting I should absolve a criminal's heinous act based on a presumption of a forgivable lapse of ethical conduct? Don't get me wrong. When it comes to leniency the courts are not immune to so-called mitigating circumstances. For instance, our laws recognize severe mental illness as a permissible defense — especially if that illness is treatable. Psychosis, severe depression, mania or evidence of such organic disorders as brain tumors, injuries and strokes can modify the sentencing by recommending psychiatric treatment in a designated facility other than prison."

M Julian breaks in. "That may be so. But what about those individuals, like Meursault, whose approach to life is one of utter dispassion? Afflicted, if you will, with neither psychopathy nor personality disorder in so far as he understands the difference between right and wrong. Meursault is portrayed as a voyeur — a bystander as you say — whose reaction to everyday events is more reflexive than contemplative. And so, my question is this. To harmonize justice with mercy in this particular case how does one assign a proper sentence if Meursault's crime was neither intended nor defensive? Who is to say? Could it not have been sparked by nothing more than the physiologic effects of a scorching noon day sun? There was no premeditation. There was, I believe, an accessory to the act — an uncalled for acute neurophysiologic switch in his brain's circuitry. Alternatively, how does one judge an action derived from a quirky personality trait for which there is no effective treatment?"

The two men sit silent. Kamel glances towards the bay. He then heaves a sigh, looks at his guest and says, "Granted, you pose an intriguing question. I confess I am not a psychologist. I am simply obliged to deal with the facts as presented. It is difficult enough to read the mind of a defendant in real time. I don't see how a court can ever acquire evidence of a defendant's mental state at the time of the offense. Can you?"

M Julian smiles for the first time. "Perhaps not. But may I prevail on your kind indulgence. Will you permit me to recreate the scene of the crime?"

Kamel stares at his guest. "I don't see how. Neither do I see what purpose it would achieve."

"Intent!" exclaims M Julian.

Kamel laughs. What an odd character he thinks. He half expects M Julian is conjuring a farce. But no, the Frenchman sits unperturbed. Kamel stops and scrutinizes his guest again. By God, he is deadly serious! Is the Frenchman on the level? What does he have up his sleeve? M Julian's expression remains unruffled. As for Kamel, curiosity wins over skepticism.

"My good friend," Kamel says. "As a magistrate I am receptive to all manner of evidence and disclosure in a criminal case. That is to say, as long as the evidence is not tainted by fanciful shenanigans or diversionary tactics. You have piqued my curiosity Monsieur. Where do we begin?"

M Julian flashes a wide grin and stands up. He hoists his satchel over his shoulder and motions for Kamel to follow him. Under a cloudless sky, the sun beats down unmercifully on the two figures as they walk silently along the beach. About two hundred yards out M Julian suddenly stops in front of a large boulder. He looks about and then reaches into his satchel. Kamel watches with interest as the Frenchman removes a large black headset. It is affixed with leather straps and blue-tinted box shaped goggles. The inner lining of the headgear is studded with numerous sensors.

M Julian explains to his puzzled host. "This is a specially designed virtual reality device. It can reproduce a scene from the past if generated from a simulative setting. Please bear with me. I will help you attach the headset. Once you have it secured you will find yourself in a three-dimensional milieu whose images will appear real to you. I should caution you that not only will your visual perception be enhanced but your auditory and tactile senses will be similarly engaged — a lifelike experience blended in with the day's environmental backdrop."

Kamel could only smile at the earnestness on M Julian's face. However, having come this far and unwilling to disappoint his guest, he feels obliged to participate in this preposterous charade. And so, as instructed, Kamel straps on the headset and stands facing in the direction of the boulder. No sooner is the image in focus when Kamel feels a shuddering sensation of profound giddiness. In the blazing heat he feels almost weightless. He is in a three-dimensional time zone. Slowly a figure emerges. An Arabic looking man is seen propped on one elbow and lying in the sand beside the large rock. He is holding a bright object. Kamel hears a voice from inside his head. It is his own voice which unnervingly is repeating a familiar passage.

I *feel the whole beach, pulsing with heat, pressing on my back. The heat is beginning to scorch my cheeks, beads of sweat are gathering in my eyebrows — in my forehead... all the veins seem to be bursting through my skin. I take a step forward. See now the figure drawing his knife and holding it up towards me, athwart the sunlight. A shaft of light shoots upward from the steel and I feel as if a long thin blade transfixes my forehead. Beneath a veil of brine and tears my eyes are blinded. I am conscious only of the cymbals of the sun clashing on my skull... Of the keen blade of light flashing up from the knife, scarring my eyelashes and gouging into my eyeballs. Everything is reeling before my eyes. I feel a fiery gust coming from the sea, while the sky cracks in two, from end to end, and a great sheet of flame pours down through the rift. I now feel every nerve in my body is a steel spring...*

Kamel reels. Flinging his hands in the air he spins around and, in a nauseous wave of vertigo, falls to the ground. Wrenching off the headset he glares at M Julian and shouts, "This is nothing but trickery! A monstrous deception, do you hear?"

"Please forgive me," M Julian exclaims as he reaches down to help Kamel. "I am so sorry, monsieur. You are right. There is no reality here. Please allow me to help you." He hooks an arm under the magistrate's waist but is shaken off. Kamel stands up giddily and tries to collect himself as he brushes sand from his trousers.

Still seething with anger, he scowls at M Julian. "Your device is nothing but a devious plaything. It will never substitute for reality. Indeed, it can never be admissible as evidence in a courtroom. Certainly not in my courtroom!"

"Please hear me out," M Julian pleads. "I simply wanted you to experience what drove Meursault to act so precipitously. To reproduce the conditions that overwhelmed him. Did you not see for yourself? There was no intent on his part. No malice aforethought."

But Kamel has already turned, and with deliberate strides, heads back to the *pension*. The Frenchman quickly bundles the headset into the satchel and hurries to catch up. His shirt collar is now wilted, his pale face damp with perspiration. From afar the scene is surreal. Played out against the backdrop of a shimmering tide, a blazing sun and a desultory stretch of beach, two figures are seen running awkwardly through the sand. One appears to be in pursuit of the other. M Julian's cries go unnoticed. "I am so sorry, monsieur. But I beseech you. Would you not agree that for just one instant, you experienced the sensation of a plausible mitigating defense?"

What with the heavy satchel, his sweat-drenched shirt and sand-clogged shoes, M Julian struggles to catch up. He shouts ahead, "Surely, as a magistrate, you may have occasion to judge a crime scene, if not through your mind's eye, then as fabricated by prosecutors, defense attorneys and witnesses. Are they not all distortions of false memories?"

Gasping heavily, M Julian finally catches up to Kamel on the terrace of the *pension*. He places the satchel on the floor and turns to his host who seems to have regained his composure. M Julian is wringing his hands in supplication. "Forgive me once again, sir. I beg of you. My purpose for that so-called travesty was honest and sincere. I simply wanted to recreate a scenario which helps narrow that formidable gap between justice and mercy. I ask you. If leniency can only be ascribed through the portals of mitigating circumstances, do you not agree that intent can only be construed by reproducing the circumstances at the time of the alleged misdeed?"

Kamel fixes his guest with a vindictive stare. "No. I emphatically do not agree. Look, I marvel at your efforts in attempting to reproduce a fictional crime scene in real time. But this sham won't convince anyone. I understand what you are trying to do. But it is futile. You should know, given your profession, any recommendation you advise the court must be delivered within the framework of the law. That meaningless exhibition of yours will not convince anyone, let alone be admissible as evidence. You have substituted a contrived re-enactment for reality and it won't work. Who knows? One can program that thing to do anything. Isn't that so?"

"Monsieur, you misunderstand. That was not my intention. I simply wanted to illustrate a critical time warp. One, if bridged properly, may reconcile justice and mercy. That is all. We stand in judgement of past events without reliving them. By failing to be at the scene of a given crime we are unable to know what goes on in the mind of an alleged perpetrator. The final judgement is a guessing game. Clemency is the single joker in a stacked deck. Why should a person's life be dependent on the luck of the draw? Besides, why should the sentence in the case of Meursault fit the person rather than the circumstances at the time of the crime?"

Just at this moment Kamel excuses himself as he slips away to answer a phone call. M Julian, meanwhile, turns and looks out at the sea. Lost in thought, he wonders if his attempt at fusing that breach in time between judgement of an event and its actual circumstances is nothing more than applied histrionics.

When Kamel returns he seems to have calmed down. Without offering a chair to his guest he says, "I am afraid I am called away to a meeting. But before I go let me say this. In a simplistic way there are only two sentencing options in a murder case once the guilt of the defendant has been established with certainty. One is a pure tit for tat — an eye for an eye if you will. No room for mercy, if for no other reason at least, the scales of justice are balanced. Equilibrium is restored, retribution is acknowledged and a life is forfeited for a life. The second option is to hear and respond to arguments of mitigating circumstances — an acknowledgement of clemency. Here, your preposterous charade may play a vital role — except for one thing." Kamel, with a glint in his eye, stares at his guest. "In Meursault's case it would have made no difference. You see, he was condemned for who he was, not for what he did. And so, my good friend, what you need is a device to unscramble the absurdity of life itself." With that, Kamel bows and bids the Frenchman adieu.

The Gap: Cognitive Dissonance and Rational Thought

If our survival as a species, hinges on our brain's unfaltering coherence, why are we afflicted with so many irrational thoughts and actions? Why do we suffer ourselves to think clearly? Are snap opinions the default mode? Distortions of reality seem effortless. Take the case of *post hoc ergo propter hoc* — a warped thinking process whereby a chance occurrence following an event is interpreted as a cause for that event. For example, the temporal relationship between a child's vaccination and a subsequent diagnosis of autism confirms, in some parents' minds, a causal link. Once they gain hold such thought processes are tenacious. Conspiracy theories, devoid of concrete evidence, can be contagious.

Beware the slippery slope. In this instance, an action or declaration is perceived to set in motion a series of catastrophic events despite little or no evidence of causality. To wit: 'If we allow one refugee into our country the flood gates will open and all our jobs will be taken.' How about the either/or fallacy? Here the illusion is to oversimplify a complex problem by reducing its solution to just two options. 'We either get rid of fossil fuels completely or the world will be destroyed.' Take the not uncommon thought distortion known as *ad hominum* or *ad populum*? Here is where someone attacks the character, background or patriotism of another individual rather than their line of argument? 'If he wasn't an atheist, I would support his choice of...'

The different ways we avoid the effort to think logically seem endless. We are often too hasty in our conclusions regarding the actions of others. Accordingly, we are too willing to pass judgement in the absence of clarity. This idleness of thought is fraught with unfortunate consequences, not least of which is the arousal of negative emotions such as anger, hopelessness, guilt and anxiety — a costly diversion of energy. Just think of it. Since energy can be neither consumed nor destroyed, we pay a price for failing to redirect cerebral energy towards thinking logically. We are given the gift of reason and yet so often fail to use it. One could go on ad infinitum, detailing the numerous instances our so-called rational prefrontal cortex is sidetracked by capricious thought processes. At last count there were no fewer than one hundred cognitive eccentricities associated with human activity. They range from the ambiguity effect (the tendency to avoid options for which missing information makes the probability seem unknown) to the zero risk bias (preference for reducing a small risk to zero over a greater reduction in a larger risk).

These distortions are not without consequences. Aberrant thought processes when unchallenged by evidence can unleash feelings of depression, anxiety, suspicion and paranoia. How a person feels can influence how they think. Witness the logical fallacy known as 'personalization'. Here is a tendency to bear one's own responsibility for events not under one's control — a self-perpetuating mea culpa. As for hidden prejudices, most of us are repositories of uncontrolled biases. If you think you are free of such predispositions don't ever take the psychologic test known as the IAT (implicit-association test). The test measures an individual's unconscious **association** with a target stimulus. It calls for a person's rapid evaluation (good, bad) of a series of images represented by concepts (black person, white person, fat, thin). You would cry foul if you learned your precipitous judgements are so disconnected from rational thought. And yet we are constantly exposed to masses of unfiltered information without an effective fact checking means to sift out the detritus.

Who better to take advantage of our hidden prejudices than political demagogues whose slick oratory feeds on our subconscious preconceptions? Democracy is no more than a concept, shakily at the mercy of an alpha leader. Granted, it is strengthened by icons such as an independent judiciary, an entrenched constitution, a charter of human rights and a free press. But it is still a concept in need of repeated bolstering.

As such, it requires continual mental focusing and unfettered rational thinking to sustain it. It is not always clear why populist, nativist and ethnocentric rant persuade so effortlessly. Even in good times the average citizen can be easily convinced of victimhood. Who can explain the psychological factors that seem to subvert democratic values? Surely, the problem lies with the 'other'. Consider the psychologic fallacy known as the availability cascade. This is a not uncommon aberration wherein a false belief is reinforced through repetition. Preach a falsehood often and loud enough and it may yet take hold.

But among the most egregious of logical fallacies is cognitive dissonance! A uniquely human trait of harboring and even expressing opposing views concurrently. To put it bluntly, cognitive dissonance is the tendency to perjure oneself. Probing the minds of animals is a daunting task but it is highly doubtful that veterinarian psychologists have diagnosed cognitive dissonance among their most troubled patients. To create a creature with such a serious imperfection as cognitive dissonance is nothing short of blasphemy. It doesn't make sense.

Let's get rid of it.

The Fix: Oops!

It was the monocle dangling from his waistcoat that drew my attention. Aware of my stare, he smiled and introduced himself. Professor J Lewis Osberg, an odd intense fellow with puckish features, pale blue eyes and a curly mop of darkening gray hair. He stood six feet tall, lean and angular with a hinged posture. We had each been looking at prehistoric bone fragments displayed in a glassed-in Victorian cabinet. We seemed to be the sole visitors in this skylit vaulted room of Oxford's Museum of Natural History. Professor Osberg had a disarming, almost hypnotic personality. He exhibited what I can only describe as a subliminal excitability. I was struck by an uncanny resemblance to Charles Dodgson — aka Lewis Carroll — who, it so happened, was a not infrequent habitué of this very museum.

Our conversation began innocently enough. References made to the diversity of mammalian specimens on display. He said he was a retired professor of mathematics who dabbled in paleoanthropology and, with a wink, confessed to a fascination in bestiaries. "Where relics are in the mind of the beholder," he chuckled.

Including the dodo bird, I wondered silently.

He turned to me as if reading my thoughts. "The time has come to speak of fascinating things," he whispered and motioned for me to follow him. I was Alice in his hands. We made our way to the rear of the museum, past the pathology wing, through a warren of tall stacks and out a foreshortened side door. A rabbit hole? We materialized (there is no other word for it) on South Walk in neighbouring University Parks without having passed through any of the standard entrances. He led me to a bench where we sat undisturbed save for muffled sounds from the cricket field and cries of distant children at play. I was half expecting him to launch into nonsense verse. Instead, he began a sober dissertation so engrossing I could not help but sit back and be captivated.

"Let us visualise ourselves on a voyage back through time." His voice was deep and sonorous, interrupted at times by a slight stammer. "A mission which enables us to contemplate how and whence we evolved as a species so exasperatingly distinct from our fellow creatures. This specialness, I am convinced, can hardly be explained by any breakthrough discovery from the fossil record — let alone biblical exegesis. The bony relics you and I have just been viewing are insufficiently illuminating to explain either our origins or our privileged status on this earth. Evolutionists are on the defensive these days. By adhering to the precarious theory of natural selection they are forever trying to score points in their fractious debate with proponents of Intelligent Design."

The good professor paused to wipe his eyes. "You see, my friend, the key question is not how *Homo sapiens* evolved as a branch of the simian tree but rather what extraordinary process, adaptive or otherwise, accounts for that distinction which sets us so far apart from other species. Does the fossil record help differentiate this sentient creature from other apes?" He paused for emphasis and leaned towards me. "Not likely. After all, we are the only hominid that survived! Imagine that. Can you think of any other genus of mammals with only a single species?"

I took this as a rhetorical question and simply shrugged. Professor Osberg smiled, shook his head and went on. "Conjectures based on fossilised bone fragments abound. Interspecies dissimilarities, no matter how subtle or finite, are for the most part quantitative. Take cranial capacity for example. Whether the trajectory of simian evolution was anagenic — that is to say linear through multiple mutations over time — or cladogenic, a branching process through adaptation, there is a clear record of an ever-enlarging brain vault. And I say so what!

"Does the size of our skulls really offer any clues? Think of it. One can trace this volumetric increase all the way from our earliest known ancestor *Ardipethicus ramidus,* aka *'Ardi'* who lived over four million years ago with a tiny brain weighing no more than 300 cc.

Would cousin Lucy of the *Austraopithecus* species have been smarter with a brain size of 450 cc? The hominid skull capacity continued to increase all the way to our most recent contemporaries, *Homo Neanderthalus,* who sported a cranial vault of 1150 cc or *Homo Heidelbergensus* at 1200 cc. And what, pray tell, is the average size of an adult male *Homo sapiens* brain?"

Without waiting for a reply, he shifted his gaze to the side of my head and exclaimed, "A mere 1350 cc! Hardly the critical distinction that sets us apart as God's chosen. And so, to account for our special place on this earth, little can be gained from desiccated bones or other unearthings. Oh sure, paleoanthropologists get their kicks when projecting these delicate bony fragments into crystal balls. For instance, there was a recent discovery of a small bone seen within a foot tendon in one of our hominid ancestors. It has been interpreted as a mutation, not found among any of the ape lineages. It is speculated that this newly acquired bone conferred the exceptional ability to walk upright. It is further postulated that this bipedal acquisition enabled our ancestors to forage for food in the open savannah. Natural selection then dictated how best to take advantage of hands now freed from grasping tree limbs. Here, suppositions run amok. With that newly acquired foot bone, an opposable thumb, flexible wrists, and smaller canine teeth, what was a poor defenseless creature to do with those idle hands?"

"Evolve an effective defence weapon?" I chimed in. Osberg frowned. I sensed he was about to shift gears and so I added, encouragingly, "So much for the fossil record?"

"I am afraid so. The trail ends here." He waved his hand in the direction of the museum although I sensed he was including the 'dreamy' spires of this heavy-lidded town. He looked out over the rolling grassland and flowerbeds that dotted the landscape. "The question remains unresolved. Or does it? Aristotle taught his inquisitive charge, the young Alexander, that every natural phenomenon has a cause. Or, as the Duchess said, 'Everything's got a moral, if you can find it'. He smiled and winked. Was he setting me up?

He rubbed his chin and then fingered his monocle briefly. He turned to me and, in a more serious vein, posed this question. "Tell me, my good friend. What do you believe are the unique traits that set humans so far apart from his fellow creatures?"

Caught off guard I shook my head and blurted, "I assume it is not that bony foot fragment. Seriously, I can only offer up the usual suspects: superior intelligence, a memory to reinforce knowledge, language as a more nuanced form of communication." I paused to gather my thoughts. "How about abstract thought, metaphorical reasoning, a sense of irony? All of the above?" I was groping. "I doubt the answer is forthcoming from either philosophy or science. As for literature, Jorge Luis Borges once said, 'Man lives in time, in succession, while the magical animal lives in the present, in the eternity of the instant'.

J Lewis laughed. "I regret to say that every attribute you cited has its counterpart, one way or the other, in many creatures. They are, to put it mildly, mere differences in scale. I agree that neither philosophy nor science, let alone literature, has provided a satisfactory answer. As for unvarnished faith, our religious leaders and proponents of 'intelligent design' are only too happy to step into the breach and attribute the special uniqueness of humans to the hand of a cosmic designer. If there was neither intent nor purpose, they argue, how else can one explain the evolution of so complex an entity as the human neocortex over such a narrow expanse of geological time? But — and here is the rub," Osberg's eyes flashed. "If there was intent and the human body was made whole it presupposes a perfect harmony — a creation that must of necessity be flawless. In other words, we, the chosen, must assuredly be either an anthropomorphic replica of our creator or prototypically unblemished. Otherwise, why go to the trouble of creating a flawed original?"

I dared not reply this time but waited as, eyes gleaming, he was about to pounce.

"My friend, it stands to reason that those who fiercely support the notion of purposeful design must accept the uncomfortable fact, notwithstanding original sin, that serious design flaws were made on the celestial drawing board. And in abundance! Let me choose one that unquestionably distinguishes man from his fellow creatures. I call it the 'Oops' factor!"

He widened his grin — like a Cheshire cat. I feared he might disappear through it. But no, he was serious. "If this singular, oh so human imperfection, evolved by way of natural selection — part of a quirky mutation that occurred at random, then we have no one to blame and we can hopefully await its antidote. And what is this flaw — this inimitable characteristic that is so painfully human?" Here, the good professor paused. His stammer had disappeared. With a riveting wide-eyed stare he said, softly, "I am referring to that uniquely human trait known as cognitive dissonance."

"Cognitive what?" I exclaimed somewhat loudly.

"Dissonance!" he whispered hoarsely, as if the very word was profane. "It is the uncomfortable sensation of having to lie to oneself." He sat back and grinned. "Whenever you or I happen to hold and defend opposing or incompatible views, we experience a disquieting sensation that begs for relief. Why should we feel uncomfortable? This psychological aberration occurs whenever, in an attempt to reduce the dissonance, we rationalise the discordance so as to preserve our self-esteem. There is nothing sub-conscious about this behaviour.

"Take the evangelical Christian who rails against sacrificing the life of the unborn while in the same breath supports the death penalty for capital crimes. In both instances there is a deliberate premeditated taking of a human life. Politicians and pamphleteers are notorious for espousing causes that run counter to their own beliefs. Corporate executives rationalize harmful products in the name of expediency. Many are those who still defend the decision to unleash the atomic bombs on Hiroshima and Nagasaki. 'Think of how many American lives were saved,' they argue, failing to acknowledge that no nation needs ever be accused of being the first to deploy this horrific weapon of mass destruction.

"On a personal note, how often have you purchased an overpriced item only to realise you had no need for it? You are upset. You feel you had been suckered. You resolve this uncomfortable sensation by rationalising the purchase so as to preserve your self-respect. You seek vindication. 'Why of course' you say to yourself. 'Come to think of it I could use the bloody thingamabob as a paperweight'. There are numerous examples. Each fraught with the justifications we invent to convince ourselves that the choices we make cannot afford to be wrong. In other words, we are compelled to alter our choices and viewpoints to maintain our self-esteem. I may be stuck with this malfunctioning car, cell phone, job, house etc. but I look upon it this way… and so on."

Professor Osberg stopped to dab his eyes again. He looked forlorn, as if grappling with an insurmountable puzzle. He said, "Find me any living creature that is afflicted with self-delusion. It is not the discordant views that trouble me so much as the uncomfortable sensations they invoke. We feel the dissonance as guilt, shame, frustration, embarrassment or anger. To overcome this unpleasantness we engage in self-deception, self-justification and self-rationalization. We are constantly fooling ourselves in an effort to maintain our sanity.

"In its most extreme form the pain of dissonance can lead to suicide. For instance, in times of warfare, people clinging to a losing ideology can become so fanatical in their devotion they would rather choose martyrdom than accept conversion. If this isn't a major design flaw then I do not know what is. It is bad enough to lie to others, but to lie to oneself is nothing if not sacrilegious. And yet we do it all the time."

Suddenly, he stopped and focused his gaze on some shrubbery nearby. He appeared to be distracted. He then swung around as if he saw a fleeting image out of the corner of his eye. I could see nothing amiss. He stared at me in a strange way and then continued where he left off.

"Self-justification to appease our jumbled thoughts may serve as an ego defense mechanism but how is it an evolutionary advantage? The irony is that our superior intelligence expends inordinate energy, effort and time rationalizing our discordant attitudes because we have lost any instinctual pathway to make the right decisions. We are never satisfied. We are prisoners of our own cognition — a constant battle to preserve our self-image in the light of competing thought processes. A serious design flaw, don't you think?"

"At the risk of feeling dissonant," I countered, "shouldn't I prefer the liberty of dispute and risk the suffering of dissonance then automatically agree with everything you say. Pity the poor sap whose beliefs are so hard wired that he or she is a victim of dogma. Given the choice, a free thinker could surely withstand the occasional rattling of so-called dissonance."

The professor smiled. "Ah yes, free will. The ability to make choices unimpeded. Were it truly free it presupposes that each so-called 'freely' made decision will be a correct one. But clearly this is not so. Hence, to guard against an imperfect outcome what do you do? You make excuses. And in so doing you feel that niggling sensation of disquiet and doubt. I grant you this. Freedom of choice, unlike the restrictive compulsions of dogma, offers hope insofar as it is endless in its quest to deliver life-sustaining benefits. But at what price?"

Osberg looked around again as if trying to spot an intruder. He then turned to me and said, "If we are to believe in intelligent design then we are obliged to acknowledge the 'Oops factor' — the blueprint flaw. Why would the grand designer go to all the trouble of perfecting the human brain with all its complexity and yet fail to untangle the wiring that perpetuates this wasteful defect? Was it to protect us from the dread of having to face our own exodus? Is it a defensive strategy to rationalise our wayward behaviour? Or, is it a self-deluding mechanism to expiate our sins? To create a creature with such a serious design flaw as cognitive dissonance is nothing short of blasphemy. And yet I myself am accursed with an uncompromising dissonance. You see, I believe there is no other salvation than to be reconciled to God."

Suddenly, Osberg pointed down the path to where it forked. "Did you see him?" he cried. I looked but saw nobody. Perhaps it was my imagination but I thought I caught a glimpse of a black tailcoat disappearing behind a hedge. We waited.

And then he sprung, or rather galumphed, landing a few feet before us.

A curious creature, he was short, lean and bouncy with a wide-grinned deeply lined face. He wore rimless glasses behind which were saucer-like eyes. He displayed a broad toothy smile and there in the corner of his mouth dangled a cigarette. His fingers, which he fluttered before our eyes, were stained with dark yellow and brown splotches. Wrapped around his midriff was a black cummerbund partly covered by a frock coat to which were stitched three outsized medallions. His greyish curly hair was half hidden by a rumpled top hat. I could almost swear I saw a price tag attached to it. He had the unnerving habit of hopping from one foot to the other.

He blew a perfect smoke ring, and in a high-pitched, yet cracked, throaty voice, he exclaimed,

"Forgive my intrusion, good sirs. I couldn't help overhearing your conversation." Turning to the professor he winked. "May I be so bold to ask whether you said what you meant or did you mean what you said?"

Osberg smiled, appearing to nod in recognition. "I suppose it was both. But, as you surmised, we are in a fog. Judging from your whimsy, are we to assume you have somehow come to terms with your chain smoking. Or are you here to unburden yourself of the many excuses to justify your vile habit? If so, pray tell us. Is there a resolution to the curse of cognitive dissonance?"

The weird hatter spun around a full circle, alighted nimbly on one foot and faced us with an even broader grin. "There is indeed a resolution. But first, allow me to pose this riddle. Can either of you name a substance that — are you ready for this? — improves cognition, potentiates relaxation, accelerates cerebral reaction time, reduces the effect of disturbing stimuli, improves information processing, reduces aggressive behaviour, increases the pain threshold and suppresses weight gain?"

He advanced one step and croaked, "And yet it is neither a euphoriant nor a psychotoxic agent."

Before either of us could respond he shouted gleefully, "Nicotine!"

He spun around again and then shouted, "Aha, fooled you. But bear with me as I explain why the chronic smoker is obliged to make excuses, as I just did, when defending this revolting habit. It turns out that most addictive substances, whether we imbibe, snort, shoot up or ingest, exist naturally, in one form or another, in our bodies. Endorphins, for example, are substances in the brain that serve as our natural pain relievers. They are opioids, chemically indistinguishable from those such as morphine and heroin. And yet they serve a similar function by suppressing the intensity of painful stimuli while at the same time giving us a jolt of good cheer when we need it. In other words, we would be in constant misery without them. Are you following me?" Without waiting a reply, he went on.

"Alcohol dehydrogenase is a natural enzyme in our guts that oxidises, or de-ferments ingested ethanol. Why should we have a specific enzyme for alcohol when most non-addictive drugs get a free pass through our intestinal lining only to be contained by a factory of enzymes in our liver?"

He gave a whoop and danced on his toes, never once allowing his cigarette stub to dislodge. He stopped, blew a puff of smoke and wrinkled his brow. "And then there is nicotine. A clever imposter, it sneaks into the gap between our neurons and substitutes for acetylcholine, one of the most ubiquitous neural transmitters in our body. Virtually every message that jumps a synapse from one nerve to another is mediated by this charlatan. Are you paying attention?"

Before either of us could respond he cocked his head and cupped his ears. "Think of it this way. As I puff away on my cigarette, my body says to the inhaled nicotine 'Hey, I know you. Welcome and thanks for the break. Since there is no need for double dosing, I'll just give my own overworked neurotransmitters a respite'. However," and here our dipsy-doodled friend threw up his arms and exclaimed, "at certain times the infernal weed, for one reason or another, may not be readily available. In which case one's natural neurotransmitter, now in deep slumber, is suddenly called upon. This wake-up call may come too late for the system to mount a comeback and all hell breaks loose. The result?"

We knew better to remain silent.

The merry hatter shot a glance at both of us and shouted, "Withdrawal symptoms! With all its painful manifestations — irritability, anxiety, sleep deprivation, inability to concentrate and feelings indistinguishable from the common flu. And to compensate for these nasty symptoms, the average smoker invents a host of excuses. For example, he or she chooses to deflect the argument by citing the miniscule risks of smoking when compared to other hazards such as booze, obesity, traffic accidents, environmental pollutants and natural disasters."

He clapped his hands. "But not me! Why? Because the so-called dissonance of which you speak is nothing more than the feeling an addict has when craving for relief." He gave a high cackle and spun around once more.

Professor Osberg, who I gathered was not unfamiliar with oddball creatures, emitted an exasperating sigh. "And how, may I ask, does your explanation help to resolve the discordance between opposing beliefs?"

Our excitable intruder broadened his grin, puffed on his cigarette and again blew a smoke ring. "It is simple. Think of dissonance as a craving. Think of a hard held belief as an addiction — a biological dependence if you will. There is no dissonance as long as the belief is not challenged. The truth lies dormant just like our natural neurotransmitter. Whenever that belief is challenged by a rational explanation you are faced with the possibility of a withdrawal reaction or dissonance."

He gave another whoop and hopped around our bench. As he settled in front of us once again, he cried, "Et voila! The solution follows logically. Don't you see? For every addictive substance there is its antidote — if you can find it. Alternatively, to eliminate the dissonance all you have to do is wean yourself off the addiction." With that he clapped his hands twice and disappeared into thin air.

We sat silent for a long time. Neither of us, it seemed, were prepared to grant credence to what we had just witnessed. I stole a glance at Osberg and noticed he was smiling. He then applied his monocle to his right eye. He squinted at me, fish-eyed.

"You see this looking glass I have in my eye? It functions as a two-way lens. I can see through it and enjoy the sensory delights of these bucolic surroundings. Or I can have it reflect back inside my cranium where, like a peeping Tom, I observe a kaleidoscopic display of neural activity that epitomises my thoughts, my imagination and my confusions — a warped and fruitless mind searching expedition. I would much prefer, as Goethe urged, to look outward and trust to my senses rather than wonder if my non-existent soul is content or not."

A light breeze rustled through the leafy branches. As if on cue I marvelled at the myriad shades of green among the trees, shrubs and plants. I could make out the Scots pine and hawthorns along an adjoining walk. I took a deep breath and inhaled the fragrances of flowering honeysuckles and other scents unidentified. I suddenly was in thrall of this idyllic setting.

I then looked down the path and saw a gathering of school age children. They were staring at the professor — expectantly. As they approached, I had the distinct feeling it was I who was intruding. And so I rose and thanked my companion for the stimulating talk. I then excused myself and walked slowly towards Norham Gardens. When I looked back, I saw the children had settled themselves in a rudimentary semicircle around him. The professor wore a jubilant smile. He appeared to be in his element as he held forth before his captive charges.

I could barely make out his words but I am sure I heard,

...and then there are those clever creatures — the bandersnatch, the jubjub bird and... who among you could ever forget the slithy tove?

The Gap: Vengeance and Forgiveness

Are we hard-wired for cruelty? Our capability of inflicting harm on others is not a trait unique to humans. But vengeance, shy of personal endangerment, is surely inimitable to our species. What possible evolutionary gain can come from settling scores, be they feuds, vendettas or meaningless squabbles? It is difficult to imagine other creatures obsessed with rancor. George Santayana's oft quoted phrase, *Those who fail to remember the past are condemned to repeat it*, neglects to recognise those whose violent attacks on others often occur because they remember the past only too well. A case in point is the senseless ethnic cleansing committed during the Balkan conflict of the 1990s. Once the canopy of Yugoslavian nationalism was lifted, the old animosities between Roman Christian Croats, Eastern Orthodox Serbs and Bosnian Muslims seethed to the surface. The same can be said for so many other atrocities throughout the ages.

Despite no evidence of threat there is suspicion of the 'other'. Harboring xenophobic tendencies, many of us are blindsided — wary of the others' alien habits, cultural mores, bizarre customs or religious observances. It may once have had an evolutionary *raison d'être* but in today's shrinking globalism the 'us' versus 'them' mindset continues to feed on ethnocentricity, racism and bigotry. Of note, the cruelty which arises from such negative traits finds support in a collective conspiracy shared through a tribal sense of vengeance.

It is doubtful the survival of other living creatures is driven by a need to destroy another simply out of vindictiveness. And yet, among humans, the violent settlement of scores based on suspicion is commonplace. It is noteworthy that in civil wars we see the deadliest violence that just happens to be between humans who know each other best. Whether the vehemence manifests itself locally as in family disputes, in communities of mixed ethnicities or on a wider scale between and within nation states, vengeance is a powerful motivator. The film industry thrives on it.

Another feature of our aggressive nature is what may be referred to as lip-smacking, heart-pounding spectatorship. The vicarious delight in witnessing mayhem between one human combatant and another. Although not unique to our species in a strict sense, the contrived spectacle of humans pummeling each other in a staged display seems to excite our base instincts. We cringe when reminded of the barbarity of gladiatorial fighting in ancient Rome. How could they have been so bloodthirsty? Imagine cheering on some hapless swordsman as he fights to a bloody death. But in

Rome's Colosseum, death was understood to be the end-game, not a by-product of the sport.

Today, in our modern colosseums, gate receipts have increased with the increasing ferocity of body-to-body contact, a side show having little to do with the objective of the match. Take professional ice hockey. During a game on November 1 1959, Jacques Plante, the goalie for the Montreal Canadiens, suffered a blood spattered facial injury as a result of a flying puck. With singled-minded resolve he skated off the ice and returned moments later wearing a protective mask — a first in The National Hockey League. Until then, organized ice hockey was, more or less, a fast balletic game where bare headed players wearing unobtrusive padding, dazzled the spectators with speed, dipsy-doodling, finesse and the occasional sharp elbow or shoulder jab for good measure. In stark contrast, today's players are barely identifiable in their helmets, visors, masks and oversized padding. Spectators are now treated to bone crushing body checks, fisticuffs, and pileups in the corners. Some players are even recruited as 'enforcers' to ensure a steady diet of brawls and fisticuffs. Spare the cynic who dares suggest that in the case of ice hockey and professional football, the heavier the equipment worn the greater the license for concussive combat. Team owners foster these gladiatorial displays since it draws a crowd. This vicarious streak of bloodthirsty-ness is evident even among fans of staid major league baseball whenever a soporific crowd is suddenly aroused by a bench-clearing brawl.

The flip side of cruelty is compassion, a trait best defined as an emotional response to another's suffering — a genuine desire to help and/or forgive without expectation of reward. Here it can be argued that such displays derive from an evolutionary drive essential for survival. For instance, the capacity for compassion is most manifest among animals reliant on prolonged post gestational care. As a social species, humans survive within interdependent groups because we have evolved the ability to forgive, to cooperate with and care for those in need. As Darwin once postulated, sympathy is our strongest instinct.

From a physiologic perspective, it has been established that the parasympathetic (or vagus) nerve and the pituitary hormone, oxytocin, qualify as 'the better angels of our nature'. Informally known as the 'cuddle hormone', oxytocin is secreted into the bloodstream of the brain, where, among other functions, it enhances social interaction, nurturing and romantic love. Both vagal neural activity and oxytocin serve a vital role in calming us down. They give us that warm self-reinforcing sensation that all is right with the world. The phrase 'take a deep breath' may be construed as a literal instruction in so far as it helps stimulate vagal nerve activity.

Another phrase is the 'laying on of hands' — both a metaphorical and tactile reference to a calming influence. In one University of California Berkeley study, pairs of subjects, unknown and unseen to each other, were separated by a solid barrier. By simply touching one another through a hole in the barrier these 'blinded' strangers were able to transmute feelings of sympathy, gratitude and compassion. Compassion and forgiveness are assuredly hard-wired into our brains. But is it changing over time? Are humans, as a species, becoming less aggressive and more forgiving?

In 1879, Richard Maurice Bucke, a Canadian alienist (psychiatrist), wrote a two-hundred-page polemic entitled *Man's Moral Nature*. In a painstaking, albeit unscientific approach, Bucke claimed that humans were acquiring a sixth sense wherein the negative attributes of hate and fear were slowly but irrevocably tilting towards love and trust. He postulated that man's moral nature had advanced and matured since ancient times. He took great pains to support his thesis based on both phylogenic and ontogenetic sources. A quarter century later, Bucke published his magnum opus *Cosmic Consciousness*. In this rambling mystical work, he visualized human consciousness as an 'illumination', one that is somehow evolving. He defined this so-called illumination as a state of moral exaltation — an indescribable feeling of elevation, elation, and joyousness — a quickening of the moral sense that will inevitably control our base instincts. Alas, in 1902 he took these lofty thoughts to his grave, and so was spared from witnessing the man-made atrocities of two world wars and the detonation of the atomic bomb.

Nevertheless, Bucke's optimism of an evolving moral nature continues into the twenty-first century with the writings of eminent thinkers such as Steven Pinker, Professor of Psychology at Harvard University. The central thesis of Pinker's book, *Better Angels of our Nature*, proclaims that our era is less violent, less cruel and more peaceful than any previous period of human existence. The decline in violence, he writes, is seen at every level of human existence — the family, neighborhoods, among tribes and between nation states. When compared to people living in any previous century, Pinker contends that those living now are less likely to meet a violent death or suffer from violence or cruelty at the hands of others. He sees this change as part of the 'civilizing process', a term he borrowed from the sociologist Norbert Elias. Both attributed this process to the consolidation of state power and the spread of commerce rather than to a genetic glitch.

Throughout the Enlightenment of seventeenth and eighteenthcentury Europe, people were beginning to look askance at forms of violence which had previously been taken for granted. These included slavery, torture, despotism, dueling and extreme forms of punishment. Some still exist but by and large they are universally condemned. More voices are now raised against cruelty to animals. Pinker refers to these trends as the 'humanitarian revolution'. Our 'inner demons' and 'better angels' may be hard-wired but Pinker is careful to ascribe our more beneficent nature to material circumstances and cultural inputs. This avoids the problem of having to explain these incremental improvements on an evolutionary basis.

But let us pause for a moment and consider whether this waning in violence is truly happening. What may be occurring is unfettered advances in human ingenuity. Perhaps we have simply substituted less bloodthirsty ways of venting man's violent nature. For instance, our technical expertise has now erected a shroud to cover our gruesome displays of bloody mayhem. In other words, we are becoming less ferocious as we substitute death at a distance, for hand-to-hand combat. Are we evolving as a compassionate species when we exchange trench warfare for drones, missiles, rockets and bombs ? What does it take to push a button of annihilation from a remote site?

It takes authority and obedience. In 1963, Stanley Milgram, a social psychologist at Yale University, conducted a study to determine to what extent an individual would go in obeying authority even if it meant harming another person. The set-up was intricate. A subject was assigned to be the 'teacher' who instructed a so-called 'learner' to recall a given word/pair from a prepared list. The learner, strapped with electrodes on bare skin, sat in a chair. The teacher was instructed to administer an electric shock every time the learner made a mistake when recalling a word/pair. It so happened, unbeknownst to the volunteer 'teacher', the 'learner' was a foil — a member of the investigating team, a good actor who deliberately made mistakes and, of course, cried out in agony despite feeling no shock. Two-thirds of the so-called 'teachers', volunteers from all walks of life, continued to obey instructions to administer stepwise shocks up to the highest level of 450 volts despite agonizing screams from the so-called 'learner'. Needless to say, this controlled experiment, despite its flaws, captured the essence of that oft quoted reply, "...I was just following orders."

Another worrisome trend, characterized in Chapter 1, is the widening gap between the rapid pace of our ingenious technology and our ability to comprehend the consequences of its deployment. In the opening scenes of Stanley Kubrick's masterful film, *2001: A Space Odyssey*, a black monolith suddenly appears among a tribe of hominids. We watch as our ancient ancestors become mesmerized by this alien totem. Imbued by some magical transference emanating from the monolith, the hominids acquire both the notion and skill of weaponry as they pick up bones and proceed to attack members of an opposing tribe. Note that the 'message' of intelligence is not employed for domestic use of the bones but rather for aggression against others.

So many new discoveries, regardless of their original intent, have been weaponized. Drones, drugs, cyber technology, Artificial Intelligence, nanotechnology, space exploration, genetic engineering — the list is getting longer. As for atomic weaponry, deterrence as a principle is a shakier concept than preemption in a world where more and more nations acquire nuclear capabilities. The 'better angels of our nature' are barely keeping abreast.

The Fix: The Good is Oft Interred... with their Bones

Shakespeare's Julius Caesar Act III, Sc. II

My good friend, Lou Grobes, spins fanciful yarns, minced at times with kernels of truth. You never know. When I came upon him the other day he was sitting, or rather draped, on his favorite park bench. Squinting into the early morning sun he seemed lost in thought. As I approached, he brightened and beckoned me to sit beside him. Instead of the usual pleasantries, he abruptly posed this rather curious question.

"What do you think Shakespeare meant when he had Anthony declare at Caesar's funeral, *The evil that men do lives after them. The good is oft interred with their bones?*"

I knew better than to indulge his rhetoric so I simply shrugged and girded myself for a stirring narrative. Lou did not disappoint. He turned to me, smiled and began. "I once heard of a man afflicted with an uncompromising bounty of innate goodness. His beneficence, his compassion, his generosity were so uncontrollably chaste he was, to all intents and purposes, an amalgam of Jesus Christ and the Mahatma.

And yet he was neither pious nor spiritual. He was too self-effacing to harbor any transcendent ideology. Having eschewed all religious affiliation he regarded his agnosticism, less as heresy than an ironic blessing. What need did he have to atone for any of his actions when he had nothing to confess? Simply put, he was born reflexively virtuous, decent and just. Or so it seemed."

Lou looked at me and lowered his voice. "Forgive me for overstating his case but I do want you to get a full picture of this extraordinary freak of nature. You see, his very soul was purged of malice and so he was incapable of committing a sin, venal or mortal. For the sake of this story, let us call him Ben — after the Latin for goodness -*benevolentia*.

"Ben possessed a natural immunity to all seven cardinal sins. Take lust. Who among us can deny having lascivious thoughts from time to time? Yet Ben, quintessence of virtue, took his marriage vows in earnest — never once coveting his neighbor's wife, nor any other woman for that matter. He was parsimonious in his eating habits and impeccably well groomed. As for acquisition of material goods, he regarded them less as objects of self-indulgence than as means of subsistence. Neither greed nor usury tempted him. On the contrary, his philanthropy and generosity towards others were legendary. Rarely would he pass a panhandler in the street without dropping a coin or two into outstretched hands. If you were ever to barge in on him at his house, unannounced let us say, he would greet you with a disarmingly hospitable smile, express a genuine eagerness to see you and welcome you in. He was agonizingly polite without being ingratiating. As for guile, he had none."

Lou narrowed his eyes. "What is most startling is the fact that Ben appeared incapable of harboring opposing views on any subject. Simply put, there was no need for self-justification. His thoughts were pure and riven of complexity and doubt. Just think. When prodded by his co-workers to take sides on controversial issues he would politely feign ignorance or offer mediation. He couldn't conceive of being trapped into any entanglement which could result in self-deception."

"Are you kidding me?" I interrupted. "Surely there was an imperfection hidden somewhere. And why am I, like you, using the past tense?"

"There were no imperfections. He was an unflawed diamond," replied Lou. "And yes, this is a tragic tale. But let's not get ahead of ourselves. Allow me to begin by taking the measure of the man.

"Ben worked as a business analyst in a large corporation. He was neither tardy nor lax in his work. He never failed to earn an honest day's wage. He was happily married with two pre-teenage daughters. If you want a portrait try picturing him as that clean-shaven, clean-cut idyllic father figure stepping out of a 1950s TV family sitcom. No one ever saw Ben display anger. He was a veritable King Solomon when dealing with interpersonal disputes, erring more often on the side of mercy over justice. Incredible as it sounds, he never once evinced envy even when others achieved advantages at his expense. On the contrary, pride was externalized in so far as he never failed to praise the achievements of others — even if such actions encroached on his own advancement."

Lou paused and chuckled. "As for admissibility into Dante's circles of hell, our hero would be declared *persona non grata*. Save perhaps for the sixth circle." Lou winked at me with a crafty grin. "You remember the sixth, don't you? A spacious plain of flaming sepulchers full of sorrow and evil torment where dwelt the heretics. I suspect our hero would have also qualified for the first circle — a seething limbo for the unbaptized. But at least there he would be in the company of the great pagan poets. Yes indeed, high above Dante's nether regions, Ben would be accorded an Easy Pass through heaven's gate. No need to queue up and be questioned by a testy St Peter.

"But seriously," Lou recovered his composure, "Ben had to contend with life on earth. Here to suffer the abuses and exploitations of his fellow man. Needless to say, Ben's irrepressible goodness exposed itself like an open sore — vulnerable to all sorts of social contaminants. People took aim at his defenceless good nature. Numbered among his friends, relatives, neighbours and co-workers were the borrowers, the schnorrers, the ambitious and the avaricious. As you can imagine he was constantly besieged for handouts, favours, sacrifices and overblown recommendations. His beneficence was so predictable that perfect strangers came calling to share in the largesse. And yet, ironically, he was dubbed a social pariah — a bore whose angelic nature branded him as a wet blanket. And so, he was rarely invited or asked to join social gatherings. Ben's wife took this ostracism hard but in deference to her husband she kept silent.

"As the years went by Ben's irrepressible altruism slowly took its toll. He became painfully aware that others were gaining ground — professionally, socially and economically. He was caught in a vortex — spinning, yet unfulfilled. His compassion and generosity brought neither solace nor happiness. Eventually, he slipped into a chasm of despair. Although it was not in his nature to blame anyone in particular, he realized that his instinctual good nature was a serious impediment to a fruitful and meaningful life. His family became the unwitting foils for his beneficence. He had to do something. But what?"

Lou paused, allowing this stark portrait to sink in. I tried to conceive how someone with such supernatural magnanimity could be so entrapped. "Surely, there were options for him," I said.

Lou nodded. "At first, Ben tried to rationalize his predicament in quasi biblical terms. For instance, he anticipated some form of redemption for a blameless life. After all, is not the expectation of deliverance a fundamental underpinning of all self-abnegating beliefs? Think of the Book of Job, *Don Quixote* or *the Divine Comedy*? Is it not taught that retribution can be gained out of suffering the hardships of hell on Earth? Without a heavenly father figure, or crystal ball gazer to promise and console, Ben quickly dismissed this fiction as a self-delusional stratagem."

Lou's eyes suddenly widened as he held up his hand. "It was during a Christmas office party one year that a curious incident took place. One of Ben's co-workers, in a state of inebriated bluster, insulted Ben's wife within earshot of everyone. Ben quickly chose honor over civility and struck the man, knocking him to the floor. Although this violent act was alien to his nature, Ben experienced an unfamiliar glow of righteousness as he basked in the approving stares of his fellow workers. Surprisingly, Ben experienced neither guilt nor remorse. He asked himself whether such uncharacteristic spontaneity was an acceptable resolution to a conflict situation. He was already aware that whenever a real-life ethical dilemma demanded decisive action, he and only he, had the instinctual ability to choose the lesser of two evils.

"Think of it. Humans as obligate social animals are constantly interacting with each other. And yet, most confrontations, ethically speaking, are rarely defined in terms of absolute good versus evil but as varying tones of gray. In other words, given a conflict situation, Ben could intuitively differentiate between subtle shades of malevolence and act accordingly. What an epiphany! Surely this explains how his own deep-seated, bred-in-the-bone sense of goodness and fair play had no difficulty in choosing what action to take when he flattened the obnoxious lout? Was this a breakthrough he asked himself?

"Just imagine," Lou pursed his lips and gazed up at the sky. "If life is comprised of successive decision points perhaps he was blessed with a distinct advantage. Unfortunately, in his circumscribed world, spontaneous episodes of such blatant conflict rose infrequently. Moreover, it was clearly antithetical to his nature to contrive them at will. And so, in the fullness of time, with nary a conflict to display his corrective intervention, the esteem from his co-workers wore off and, once again, he was easy prey to their wants. Ben needed a different tact. He had to do something. His job was now threatened. Thanks to opportunistic philanthropies and like-minded scavengers his hard-earned savings were shrinking. Financially, he was being bled dry. What to do?"

Lou looked at me. I could sense from his demeanour that a calamity was about to unfold. Reading my thoughts, he nodded. "At first our hapless hero sought refuge in the teachings of the ethicists. He delved into philosophical texts desperately seeking workable formulas to complex questions of moral behavior. He rejected both the consequential ethics of Jeremy Bentham and the categorical ethics of Immanuel Kant for the simple reason that each proposed a rational basis for human behavior. Remember, Ben's actions were instinctual, not rational. And so could you guess who among all the philosophers did he seek guidance?"

I shook my head.

Lou cried "Why, none other than that inveterate madman, Friedrich Nietzsche. Who else offered such a cockamamie view of ethical behavior? Ben was inspired. Nietzsche professed that 'goodness', if acquired, is nothing if not self-defeating — a true sign of weakness. Conversely, innate goodness is genuine. By contrast Rousseau maintained that while man is born innocent, pure and unblemished by sin, he inevitably becomes contaminated by the temptations inherent in societal interactions.

"Ben was reassured by Nietzsche's reference to the *non-egotistical instincts of compassion, self-denial and self-sacrifice.* However, on reading further, Ben became confused, disillusioned and befuddled. The so-called 'good' man, according to Nietzsche is nothing but retrogression — a flaw or danger insofar as he advocates from a position of helplessness. Moreover, Nietzsche recognised inherent goodness as possessed only by those of nobility. He argued that goodness is an historical necessity, *embracing nobility of mind and spiritual distinction.* As for the common folk, Nietzsche, in fact, abhorred altruism as a moral value. He slammed the door shut for Ben when he claimed altruism leads to a bad conscience and is therefore unredeemable by any act of atonement.

"But Ben did not possess a bad conscience. Neither did he ever exhibit rancor — that most perilous of vices. Ben could not visualize himself strutting about as a self-fortified hermit oblivious of others in need. Ironically, the primary source of Ben's exploration of Nietzsche's writings was *The Geneology of Morals*, a book written in 1887 when Nietzsche's brain was already steeped in lunacy.

"And so," Lou continued with a helpless shrug, "Ben derived neither comfort nor enlightenment from forays into the philosophy of ethics. Nietzsche was mad. Rousseau promoted the idea that man, while born timid and peaceful, grew up quarrelsome and ill tempered. The more Ben's brain struggled with all this humbug the more dispirited he became. Who had the audacity to construct value judgements? Ben was left dazed and confused. As his situation grew more inconsolable so did his hunger for self-help talismans. He waded through countless testimonials of life affirming remedies. He found himself inundated by all manner of wondrous claims for a satisfied life. These ranged from TV snake-oil charmers to a plethora of articles extolling the virtues of one panacea after another. It was hopeless. Nothing clicked." Lou sat back and grinned. I sensed he had something up his sleeve but was now waiting for me to offer any suggestion.

Half-jokingly, I said, "Perhaps Ben should have declared himself a monastic. Why not head for the hills and sever all connections with human society?"

Lou dismissed this lame offer with a wave of his hand. "No, Ben wasn't ready to toss in the towel. Neither was he about to accept his fate."

Lou leaned towards me, his eyes narrowed. "And now the story takes a strange twist. One night, Ben had a disturbing dream. One in which he felt curiously possessed, as if afflicted with a mental disorder. He sat bolt upright in bed. His eyes lit up. 'Wait a minute,' he said to himself. 'Is it possible I have an organic defect? Is my instinctual goodness nothing more than a quirky pathologic lesion in my brain? And, if so, could it be treated?' He imagined further. 'Perhaps I have a rare neurological disorder that is reversible'. Considering his miserable state, he would settle for any remedy be it electroconvulsive shock treatment or mind-numbing drugs or — perish the thought — surgical excision. Think of it. If he was born hard-wired for beneficence, was it nothing more than a cerebral malfunction — a localized glitch possibly identifiable by modern imaging technology?

"He reached for his laptop. With hope and anticipation, he delved into the burgeoning fields of behavioral science and neurophysiology. His mind was in free flight. To his amazement, he discovered that certain behavioral activities can indeed be visualized electronically as flashing colors from distinct regions in the human brain. Thanks to the use of functional magnetic resonance imaging (fMRI), discrete and reproducible patterns of cerebral activity can be identified while subjects undergo provocative psychological testing. Just think. Isolated sites for selective emotions are chromatically highlighted during induced provocations. He learns, for example, that within the prefrontal cortex, sits the command-and-control center for cognitive influences on moral decision making. It shouts 'Here is where my moral center lurks. Come and get me!'

"Ben learned that our emotive or affective centers — comprised of the limbic system, amygdala and insula — are located deep within our mid-brain, remnants of our ancient instinctual nervous system. The prefrontal bulge that comprises our staid executive functions is a late acquisition of simian evolution. It performs an inhibitory brake on unfettered outbursts of emotional sensations.

"Ben was driven. For the first time he felt a breakthrough was imminent and so he dug deeper. He wondered whether man's moral nature is nothing more than a continual struggle between these dichotomous regions. He became obsessed with the notion that his innate goodness was no more than a brain lesion which could somehow be functionally and/or anatomically identified by modern day imaging modalities. Perhaps his 'goodness' or 'compassion' centers were abnormally developed — not unlike Einstein's expansive parietal lobe, the site of spatial and visual perspective. Could parts of Ben's brain be so disfigured? Was his head ahead of his time? He had to find out.

"In the meantime, his personal life was disintegrating. His wife had now left him, taking their daughters with her. His life savings were depleted. He was barely able to concentrate on his job. His only salvation lay in the discovery of a psycho-neurologic defect somehow amenable to treatment. He was desperate.

"Once again, he reached for his computer. He made contacts with several leading centers in cognitive and behavioral neurosciences. 'I'm a man trapped in a state of ineffable goodness,' he pleaded. 'Can you help me?' In his appeal, he carefully and meticulously described his predicament as a defenseless paragon of virtue uncontrollably driven to perform good deeds. He confessed to having lost all power of free will. By describing himself as a curiosity, a human guinea pig, he offered his suitability as a unique candidate for observation and testing. He would readily acquiesce to any experimental intervention. Sounds far-fetched?" Lou shot a glance at me.

"To a desperate man, I suppose it was worth a gamble," I said

Lou cocked his head and nodded. "Now, it so happens that requests such as Ben's were not unusual in those centers probing the inner workings of the mind.

Most unsolicited offers were dismissed as crackpot attempts to have a high-tech machine 'read my mind-please!' Conversely, many centers were experiencing difficulty in recruiting study volunteers, thanks to a widespread wariness of personal infringement. And so, weeks passed without so much as a terse reply. Our hero became a nervous wreck."

Lou paused and shut his eyes. I couldn't tell if this signaled the end of the story or if I was to be privy to a therapeutic enlightenment. Lou glanced at me as if reading my thoughts. He smiled and went on.

"Finally, one day Ben received a brief letter from an acclaimed center of cognitive neuropsychology. It read:

You have piqued our curiosity. We do not know if we can be of any help. However, would you be interested in participating in an experimental protocol?

"It was clear the investigators were fascinated with Ben's unusual condition. And while they could promise neither a definitive diagnosis nor specific cure, they probably considered Ben a useful outlier for their registry. What was there to lose? Ben promptly accepted with a mixture of alacrity and guarded hope.

"At the center's research clinic, Ben was subjected to extensive pre-test scrutiny including a detailed history, physical examination and routine blood tests. He then sweated through a battery of psychological tests which did not fail to raise eyebrows among the investigators. Finally, he underwent functional MRI imaging with and without provocative stimuli. After all tests were completed, Ben was told to return home and await the results.

"Two agonizing weeks went by without a word. Anxious and distraught, Ben could be seen walking about in a daze — hopeful and despondent at the same time. Acquaintances and co-workers kept their distance. Ben wondered. Did this mean the investigators found nothing out of the ordinary and had simply forgotten him?"

Lou sat back and was silent for a moment, as if collecting his thoughts. He then turned to me and in a grave voice continued.

"At last, on a brisk gray winter morning Ben received an urgent call to come and meet with the neuropsychiatrist who was head of the investigative team. With a strange mix of fear and hopefulness Ben set out for the research facility. The tension in the room was uncomfortably solemn as Ben sat facing the scientist.

"And then the bombshell!"

Lou raised his hands in dramatic fashion and clasped them together in a reverential pose. "Ben was told, in hushed tones, that the fMRI images revealed neither overexpansion of his cognitive centers nor heightened activity in any zones of positive emotions. If there was a so-called compassion locus it failed to light up. And then, to Ben's utter dismay and shock, he learned that what did light up was an unequivocal buzz of activity in a pinpoint region of his prefrontal cortex. Specifically, this signal was situated within that zone responsible for *inhibiting* negative emotions. In short, that vivid pulsatile glow represented a continuous effort to suppress and inhibit an abnormally overactive locus deep within his limbic system.

"Ben was confused. 'What is that locus?' he asked.

The neuro-psychiatrist hesitated. He sighed deeply, shifting uncomfortably in his chair. This is what he said. 'I am sorry to inform you that we discovered an overactive site in your limbic system that is in continuous need of suppression. That locus has been identified as the center for *guilt*'."

"Guilt?" cried Ben. "I don't understand. What does guilt have to do with my behavior?"

The doctor spread his hands on the desk as if to indicate he had nothing up his sleeves. He leaned towards Ben. "I must say we have never seen that degree of cortical inhibitory activity before. My colleagues and I have discussed this singular phenomenon long and hard and we can only conclude that your so-called benevolence is nothing more than a manifestation of a powerful compensatory reaction."

Ben was beside himself. "What do you mean compensatory? What is going on?"

"You see, sir," the doctor explained. "Based on the unusual fMRI images together with all your test results we believe your behavior — your kindness, generosity and compassion — is actually a sustained effort of a cognitive center in your prefrontal cortex to hold in check your powerful guilt complex. It is a protective strategy. Otherwise, we fear that hot spot of guilt, deep in your mid-brain, is perilously close to a nuclear center that releases adrenaline. If left uninhibited it could cause irreparable harm to your cardiovascular system."

Ben was shocked. He stared in bewilderment. Half-crazed, he shouted, "Are you telling me that my natural goodness is nothing more than an overcompensating effort by my rational centers to spare me from having a heart attack or stroke? Death by guilt?" The doctor nodded. As a final blow, Ben was informed that the inaccessible site of the lesion precluded any attempt at surgical removal or any other form of treatment.

Lou shook his head. "Can you imagine the irony? For the better part of his life, Ben's immaculate behavior, his anointed saintliness, was simply a cover-up to mask his powerful guilt complex. What to do? Well, there was one option left and it came to Ben reluctantly. Why not attack this pervasive guilt with the one weapon believed to be effective?"

"Atonement?" I offered.

Lou clapped his hands. "Bingo! And so, Ben turned to spiritualism as a means to expiate if not exorcise his non-existent sins. You recall that his disdain for religion stemmed from a disconnect between deed and professed faith. Who permitted such transparent perjury? Regardless, his only hope lay in a prescribed religious ritual with its promise of redemption, absolution and, above all, guilt-squashing. Ben would submerge himself wholeheartedly in the daily rites of a professed faith in the hope it may ultimately douse the fire in his guilt locus. Or so he believed. He prayed that his rational centers, if liberated, would not rebel against what he felt was religion's mumbo jumbo. Ben was in a corner. Once again, he had no choice. He had to surrender to religious dogma. It was his only hope.

"Ben chose Catholicism as the one religion that offered divine intervention — thrice blest. First, its transcendent spirituality promised defeat over self-doubt. Second, the *causa prima* or concept of original sin readily absolves oneself of a personal guilt and, finally, unlike Judaism where atonement is an annual act in anticipation of sins yet to be committed, the Catholic church confessional, like the ATM machine, is readily available whenever the tortured soul is in need of a quick fix. And so, our despondent hero proceeded to plunge into all the obligatory rituals for his conversion. He began with the rite of Christian initiation for adults. He then donned a white robe and knelt in a shallow pool for his baptism. He attended special mass and took the catechisms. In short, he forced himself to be devout. And so, he was.

"Alas, the effect was short-lived for he had no need to confess. Sins were hard to come by naturally, let alone forced. His stubborn selflessness was too powerful for even the tiniest transgression. When he tried to commit the slimmest of infractions, his guilt center would pulsate uncontrollably necessitating an equally powerful corrective response from his higher centers — enough to cause a splitting headache. This rapid neuro-reflexive compensation was always faster than any trip to the confessional. In the meantime, his personal life was in shambles. He was hopelessly forlorn and had run out of options.

"One fateful day he was seen standing on a subway platform when suddenly he hurled himself onto the tracks in front of a speeding train. Witnessed accounts were divisive. Some who recognized him contend that he was attempting to save a child who was standing perilously close to the edge. Others commented on his despondency, his pitiful demeanor and unkempt appearance."

Lou Grobes sat back and sighed. "And there you have it, my friend. Ben finally succeeded in committing a wilful act — the ultimate sin."

Lou stood up, stretched and was about to take his leave.

"Hold on," I said. "Is that all? And what, pray tell, does all this have to do with Shakespeare's quotation?"

Lou nodded and replied. "Ah yes. Tragedy in the literary and theatrical sense defines a hero's fateful outcome in terms of innocence misconstrued. In Ben's case it was nothing more than irony. You see, by committing suicide Ben finally expunged that fiery lesion in his brain. However, the church pronounced the act a suicide. Absolution was denied. And so, you see, my friend," Lou shook his head. "While Ben's soul may have been condemned to an eternity in hell, his goodness was interred with his bones."

The Gap: Perception and Reality

If psychologists thrive on the treasures of our psychic frailties, philosophers excite themselves with the mysteries of human consciousness. One of their nagging disputes is the interface, or lack thereof, between perception and reality.

In his *Allegory of the Cave*, Plato tempts us to differentiate between what we see (a sensory perception) from what is real. In his cave are three prisoners. They are permanently bound to chairs, forced to face the back wall of the cave. All they ever see are shadows flickering on the wall. Behind the prisoners a flame burns. The shadows they see are reflections cast from moving objects and individuals parading in front of the flame. Hence, the prisoners' sole concept of reality is that of a two-dimensional world. One day, one of the prisoners escapes, and suddenly finds himself confronted with a multicolored world full of depth and partially devoid of shadows. Infused with this new-found reality he returns to the cave but fails to convince his former mates that what they see on the wall is nothing but illusions. Plato distinguishes people who mistake sensory knowledge of the truth from those who see truth in a broader philosophical context. If you believe what you see is the truth, who can say you are seeing but a shadow of what is real? However, any instance of distorted perception, or *trompe l'oeil,* is not unique to humans. It is no less a biological quirk of nature than that of a bird crashing into a plate glass window.

From a neurobiological perspective, the brain's operative depiction of a viewed object is not a mirror image. Nor does the eye function as a camera. It is far more complex. In its simplest representation each viewed image is transmitted by the optic nerve to the visual cortex at the back of the brain. From there the image is reconstituted, processed and sent through multiple neural pathways to different parts of the brain. The ultimate reconstruction of the image may reflect what is real or an interpretation of reality. In other words, the final image of any object may be no different than the shadows on the wall of Plato's cave.

Let us consider a different thought process. One that is unique to humans. I am referring to the thought experiment of knowing (or pretending to know) what you don't know. On September 30, 1942, the classic radio series *Suspense* aired a titillating drama entitled *100 In the Dark.* During a dinner party hosted by an elegant society lady, her precious sapphire ring is stolen. In the lead up to the theft we overhear snatches of gossip, sordid intrigues and other whisperings among the guests. It is clear that one of them took the ring. To retrieve her jewel, the hostess, not wishing to embarrass her friends, embarks on a soul saving stratagem. She orders all doors locked and all candles extinguished. She instructs her guests that she will count slowly to one hundred in the dark. During this interval the thief will have an opportunity to restore the ring without being identified. She warns her guests that if the ring is not returned, by the time she reaches one hundred, the police will be called and everyone will be searched on the spot.

As listeners we are transfixed while the hostess counts, deliberately and slowly, all the way to one hundred. There is heard the occasional shuffle, a suppressed cough, a bump here and there. The count continues. The tension mounts. Finally, she reaches one hundred. When the lights go on the ring is restored.

That's it! End of story. We never know who took the ring.

This narrative was shared among a group of men sitting around a table at their private club. They did not know what they did not know. But, given their individual biases and preconceptions — their inner eye so to speak — the unresolved ending did not prevent them from speculating on the identity of the thief. No animal need bother with such uncertainties, since it is doubtful they worry about what is not there.

Donald Rumsfeld, the former United States Secretary of Defense, achieved some notoriety for his famous speculations on 'knowns' and 'unknowns'. There are known knowns — in other words things we know we know. The world is round, the sun rises in the east. There are also known unknowns. That is, we know there are some things we do not know. Finally, there are unknown unknowns — things we don't even know we don't know. A number of philosophers, among them Slavoj Zizek, maintain that beyond these three categories there is a fourth — the unknown known. Here we are dealing with either suppressed memory or avoidance — a refusal to face an unpleasant outcome by acting as if the outcome (the unknown known) is too remote for it to interfere with our immediate satisfaction. Our non-perception of a problem can be an obstacle to its solution.

Take climate change. There are those who deny its scientific basis, first described in 1858 by John Tyndall. He demonstrated that the reflected rays of infrared radiation from the earth's surface can be trapped by certain gases in the atmosphere. It took one hundred and fifty years before another reality was confirmed. Since the beginning of the Industrial Revolution in the late eighteenth century, there has been a steady rise in the earth's temperature coincident with an exponential accumulation of atmospheric carbon dioxide derived from widespread deforestation and the burning of fossil fuels.

How was it that we energy hungry humans substituted the remnants of subterranean non-renewable deposits of oil and gas for the clean renewables of readily available wind and solar energy?

What was the perception that led us so far astray? Are the emissions from smokestacks nothing more than shadows on the walls of caves? We laughed at Don Quixote when he charged at windmills, a source of power for the poor inhabitants of La Mancha. Now we laugh at ourselves for having substituted the smog ridden air of carbon emissions for the gentle breeze of a wind turbine. There are so many attempts to distort perception in the face of reality.

The Fix: Assignment in Dystopia

"You could always hitch a ride on the Hale — Bop comet" smirked the Alpha-Draconian. The Tall Grey stood motionless, smarting at the rebuke.

"Now, let's get serious," the A-D continued. "This is to be an exploratory mission to the planet earth. You have been appointed our special emissary. Our UFO-naut so to speak. Despite the intergalactic distance separating our wet rocky planets — Tau Gruis and Earth — we share similar coordinates in space. We are cosmic cousins." The A-D's bulbous eye clicked back and forth as it attempted to fixate on the Tall Grey.

"Now, here is your mission. You will be speedily transported to Earth. You will return with answers to three critical questions. Is there life on Earth? If so, what are the sources and uses of energy that sustain their vitality? Finally, are any life forms on Earth sufficiently advanced to justify and establish formal communication?" The Tall Grey's barely perceptible nod signalled a grudging assent. And so, armed with a celestial camcorder and a microsecond supply of angel dust, the Tall Grey sped toward Earth — a hundred light years away.

Time flew. Facts were gathered.

Returning to Tau Gruis, the Tall Grey was quickly shepherded into an underground debriefing room. The Alpha-Draconian presided while a mix of Altairians, Spiny Reptiloids, a Six-Fingered Green Dwarf, two scaly Reticulans, a scattering of Cyborgs and a few Greys comprised the elite council. The final report, considered an extraordinary fabrication by some, was eventually filed in an abandoned ziggurat. However, if it piques your curiosity, here is what the Tall Grey reported.

"The answer to the first question is yes," it began. "There are plentiful multi-cellular life forms on Earth. Bizarre as they may appear, they all share with us a DNA helical template as the basic unit of life and reproduction." Murmurings of interest echoed through the hall.

The Tall Grey continued. "As to how these life forms utilize energy boggles the mind. Allow me to explain." A few disheartened grunts from the Droids. Ignoring the slight, the Tall Grey went on. "Among the more ubiquitous life forms on Earth are so-called green plants and small flying creatures. Both share a unique symbiotic relationship in so far as they thrive on two sources of renewable energy — solar from their star and wind currents. The green plants and trees have cleverly devised a system called photosynthesis. Simply put, these green organisms contain a special pigment called chlorophyll that captures the electromagnetic energy from their sun."

"Sounds like a pigment of your imagination," guffawed a disarticulated Cyborg. The A-D fixed the interloper with a fearsome stare and urged the Tall Grey to continue.

"Through a series of chemical reactions, mediated by an atmospheric gas called carbon dioxide, the packets or quanta of solar radiation are converted into potential energy sources equivalent to our celestial nectar — a sweet substance they call sugar. As an essential nutrient, this nectar is ingested in one form or another by all living creatures. From their aquifers, these same plants and trees suck up water through their earth-bound roots. The water is composed of a vital gas called oxygen. This gas makes up only twenty percent of their atmosphere. And yet all non-plant creatures, whether flying, scurrying about on land or swimming in their waters, rapidly succumb without it.

"So you see," the Tall Grey explained, "there exists on Earth an intricate, albeit perilous, quid pro quo wherein the survival of both the carbon dioxide exhaling animals and the oxygen exhaling plants depends, in part, on them inhaling each other's discarded gases." An uproar ensued as the silence in the hall was breached by a collective flapping of tentacles and loud snorts. The A-D clicked a warning signal and motioned the emissary to proceed.

"Now, here is where it gets interesting," said the Tall Grey. "For reproduction, the sessile plants cannot wander about to find a mate. So what do they do? They set a snare in the guise of their multicolored flowers — a lure for flying creatures such as bees, butterflies and birds. While these beasts are taking their fill of nectar from the flowers, the wily plants are smearing pollen on the creatures' hind quarters — a stowaway ruse that guarantees cheap transportation of their seeds to other flowers."

An irritable Short Grey shrugged what passed for its shoulders and exclaimed, "If the bee, butterfly or bird can get its fill from one flower why would it ever bother to visit another? That doesn't sound as clever as you make out."

"Ah, good question," replied the taller Grey. "The balance of nature and the evolution of most species on Earth are held tightly in check — more or less — by a process called natural selection. You see, the successful plant survives by yielding only enough nectar to barely satiate these flying creatures. Always leave them hungry is their modus operandi. In this way nature's equilibrium is maintained." Satisfied that it has squelched its shorter cousin the Tall Grey went on.

"Let us now consider energy sources and their transformation. After it is ingested, the sugar undergoes a cascade of metabolic steps — a cycle that ultimately requires oxygen before any kinetic energy can be liberated. The wind currents promote both random seed dispersion as well as transport for those flying creatures. This symbiosis pertains throughout the animal and plant kingdoms. It allows energy to constantly flow so that nutrients such as sugars, proteins, fats, ketones, gristle or whatever are exchanged and transmuted within and among species along a hierarchical food chain."

"It sounds too pat to me," cried out a gnome-like Altairian in the front row. "Surely, even on Earth, the second law of thermodynamics must obtain. Would you not agree that with any transformation from one energy source to another there has to be some loss of energy? Is the planet Earth completely devoid of entropy?"

"Nothing so faultless," replied the Tall Grey. "As tight a symbiosis that nature provides there is always some frictional waste. Surprisingly, it is held at a minimum among most living forms. However..." and here the Tall Grey rolled its vertical eyes skyward "there is one errant species hell-bent on savaging the energy equilibrium. I refer to a rather eccentric collection of bipedal wonks that have the effrontery to call themselves sapiens — or knowledge bearing. Talk about ugly!" Here the emissary flashed a photographic composite of humans gawking while at a political rally. The assembled reptiloids recoiled in horror. Save for the Green Dwarf who blushed a luminescent jade.

"These so-called Homo sapiens are omnivorous," the Tall Grey continued. "They will eat anything. Moreover, they seem unwilling to be satisfied with the energy transformation of their food sources. They are constantly in search of external sources of energy to power their indulgences. Would you believe it?" the Tall Grey honked excitedly. "These 'saps', unlike their fellow creatures, are afflicted with something called free choice — a mutated substitution for instinctual behavior. So what do they do with this precious gift? Well, instead of exploiting the freely available, inexhaustible, ubiquitous and safe renewable energy provided by their star and wind currents, these creatures expend inordinate energy to dig deep into their earth to extract a pair of non-renewable sources called fossil fuels and uranium. Both these substances are exhaustible, geographically isolated, costly and toxic." A snort from a paradisic Cyborg in the second row sparked an audible tittering by others.

"I agree it defies logic," said the envoy, stifling a chuckle. "These sapiens literally and figuratively turn their backs on their own star and wind as they drill deep inside mountains, beneath the desert sands and into the ocean floor — all in an effort to extract the remains of microscopic carbon laden organisms that were trapped billions of years ago in watery basins. These hydrocarbon-containing fossil fuels are extracted, pumped or blasted out in a variety of crude forms they call oil, gas and coal. After extraction, the crude hydrocarbons are transported, refined and converted into different forms of energy, none of which is metabolically useful for their own sustenance. Rather, they are exploited for external uses such as transportation, shelter, illumination and temperature regulation.

"Talk about entropy! For instance, to remove the oil they dig a hole thousands of meters into the Earth's crust and pray the oil will gush freely. However, the oil has a mind of its own. You see, it will only oblige if it is under considerable pressure and that only occurs when there is a plentiful supply. But here is the catch. If the oil is too thick or its pressure too low by virtue of its depleted state, the saps then drill a second hole and either jack pump it out or force it under steam pressure — a process that requires almost as much energy as that contained in the oil itself." The assembly erupted in pandemonium.

It was the A-D's turn to respond with a cynical snigger. "And what possible use is all this exploration?"

The Tall Grey emitted a sonorous sigh. "I can only report what I witnessed. After it is extracted, packaged and transported the oil undergoes refinement into various liquefied states called gasoline, jet fuel and diesel oil. These fuels serve to power their various means of transportation. Other hydrocarbon sources such as sticky bituminous oil mixed with sand are dredged from fields laid bare in frozen tundra. Pressure forced natural gas is obtained by blasting through shale rock, thereby emitting toxic fumes while entire mountains are stripped of green forestation so that coal, another hydrocarbon, can be mined. Both the coal and natural gases are burned in several transformative steps to power their electricity. And so, to answer the question on entropy, there is indeed wasteful loss of energy on

Earth and its major contributors are these addled bipedal creatures."

"I don't get it," interposed a Bristly Hairy Dwarf. "You mean to tell us that to obtain energy these woeful creatures have ignored both the heat from their star and the power of their wind to savagely strip the land bare of the same vegetation that provides them with oxygen and nutrients? And then by doing so they have concocted an increasing number of transitional steps in energy production that is rapidly becoming a zero sum game in terms of thermodynamic equilibrium?"

"Brace yourself. You haven't heard the end of it," said the Tall Grey who paused momentarily to sip a galactic thirst-quencher. "To make matters worse the supplies of oil and natural gas are being slowly depleted. Furthermore, the most abundant sources are located in what can only be described as hostile territories."

Two Reticulans were suddenly aroused. Murmurings broke out.

"It turns out," the Tall Grey went on, "these sapiens are social animals who seem to have a difficult ability to socialize. They are forever fighting each other — primarily over land acquisition. It appears that the richest supplies of oil happen to be buried in lands whose occupants are distrustful and wary of those who lust after it the most.

"It gets worse," cried the Tall Grey, trying to be heard over the babble and laughter around him. "A major problem is disposal of the waste and burnt residue from these hydrocarbons. These, it so happens, emanate as gaseous emissions, spewed into the atmosphere mainly as carbon dioxide — less so as methane gas, and toxic nitrous oxide. Included are particulate matter that stick in their craws."

"In their what?" asked the Alpha-Draconian.

The Tall Grey blushed and flapped one of its tentacles. "Sorry. By craws I meant that which serves as their breathing tubes. But allow me to continue. The more ominous and long-lasting quandary is the cumulative effect of these pollutants on their climate. A doomsday scenario called the greenhouse effect. Allow me to explain. On our planet, as on theirs, the shorter wavelength from our stars' ultraviolet radiation passes through each of our atmospheres and is absorbed by our planets' crusts. This provides a welcome warming effect. Here on Tau Gruis we make every effort to ensure that the absorbed energy is unimpeded when reflected back into the atmosphere in the form of infrared radiation.

"However, because these asinine sapiens emit so much carbon waste into their atmosphere, these gases have formed a canopy, trapping the reflected radiation which is then redirected back to heat their lands and oceans. The result is a perfidious increase in surface temperature resulting in a polar ice meltdown, a steady rise in sea levels, acidification of their oceans, extreme weather conditions and an accelerated extinction of many species."

A few Droids slapped their bulbous noggins in befuddlement. A loud hoot was heard from the assembled members prompting the A-D to call for order. The Tall Grey, gratified that it had a receptive, albeit bellicose audience, continued.

"Instead of abandoning this ludicrous exploration for subterranean carbon sources and turning to the freely and constantly available clean sources of solar heat and wind, what do you think is their second choice of energy?" This was met with irritable shrugs.

"Well, it is something called 'nuclear' energy." To let this sink in, the envoy paused and took another drought of celestial elixir. "Here, the sapiens indulge in what is called open pit mining — yet another underground folly. Using a leaching method they extract uranium, a heavy metal that is unstable because it possesses an excess of neutrons in its tightly overcrowded nucleus." The Tall Grey ignored a cynical grunt from the Green Dwarf.

"First, they grind this crude ore, so-called pitchblende, down to a fine powder they call 'yellowcake'. They then separate and convert this uranium oxide salt to a gaseous uranium hexafluoride, a process these sapiens euphemistically refer to as enrichment. Translation? The gas is now charged with deadly potential. But first, permit me to digress. There happened to be this strange creature called Albert Einstein. In a fitful moment of epiphany, he postulated that the atom contained energy equivalent to the product of its mass and the square of the speed of light. A perfectly safe theoretical conjecture since no one at the time imagined that the atom could ever be split to release that enormous energy. And guess what? Thirty years later, a couple of German scientists blew theoretical physics out the window when they smashed uranium atoms to smithereens using slow neutrons in a crude reactor.

"So, now there are these giant nuclear reactors in which the uranium hexafluoride mixture is 'enriched' as a fissionable isotope by either gaseous diffusion or gas centrifuge. The process separates the lighter atoms of the more unstable U^{235} isotope from its slower stable parent U^{238}. The U^{235} atoms are split apart in a controlled chain reaction. And I do emphasize the word 'controlled'. You see, if uncontrolled, this chain reaction can clickety-clack to a 'critical' state and 'POOF' — there goes an entire city!" Once again pandemonium broke out and once again order had to be restored by the A-D who couldn't believe his auditory appendages. He motioned for the Tall Grey to elaborate.

"The controlled chain reaction produces heat energy which enables water to convert to steam whose energy is then converted to electricity." Anticipating the next question from the learned assembly the Tall Grey quickly went on. "Ah yes, what to do with the dangerous spent fuel you may ask? Well, why not simply dig more holes in the earth and bury it where it can slowly decay over millions of years!"

The Alpha-Draconian held up a withered claw to quell the groans. "My esteemed fellow council members, may I intervene at this stage? I believe we have the answer to the first two questions. There is life on Earth. And it appears that all species on Earth, save one, utilize energy efficiently and economically with minimum entropy. Are there further questions for our brave messenger?"

"Yes." This from a Spiny Paradisic. "Do these so-called sapiens ever use their star's solar power and wind currents for anything?"

"I can only speculate from their peculiar behavior," replied the Tall Grey. "For what it is worth I did notice many of them sprawled on sandy beaches taking in their star's solar rays. Even here they are so suspiciously averse they smear their torsos with gobs of horrible smelling emollients — presumably to insulate themselves against the ultraviolet rays. As for wind, it seems that sailing and kite flying is rapidly giving way to motorised propulsion. Although it is said that Einstein was fond of drifting aimlessly about in a sailing boat."

"If they are so dumb how come they built all those grand cities, elaborate transportation systems and electronic devices?" interposed the Short Grey.

"I didn't say they are dumb. I would say they have substituted misguided ingenuity for intelligence!"

A grumpy old Cyborg waved a spiny claw and asked, "You told us how sapiens use energy for external purposes but failed to mention how energy is utilized for their bodily functions."

The Tall Grey sighed. "Ah yes, once again those sapiens, unlike their fellow creatures, have a tendency for self-destruction. You see, like us, all non-sapien life forms on Earth utilise energy efficiently. That is to say we all abide by the law of optimisation — performing our tasks with the least amount of expendable energy. And so, on Earth, all non-human, non-domesticated species convert one part of their hard-won food into that portion of kinetic energy required for day-to-day survival and the other part stored for future use in case of want or starvation.

"Most sapiens however, inadvertently shift their optimization point so as to expend less energy than they take in. For example, a typical sap can be seen driving his or her car — rather than walk — to an emporium called a supermarket. A large store glutted with processed food packages — all colorfully displayed along endless aisles. These portly human specimens purchase more food than required. They then drive home, plop down into an adjustable recliner in front of something called a television screen and proceed to consume an excess of calories over expenditure. As for internal energy transformation, the sapiens' metabolism is tricked into storing the unused energy into fat cells. These cells release floating lipid particles that go on to coat and rust their inner pipes."

A hilarious uproar exploded from the council members.

It was then the Alpha-Draconian intervened to draw the meeting to a close. "My fellow reptiloids," it announced. "Please contain yourselves. May I conclude? As for the final question regarding formal contact with intelligent life forms on Earth, I take it that our brave envoy has effectively excluded those sapiens. However," the A-D turned to the Tall Grey, "are there any species on Earth whose success in evolutionary terms approaches our own, and therefore, warrants an effort to communicate with them?"

Without hesitation the Tall Grey replied, "I would strongly recommend communication with creatures called bacteria. They have been around for more than three billion years. They are ubiquitous and have been at war with Homo sapiens since the dawn of recorded time."

"Good," croaked the A-D. "Let us contact them"

The Gap: Empathy and *Schadenfreude*

Imagine you are walking along a street undistracted when, suddenly, you see a man with a cane trip and fall heavily to the ground. Instinctively, you rush to help him but others are there ahead of you. Your flash of empathy is pre-empted — a forfeiture of good intentions. But hold on. You now recognize the injured man. He is none other than a perennial bête noir, a former boss of yours who, just a few years ago, fired you from your job with little or no justification. Bitterness and rancor have dogged you ever since. With surprising alacrity your reflexive burst of empathy is instantly supplanted with *schadenfreude* — a feeling of joy at the man's misfortune.

If a personality trait implies consistency in a behavioral pattern how can opposing traits such as empathy and *schadenfreude* alternate so effortlessly in the same individual? Among several pat answers are those ascribing opposing traits to separate sites in our brain. For instance, using functional magnetic resonance imaging (fMRI) of the human brain, studies have shown that feelings of empathy appear localized to the anterior cingulate cortex (ACC), an area in the brain shared with that for pain sensation. To empathize is to suffer? In stark contrast, the muted self-satisfied smirk of *schadenfreude* lights up the 'reward' center in the left nucleus accumbens. To gloat is to be compensated? Or, one may choose to explain the dichotomy as a neurophysiologic switch — a mimicry wherein so-called 'mirror neurons' are seen to pulsate in response to different provocations.

Psychologists who are more earth-bound get around the snag by differentiating among subtypes of empathy and *schadenfreude*. Let us take empathy first. There appears to be both cognitive and affective means by which we unleash sympathy into action. Cognitive empathy is the ability to imagine or feel someone else's thoughts and sensations. In essence, it is the extraordinary capability of getting inside someone's head and feeling their pain. Affective empathy is less intrusive yet more purposeful. It is the reflexive drive that responds to another's plight. It is more knee-jerk than mindful. Think of it as a reflex response to, 'there but for the grace of God go I'. You were probably driven by affective empathy when you instinctively rushed to help the injured man.

Is empathy an impulse driven by altruism or self-interest? Children as young as twelve months of age not infrequently exhibit empathy when they spontaneously, and adorably, reach out to others in distress. Alternatively, they are just as prone to explosions of glee when observing another kid in helpless freefall. Unlike adults, their outbursts are often expressions of unmasked *schadenfreude*. This abrupt switch in a given child can be downright perplexing. But is it sustained? It is said we maintain the same level of empathy throughout our lives. And yet there is concern that when teenagers and young post-adolescents immerse themselves in social media they become increasingly self-absorbed and narcissistic — traits which, if anything suppress empathy.

Schadenfreude, on the other hand, is an emotion you would rather keep to yourself. Like the blush of shame, the self-conscious sensation of *schadenfreude* is often uncontrollable — eliciting pangs of self-incrimination. Unless of course it is the collective aggressive behavior shared with like-minded fans at a sporting event. 'Kill the umpire!' 'Damn the opposition!'

We embrace a mutual spirit of unanimity whenever we witness the humiliation of our adversaries. We are carried away by the exuberance of the crowd, our jeers rising in a storm, forgetting for a moment the embarrassment and pain inflicted on any of the opposing players. On June 10, 2019, during a high intensity NBA basketball championship game in Toronto between the Toronto Raptors and Golden State Warriors, Kevin Durant, a superstar for the Warriors, fell to the floor seizing his Achilles tendon and grimacing in gnaw-crushing pain. Instead of a hushed response of collective sympathy from the Toronto crowd, there was an outburst of raucous elation. It took the Raptors' players to finally subdue the crowd. One could sense a creeping aura of mea culpa that permeated the arena that night. It was empathy as afterthought.

As for wishing others harm we sometimes get carried away. For instance, in military boot camps, under the guise of self-preservation, the enemy soldier is to be perceived as sub-human. This grants justification to feel and express permissible *schadenfreude*. It is not uncommon to absolve a feeling of *schadenfreude* as a settling of scores, especially if the target individual is considered unworthy or threatening. Perhaps the most frequent incitement of *schadenfreude* stems from jockeying for one's proper niche in the social order — a zero sum game based on securing one's rightful slot in a given hierarchy.

Let us conjure an extreme example.

Picture yourself as a humble pilgrim making the trek from Canterbury to Rome. The year, let us say, is 1220 CE. You are somewhere in Tuscany, about halfway between Florence and Sienna. Just when you reach the crest of a hill you suddenly gaze in awe at a group of skyscrapers dotting the skyline. Yes, skyscrapers! The towers, about seventy of them, rise majestically above the tiny walled city of San Gimignano. You learn that these tall stone edifices, some over 150 feet high, are the living quarters of the wealthiest families in the region. They are the pinnacles of social status. It is the actual height of each building that determines the absurd benchmark by which each family vies for relative dominance within a tight social hierarchy. You are appalled to learn that one super rich family, wallowing in the largesse from their productive vineyards, enjoys a temporary *schadenfreude* as they gaze down on their neighbors. Alas, the feeling is short-lived. There, right beside them, a rival family, made rich on saffron spice production, is erecting an adjoining domicile that threatens to over-tower them.

Today, we may not exhibit such blatant ostentation. Nevertheless, we are capable of expressing our envy into acceptable forms of *schadenfreude*. It just requires a different set of circumstances. For instance, in addition to proven skills for specific tasks, ambition and competitiveness are traits highly desirable in many corporate workplaces. In a highly toxic atmosphere of tenuous job security, the rewards of advancement can easily pit one individual against another. It is a form of acceptable bullying wherein a slip of one colleague means an advantage to another. What began as envy can easily transform into a self-satisfied feeling of *schadenfreude*.

In most psychology experiments, it is attested that while envy is not synonymous with *schadenfreude* it is nevertheless a driving factor. The particular social context may actually serve to breed *schadenfreude*. What is intriguing about human emotions is the rapidity in which one experiences genuine empathy at one instance in time and *schadenfreude* immediately thereafter.

How does Aristotle's golden mean play out here?

The Fix: There but for the Budding of Blossoms

The story was told to me some time ago but I cannot vouch for its authenticity. I leave it to the reader for any hint of plausibility. The narrator recalled the story after seeing Luis Buñuel's movie, *Viridiana* — a harrowing tale in which a young novice in a cloistered convent inherits her uncle's property, leaves the nunnery and devotes herself to gathering and caring for beggars — an empathic act that tragically misfires.

As best as I can recall, here is what the narrator told me.

The origins of variolation, a primitive immunity against smallpox, are misty. According to legend its first application may have taken place during China's Song Dynasty in the late thirteenth century. Repeated outbreaks of the deadly pox were common, fierce and decimating in south-western China. It was here that alchemists, living in the caves of O-Mei-Shan, and true to their Taoist beliefs, were concocting elixirs of immortality — to no avail. It took a Buddhist nun with extraordinary powers of observation to experience an epiphany. She was a member of the Enduring Joy Convent in Ch'eng-tu, a western enclave in what is now

Sichuan Province. She was among those nuns, although unconfined as a monastic, who took her dharma seriously. She dismissed the Buddhist superstition that a person's susceptibility to disease was a manifestation of moral transgressions in past lives. Instead, she sought contingencies.

Having witnessed and presided over several outbreaks of smallpox, she noticed that survivors of previous attacks were less prone to acquire the disease when re-exposed. She was convinced the disease was transmitted by inhalation of air droplets — primarily, if not exclusively, through the nostrils. This alone was a remarkable presumption considering the fact that the germ theory of transmissibility had to await another seven hundred years to be accepted. It did not escape her that in a typical epidemic, children were especially susceptible.

One day, during a smallpox outbreak in a nearby village, this Buddhist nun was summoned to see a sick baby. He was horribly speckled with pustules over his face, arms, hands and chest. Such lesions were euphemistically labelled 'the budding of blossoms'. According to legend, the nun scraped a sample of pus from one of the open sores, quickly ground it with a pestle and then dried it in a cotton swab. A few days later, she was somehow permitted to approach a healthy child, apparently in harm's way, and blew the dried powder through his nostrils. Whatever the dose of the dried toxin, the child was spared all manifestations of smallpox when subsequently exposed during a recurrent epidemic in his village. In time the practice took hold. Word spread fast.

Back at the Enduring Joy Convent the halls were already abuzz with the breakthrough discovery. It was there that a young novitiate took the news to heart. We will call her T'an-Hui (Radiance of the Dharma). Her own family had suffered horrifically from the dreaded pox, leaving many of the survivors blind or disfigured for life. She alone was spared. Having witnessed the death and desecration attributed to this unholy disease, T'an-Hui became smitten with an uncontrollable empathy for those in distress. She had to reach out in some way to help others. She was barely twenty years old, confined within monastic walls and years away from achieving the requisite eight vows of garudhammas which would grant her ordination as a Bhikkhuni. Yet she knew in her heart she was capable of achieving nirvana.

One night, T'an-Hui awoke, startled by a mission already fully formed in her mind. She then made her own vow. She would dedicate herself to learn everything there was to know about how to prepare and administer the dried smallpox toxin to susceptible children. Once confident of her craft, she would then declare herself a renunciant, don a white robe and with shaven head leave the monastery to apply her expertise throughout the countryside. She was determined to assuage that burning fire of empathy. And so she did.

With her gentle cast, her soft eyes and aura of beneficence, T'an-Hui was permitted access to children whose skin eruptions announced the early stages of smallpox. Under the convent's supervision, she learned how to extract pus from eruptions, wrap the scabs in cotton wool and store them in dry dates with their kernels removed. After sealing the dates with yellow wax, she was taught how to preserve them in dry storage. As she became proficient in technique, she learned to harvest samples of pustular scrapings from previous inoculations as opposed to fresh lesions of natural acquired smallpox — a precaution which ensured a milder form of the disease.

One morning, self-assured of her ability, T'an-Hui left the convent and proceeded to wander the backroads of villages. Wives' tales laid the path. News of the inoculum's magic properties had already gossiped its way throughout the countryside. Mothers in particular sought anyone skilled in the technique, ready to pay handsomely to protect their children. T'an-Hui, true to her beliefs, would only accept alms and so was sought after in the poorer hamlets of the region. Word spread of her ministrations. Her skills were whetted. Her empathy rewarded. She learned that for scabs to maintain potency for three to four months her stock had to be continually replenished. On some occasions she had no choice but to extract samples of fresh eruptive lesions from children who, unwittingly, served as recycled fodder. In these instances, care was taken to obtain samples from subjects with mild disease — if she could find them.

Not everyone was convinced. To some, suspicions were allayed. To others, sorcery was afoot. T'an-Hui was careful to walk a fine line between the two. A diminutive figure with trusting gestures, she was often seen explaining her mission and the promise of lifelong protection. During the first three years of her services, she encountered two local outbreaks of the pox. One nasty attack spread through a village in which a dozen children between ages two and twelve were severely afflicted. Three of them died in agony, one became blind and the rest permanently scarred. All five of T'an-Hui's 'treated' children were spared with nary a trace of the disease. Similarly, in the other enclave, all of T'an-Hui's variolated children emerged unscathed.

In time, the young novitiate became a whispered name in the province. Sightings of her small robe-encased figure were shared among villagers and farmers as she was spotted flitting from one village or farm community to another. Whether her technique was deemed infallible, divinely attributed or blessed with uncanny luck, at no time did any of her children, once inoculated, either break out with a full-blown attack or serve as a source of contagion.

Ah yes, contagion. The deadly virus had no respect for boundaries. History attests to this. As to its galloping spread, transmission did not require an intermediate vector such as a reduviid bug, mosquito or tsetse fly. It traveled strictly by way of human-to-human contact either through air droplets or contact with body or clothing. Neither did it travel as the crow flies nor in ships laden with pestiferous rat fleas. It simply hitched a ride and journeyed wherever man's wanderlust took him, ploddingly along trade routes, military campaigns, colonizations or migrations. One can trace the lengthy trek of smallpox via the old Silk Road from Africa to China, carving a path of deadly destruction from the ancient city of Tyre, up through Bactria, and over the Hindu Kush. Thence to Samarkand, Kashgar and into China at Chang'an. A global miasma of the dreaded bug enveloped the world, sparing no niche where humans chose to settle.

Several years passed. One day, T'an-Hui found herself in a remote mountain village among a primitive people shut off from the outside world. They were mainly peasant farmers tilling a hard-scrabbled land while the women tended their goats and pigs. T'an-Hui was astonished to hear that in this secluded countryside the inhabitants heard tales of epidemics elsewhere but could not recall a single case of smallpox within their community. Neither did their folklore make reference to anything resembling an outbreak of the wily pox. T'an-Hui's burning sense of protectionism was aroused. She envisioned an impending devastation should the disease take hold among these highly exposed, unimmunised and vulnerable people. No one would be spared. She had to act.

T'an-Hui boldly approached the elders of the village and explained her mission. She was prepared to immunize the children against a terrifying disease should it arrive. A whole generation will be spared. Not surprisingly, the male elders of the community balked. Despite her angelic demeanor, they viewed her as a crafty sorceress and rejected her offer. The women, however, felt otherwise. A few, having been told of the grievous harm to children elsewhere, mounted a charge. Word had already leaked of T'an-Hui's magical deeds in other villages. A stand-off ensued.

In time, the elders gave in. T'an-Hui was granted permission to apply her technique but only under the watchful eyes of a few selected villagers. Furthermore, only one child was to be chosen as a trial case. The stage was set. In a small thatched hut, Li Wei, a rather sickly five-year-old lad, crippled with cerebral palsy, tittered as he stood shyly before T'an-Hui. She hesitated at first. She usually chose a healthy child who ordinarily would recover unblemished from the induced infection. But anticipation bristled in the air. Wonder, perplexity and expectancy were all etched on the faces of the villagers in attendance. She had no choice but to proceed.

T'an-Hui happened to have a fresh supply of scabs from a recent outbreak. She asked Li Wei to sit in a chair while she carefully removed the powdered extract from a covering of vine leaves. Before the bewildered group of onlookers, she instructed the boy to raise his head. Slowly T'an-Hui blew the powdered toxin into his nostrils. She then held his nostrils fast to prevent any sudden sneeze. The boy opened his eyes wide and looked at her blankly. The villagers could not help but laugh at the boy's puzzled expression. T'an-Hui explained to the group that in about a fortnight Li Wei will develop a mild fever and may show reddish patches in his mouth with or without flat papules over his skin. Both the fever and skin rash will dissipate over several days and our brave little boy will not only recover completely but will be blessed with lifelong resistance against any malicious outbreak should the disease ever attack the community. T'an-Hui promised to stay in her ramshackle hut at the edge of the village to wait out the incubation period. If, as expected, no harm came to the boy she would gladly inoculate the other children in the village.

That afternoon, as fate would have it, dark clouds appeared over the village. This was followed by a relentless rain storm that persisted for days on end. The flooding created impassable puddles and small lakes making it difficult to navigate within the village. It eventually washed out many of the farmers' fields. Spirits were invoked but they were deaf to appeal. And the rains kept coming. Waterlogged and drenched to despair, the villagers could only wait out the onslaught. Meanwhile, a few of the women, keeping a close watch on Li Wei, were whispering of a conceivable link between the boy's inoculation and the appearance of the rain storm.

On the thirteenth day following the inoculation, Li Wei developed a high fever which progressed to intermittent attacks of delirium. Over the next three days there was rapid spread of raised red papules across his face, hands and torso. These evolved into fluid filled pustules some of which leaked while others formed crusty scabs. When T'an-Hui was finally summoned, she was appalled by the ferocity of the attack on the poor lad. It was hopeless. Never had she seen such a malignant case. All she could do was muster the excuse that his frail constitution rendered him vulnerable to the full-blown infectious disease.

The clouds had still not lifted when two days later, to T'an-Hui's horror, two pre-teen girls who had previously fondled the boy exhibited unmistakable signs and symptoms of the deadly virus. One by one, children of all ages, together with many adults, fell victim to the onslaught. The affliction became rampant as it spread rapidly throughout the village and countryside. The virulence was especially rabid. Cries of the suffering could be heard throughout the community. Within three weeks, a full-blown epidemic was afoot. No one was spared. Several children died — including Lu Wei.

One day, the male elders, together with a few select widows and blighted mothers, convened to plan a way out of the catastrophe. Various spirits were invoked but it took little time to conclude that the cause of the outbreak was T'an-Hui and her bewitchment. Severe punishment had to be applied. Several gruesome techniques were discussed but the group eventually settled on sixty lashes with a bamboo cane, a particular macabre form of retributive torture.

On the following morning, one in which the clouds were seen to disburse, T'an-Hui was physically dragged to an open clearing in the center of the village. She was tethered to a makeshift stake and stripped bare. All the villagers, the elderly, the young, the halt and the lame, turned out and stared in silence. There was to be no preliminary indictments. Everyone knew the meaning of equitable justice. A tall, broad-chested and bearded man, wearing a traditional silk robe, stood beside T'an-Hui. In hushed silence he lifted a broad stave of bamboo and proceeded to lash T'an-Hui's backside with slow heavy strokes. She emitted loud shrieks of searing pain while the villagers looked on in silence.

If they expected any sign of contrition, they were disappointed. On the contrary, there was an extraordinary transformation that overcame T'an-Hui. Weakened, helpless and cringing with each malevolent stroke she looked out at the assembled masses, and for the first time, experienced an emotional conversion. Facing her was a sight of wretchedness. Men, women and children, each and every one afflicted with grotesque signs of the malevolent pox. She couldn't help staring. Some were blind, some heavily covered with ugly pustules. Others so ravaged they lay near death, immobile on makeshift pallets. Many were already showing evidence of permanent scarring. Even her torturer's arm was enveloped with crusted scabs.

It struck T'an-Hui that what aroused her was not pity or empathy but a realization that within this remote region only she would be ultimately spared. Should she survive the torture, the welts, wounds and bleeding she would eventually heal and in this godforsaken wasteland she alone would emerge with clear smooth untarnished velvety skin while the survivors would end up disfigured. Indeed, she would stand out as the only vision of purity in the countryside — the Enlightened One, chaste and unblemished.

She laughed! It was a derisive laugh. She was overcome by a new and strange sensation. Rather than feel pity for the villagers, she felt a sense of joy at their discomfort. She reasoned. If any of the villagers happened to feel empathy for her, it had to come at the cost of physical torture. Whereas for T'an-Hui the blows raining down on her were becoming less excruciating as she wallowed in the 'pain relieving' sensation of *schadenfreude*.

The Gap: Language, Innate and Acquired

If a dolphin or a bonobo or even, let us say, a rose-breasted grosbeak, were to be sidetracked in their wanderings and suddenly find themselves in a foreign habitat of their own species, would they be able to understand the whistles, gestures and squawks of their hosts? If human language acquisition is innate, a fundamental constituent of the brain's wiring, why do we speak in different tongues? More to the point, why do humans, despite an innate facility with their mother tongue, become so muffled when in distant lands?

At last count there were no fewer than 7000 distinct languages in the world today. Did they all originate from one Adamic dialect? There is no paucity of theories regarding the origin of language. Most linguists agree that human language owes its origin to something more complex than a simple evolutionary progression from gesturing to the discovery of one's voice. Watch a chimpanzee attempt communication with a human. The flailing of arms and the pounding of chests are not infrequently accompanied by mouth contortions and grimaces. As if the animal is trying to speak. The failure to do so cannot simply be ascribed to the anatomical site or configuration of the chimp's voice box. For human language to have evolved there had to be a transformative switch in the human brain. A complex set of mutations perhaps?

One estimate is that human language first appeared between the emergence of modern humans, 200,000 years ago, and their wanderings out of Africa, around 60,000 years ago. Evolutionary linguists narrow the gap between 85,000 and 60,000 years ago, a time when humans first acquired skills for tool making, symbolic representations, social structures amenable to integrated communication and the ability to satisfy the human bent to roam and explore.

It is doubtful that the first human to utter anything meaningful awoke one day and spoke in whole sentences. On the other hand, complicated syntax coupled with a full-bodied lexicon can be found within many primitive tribes. Take a two-year-old child out of any primitive or isolated social enclave and no matter where the child is transferred, he or she will easily learn and adopt the language of the host. Given proper exposure and time, a miracle unfolds. The child will graduate from infant gesturing and babbling to testing the reactions of others to her sounds and finally to intelligible speech.

Unique to humans is the complexity of language, a skill which not only communicates but expresses human thought. And yet, from a neuroanatomical perspective, the selective brain sites and core neural networks of our language-based system are not that dissimilar from other animals. Indeed, for both humans and non-human primates, there are but slight variations in the size and symmetry of key brain loci such as the inferior frontal cortex and Broca's area.

Moreover, there appears to be an evolutionary mismatch between the biological and cultural developments in human language — a distinction which has plagued investigators in the field. The singular innate capacity to acquire language is, for lack of a better term, a 'mind' thing, not unlike René Descartes' mind-body convergence. Noam Chomsky, the renowned linguist, refers to this ability as the Language Acquisition Device or LAD. In brief, the very structure of language appears to be hard-wired in our brain. Think of it as a composite of universal grammar. It accounts for a child's capacity to acquire complex structural elements of different languages. Is this the extraordinary acquisition that sets us so far apart from other creatures?

No amount of brain-gazing has explained the age-dependent limitation in learning a second language. Something interferes. It seems, as time goes on, we are dependent on a different set of computational skills. The inborn capacity to acquire language acts as a slate or template upon which the rules are indelibly printed. But the slate needs sensory input to enrich the acquisition. There are tragic, fortunately rare, cases of children who, from birth, were forcibly deprived of any sensory exposure to human speech. Beyond puberty it becomes next to impossible to teach such individuals to speak in whole sentences. On the flip side, the uncluttered brain of a child under ten years can not only acquire its mother tongue with ease but is more receptive to learning a second, third or fourth language compared to older folks. It appears the more immature the brain, the greater its flexibility — a condition called the Critical Period Hypothesis.

None of the above explains the origins of so many languages. Neither do they forgive God the curse of multilingualism.

Therefore, is the name of it called Babel, and the Lord did there confound the language of all the earth; and from thence did the Lord scatter them abroad upon the face of all the earth
Genesis 11:9

If we rebuild that tower of Babel, could we retrieve that original tongue — whatever it was?

The Fix: Lost in Back Translation

Where am I? Is this some kind of a mausoleum? Creepy. I look around and take in a massive atrium within which are helical tiers spiraling upward in ever diminishing loops to a barely visible patch of sky. Architecturally, it is an amalgam of the Guggenheim and a Babylonian ziggurat. Shafts of dust-sprinkled light filter in through high arched windows. A cold, grey, metallic aura permeates the place. The feeling would be tomb-like if it wasn't for a constant buzz of frenetic activity all about. A swarm of fussy uniformed functionaries, dressed in dark suits, are seen scurrying in all directions. Some are carrying armfuls of manuscripts, others are pushing carts laden with books of all sizes. Others are clacking away on antiquated typewriters. Still others are milling about, conferring in hushed tones. A feverish air of purposeful activity echoes throughout the vast emporium.

Every so often I am approached by a bustling drone. "Are they ready yet?" he or she asks.

Or, "Do you have the list?"

Or, "Hurry please, we need the titles now". When I inquire what it's all about, I am met with quizzical stares, impatient shrugs. And then off they scatter.

I look around hoping for a familiar face, a friendly floorwalker, an information kiosk — anybody. Suddenly, I spot him. A blind man, slowly groping his way along the circular railing. He is of medium height, heavyset with a slackened jaw and drooping shoulders. He is wearing a crumpled brown suit. As he approaches, I notice his eyes are gray and squinting. His thin white hair is brushed back off his temple. As I look closely, I can hardly contain myself.

"Senor Borges?" I call out. "Is it really you?"

Jorge Luis Borges stops and turns towards me. He smiles and replies, "Ah, greetings my good man. Can I be of assistance?" I am dumbstruck. What is such an iconic figure doing here?

"Forgive me, sir," I call out. "I am aware of your predilection for labyrinths but what in heaven's name is this place and what is going on here?"

Borges sighs. "Son, your use of the word 'heaven' is fortuitous as I shall explain. Come, let us sit down."

I join him on a side bench just below the iron railing. Waving his hand about he says, "My friend, you are in a giant scriptorium. Try imagining it as the interior of Peter Breugel's rendition of the infamous Tower of Babel. You may recall that all too brief entry in Genesis where God vented his disapproval with the postdiluvian rabble of Babylon. It was not so much for their brazen effrontery to build a tower to his lofty domain. Oh no. You see, the multitude of humans at that moment in time was monolingual — a unique trait which, given the circumstances, may well have ensured success in their stately mission. Consider if you will how different, how advanced I should say, our civilization would be if we all spoke in one tongue. But God had little alternative but to inflict our species with the curse of multilingualism — a far greater and lasting retribution than raining down frogs, locusts and plagues."

Borges pauses to rub his eyes. He shakes his head, leans forward and squints at me. "What you have here is a re-enactment of that ancient effort. Within this tower is an attempt to eliminate the babble by recapturing mankind's original Adamic language. How is it to be done? Believe it or not, the zealotry you see around you is nothing less than a blasphemous effort to back translate all classic texts and manuscripts to their original source. Because of the world's multiplicity of languages — more than six thousand at last count — there is a sense that the kernels of original ideas and their expression, whether scientific, literary, poetic or philosophical, have been lost in translation."

Borges pauses and smiles. "In an odd way I agree. No problem is as completely discordant with literature as is the problem posed by translation. Meanings distorted, idioms fractured, the curse of linguistic transgressions — all a garble, a lexical nightmare according to some. Here at least there is purpose, driven, I fear, by a colossal misguided assumption. What, pray tell, prevents a back translation from being any less authentic than its forward rendition? Do you not agree?"

"I think I do," I reply, hesitantly. "I am reminded of a crafty psychology experiment. Six subjects are sequestered in a soundproof room. Outside the room a volunteer recruit is shown a glossy illustration of a hunting cabin filled with all kinds of bric-a-brac and assorted curios. The volunteer is asked to memorize the scene and then verbally reconstruct the precise details of the picture to the first subject invited to leave the room. There follows a sequential pattern in which each subject describes their recollection of the previous verbal description to the next subject and so on down the line. Needless to say, by the time the last interchange takes place there is no resemblance whatsoever between the final iteration and the original illustration. If one cannot back translate a memory over such a brief period of time, how can it be done over thousands of years? Is that what we have here?"

"Quite so," says Borges. "And yet your example was verbal hearsay in a common language. A tribe's oral history when passed on from one generation to the next is forever at the mercy of the brain's limited capacity to store memory. It is one reason why writing, as a storage vehicle, was invented. Alas, only to be subverted by multilingualism and the need for faulty translations. Just as mercy and justice are so often irreconcilable, so it is with the two-headed literary attributes, of fidelity and fluency."

Borges stops. His face suddenly lights up. "I daresay there is one exception. I refer to the Septuagint — that early Greek translation of the Hebrew bible. The story goes like this. In the second century BCE, Ptolemy Philadelphus, king of Egypt, commissioned a Greek translation of the Old Testament. It was to be eventually housed in the great library in Alexandria. It is alleged that Eleazar, a Jewish high priest, was deputized to select seventy-two translators — six from each of Israel's twelve tribes. For seventy-two days, these Talmudic hair splitters were confined in separate cells on a remote island. It is alleged they had no means to communicate with each other. And yet, miraculously they emerged with identical translations!"

Borges titters. "A biblical fable, no? Contrast this with the muddled translations of St Jerome's Hebrew Bible to the Latin Vulgate or, the different versions of the King James Bible from Hebrew and Greek into English. And so, my friend, here in this scriptorium you see a massive, some say foolhardy, effort to recapture the purity of ancient source material by way of back translation. The objective appears to be twofold. One is a systematized process to resurrect the true meaning and flavor of the original text. The other, I regret to say, is no less nefarious. It is a venture to recapture that original monolingual language — a bold sacrilegious challenge to God's edict." Borges frowns. He slips a handkerchief from his pocket and wipes his eyes. He then tilts his head and listens to the cacophony surrounding us. After a brief pause, he turns to me.

"Those who are so misguided argue that language is divinely ordained as opposed to being utilitarian or conceived as abstractions of the mind. The search for hidden meaning in sacred texts is not new. Symbologists and numerologists abound. Think of the Kabbalah for instance — an attempt to flush out meanings concealed within sacred texts. The search for the language of Adam is not new. Several disreputable attempts have already been made. The Holy Roman Emperor, Frederick II, himself a multilinguist, was obsessed with discovering the voice that God imparted to Adam. Accordingly, he devised a barbaric method in which selected infants were raised from birth without any sensory exposure to human speech. Thankfully, those experiments were quickly abandoned."

Borges knits his eyebrows and sighs deeply. "It begs the question. Is human language truly innate? If so, its signals of communication must be knowledge based. Consider writing. It began as representational but then became an extension of human thought — both a repository of memory and a utilitarian vehicle. Man cogitates, ergo he summates." Borges chuckles. There is a long pause as if he is lost in thought. But he turns towards me and quietly murmurs, "I have spent my life writing in solitude and then only to realise that the written word can never replace the richness of human discourse."

"Senor Borges, is it not true that back translation, from whatever medium, has occupied scholars for centuries? Think of the Rosetta stone. Who knows whether the decryption of those markings is accurate or if the back translation is authentic given the many attempts to decode those ancient hieroglyphics? Besides, who can be assured that back translation of any text is necessarily a linear function? For all we know there is a wide hysteresis loop wherein the back translation is as distorted as its forward rendition."

Borges simply shrugs. I try a different tact. "Tell me, sir. If language is so physiologically imprinted in our genome, why is it increasingly difficult to learn a foreign tongue as we age? You who are master of comparative literature can surely break through the fog that surrounds us."

Borges peers at me and smiles. "Ah, so many difficult questions. Son, I am but a humble wordsmith. Granted, I have been moved many times when probing the classics of other cultures. Regretfully, I can only wonder at the effort being made here. The evolution of both medium and message is a fascinating trajectory that seems unstoppable. Your Canadian guru, Marshall McLuhan, had something to say about that, *n'est pas*? In prehistoric times communication was primarily oral with some pictorial representation on stone. Then there evolved cuneiform symbols on clay, Egyptian hieroglyphics on papyrus, Chinese characters on paper and, in Western Europe, manuscripts on parchment. The latter defined the scribal world of medieval Europe — heavily guarded and entrusted to the select literati of the church. In the meantime, the Arabs, using paper, were busy translating the entire corpus of Greek science, philosophy and literature.

"And presto! In 1438 came that revolutionary breakthrough — the invention of moveable type by Johannes Gutenberg. All hell broke loose. For the first time, copies could be generated and distributed among the masses. No longer was the written word the sole possession of the priesthood. It wasn't long before the literate proletariat demanded access to the written word. Throughout the thirteenth and fourteenth centuries there was a massive effort to translate the classics into the vernacular and thence into a multitude of languages." Borges sighs. "And with it, of course, you have the inevitability of shoddy renditions."

Borges is tired. He looks haggard. Once again, he rubs his eyes. I want to bring him up to date with the latest revolution in electronic communication, the slippage from analog to digital and the potential demise of print as a medium. But he rises, and with characteristic grace, excuses himself. "I am afraid I must go." He rolls his eyes. "Apparently, I am needed on the seventy-fifth tier where they are back translating a Spanish version of the *Don Quixote* to Aramaic."

As I watch Borges make his way to the winding staircase, a solemn looking emissary approaches. She asks if I have any lists to submit. From the bustle and murmurings around me I become aware I am on the tier designated 'The Bureau for Back Translation of Medical Texts'.

"Do you mean a compendium of noteworthy medical texts?" I offer. She nods impatiently. I have the distinct impression she is an automaton — an articulated component of a giant assembly line — programmed to feed the belt with modern texts that somehow have forsaken their usefulness.

With insufficient time to organise my thoughts, I blurt out, "You can start with Guy de Chauliac's *Chirurgia Magna* written in 1363. Then there is Bernard of Gordon's, *Lilium Medicinae* an encyclopedia of diseases from 1305, and, oh of course, the *Rosa Medicinae* by John of Gaddesden in 1314." She frowns with a decidedly puzzled look but quickly jots down the titles. She thanks me, turns and clicks away on high heels.

Ten minutes have hardly elapsed when I am suddenly accosted by an officious bespectacled man exhibiting an unmistakable air of authority. His silver gray goatee cannot hide compressed lips of sternness. He is short, chunky and wears a charcoal-grey suit and a crisp white shirt with starched collar. He introduces himself as the bureau chief but does not divulge his name.

"While we are grateful for your assistance in our work here," he begins, "I have to inform you of the precise order in which we operate. Let me explain. We are comprised of many learned experts — editors, translators, lexicographers, philologists, etymologists, linguists and specialists in semiotics. Our destiny (he actually uses the word) is to identify and back translate key medical texts to their source. As we progress from one language to its forerunner, we carefully, diligently and iteratively, test the authenticity with the revised text and then, piecemeal, continue the back translation until we reach the original version from which it is derived. It necessitates a process of strict orderliness."

He cocks his head and in a supercilious tone says, "Now, I regret to say, you have given us the titles of three so-called source texts. May I be so bold to say that you have simply pulled the titles out of your hat?" He has a high-pitched nasal tone, and speaks without a hint of irony. "They are derivative. Codifiers at best. No different than an amateur artist's copy of a Rembrandt let us say. Besides, your offers are fourteenth century compendia, far too obscure to be considered true source material." He is resolute, bearing a frustrated expression of impatience. I wonder whether, down deep, he also imagines this entire enterprise as quixotic.

Reading my thoughts, he continues. "Have no illusions. Our task on this particular floor is made all the more challenging because most classic medical theses were translated into the vernacular. Something to do with the foolhardy concept that medical science should be both informative and practical for the masses. We are thus compelled to back translate from many common languages — each steeped in their own peculiar idioms. It baffles me why they couldn't have restricted all medical texts to the mainstream languages of Latin, Arabic, Greek, Hebrew, Sanskrit or Chinese. Even the Carolingian minuscule crossed national boundaries and so is widely interpretable. You see the dilemma, don't you? Therefore, what we need from you is the sacred canon of medicine's source material. We'll do the rest."

He is about to bound away when I stop him. "May I ask how you can be assured of authentic recapture of the original text when a classic such as Hippocrates' *Materia Medica* has not only been through numerous stages in translation but for each rendition there was at least an attempt to interpret its pronouncements in the light of new advances?"

He stares at me with astonishment and shakes his head. "New advances are not our concern. Let me be clear how we operate here. At each stage of the process, we have multilingual editors who meticulously derive the original language from the back translation. We subordinate scientific validity to translational authenticity. Furthermore, our methods are exceedingly precise. They include no fewer than three distinct types of translation, namely: metaphrasic or word for word, paraphrasic to ensure idiomatic correctness, and machine language when needed."

I am about to interject when he waves me aside. "Our overall purpose is twofold. — First, to correct any discrepancies with regard to a translator's intent and, second, to discover the essence of the original pure language. We are expert at resolving issues of adaptation, abridgement, innuendo, and false interpretations. Our lingua franca is authenticity, pure and simple." He states this without a wink or smile. "Are you now prepared to contribute?" he asks.

I nod, uncomfortably aware that I may be embroiled in a fruitless venture. I am about to ask why they just couldn't access the rich store of medical manuscripts held by The Wellcome Trust in England but he has already scampered away.

My initial reaction is to oblige with the standard canon of ancient medical treatises. Mindlessly, I scribble the following: Pliny's *Historica Naturalis,* Hippocrates' *Materia Medica,* Galen's *Spiritus Animalis,* Celsus' *De Medicina,* The *Liber de Pulsibus* of Philaretus, Avicenna's *Canon of Medicine,* The Edwin Smith *Papyrus of Ancient Egyptian Medicine, The Ayurveda,* a Sanskrit classic of ancient India, and *the Huangdi neijing* of China. I even include, with tongue in cheek, F*asciculo de Medicina,* an ancient Roman text whose frontispiece depicts the Emperor Nero observing the autopsy of his mother Agrippina, who he murdered in 59 CE.

It then occurs to me that translations of literary masterpieces seldom capture the essence and fluency of the original — Edward Fitzgerald's *Rubaiyat* being a notable exception. In fact, with each forward translation the language shifts. There is a proportional and progressive blurring of the original prose. Conversely, in most translations of ancient medical treatises, the language is not only enhanced but the textual meanings are enriched as new discoveries came to the fore. What possible gains can back translators expect when the original text is replete with erroneous concepts of natural phenomena? It seems to me that I should be submitting a list of those astute translators who helped improve on the original texts by incorporating new ideas and evidence-based discoveries. A formidable task since in many instances there is no record of the translator's identity. Nevertheless, I feel obliged to press on.

I am reminded that while the illiterate populace of Western Europe lay dormant during the Dark Ages, the Arabs of Muslim Spain were busy translating Greek texts into a fluid universal language. Scientific texts were not only preserved but their ponderous Roman nomenclature was recalibrated into a more rational Arabic numeracy. I suddenly recall that in Cordoba and Toledo, entire schools of translators were busy sifting, clarifying, and interpreting the works of Galen, Hippocrates, and Dioscorides among others. Here, one discovers rare sightings of enlightenment. In deference to their accomplishments, I tear up my previous jottings and prepare a revised list of whatever I could remember of that select group of translators. I find a seat by the railing and, furiously, I begin writing. The list takes shape.

Gerard of Cremona, the Italian itinerant who went to Toledo and translated Al-Razi's *Recrueil des Traits de Medicine'* from Arabic to Latin. Abraham ibn Daud, a Hebraic scholar who translated Avicenna's encyclopaedic *Kitab al-Shifa'*. Andrea al Pago, a sixteenth century Italian who translated the works of Ibn-al Nafis into Latin. The Nestorian physician Hunain ibn Shaq, a writer of medical texts himself, translated many Greek medical treatises into Arabic and Syriac. And of course, how could I omit the esteemed Hebraic scholar, Maimonides. In his *Commentaries on the Aphorisms of Hippocrates* (he was using Hunain Ibn Ishak's nineth century. Arabic translation), one finds the following samples as critical emendations:

Says Hippocrates: 'He whose bowels are loose during youth develops dryness of his stools in old age...'
Says Maimonides: 'When I sought the truth I found that this assertion is undoubtedly false.'
Says Hippocrates: 'If a fever does not leave the febrile patient on odd days, it relapses.
Says Maimonides: 'This statement should read: '...on one of the crisis days irrespective of whether it is even or odd'

And so the revisions went on through two hundred pages.

I recall some translators who, using local argot, have enriched the source material without altering the intent or meaning. I include an example from the *Compendium Medicinae* of Gilbertus Anglicus, a translation into Middle English from the Latin by an unknown translator in the thirteenth century. Herewith, a reference to gonorrhea:

Gomorra, that is flowing of a manis sede agenis his wil, and this is of plente of blood, either of palesie of the stones, either of grete feblenes of a man that mai not withholden his sede, either it cometh for the sede is thinne and flowith oute lightli.

I was just about to write down this translation when out of the gloom I am startled by an intrusive courier. "Have you the list yet?" He is edgy and suspicious.

"I am afraid my list is incomplete so far," I reply. He does not budge. His eyes are cold and accusing.

I shrug and hand him my single sheet of paper. "Well, OK, if you insist. I should mention I decided to submit a list of translators rather than titles of original works."

He flinches and is about to protest when I add, somewhat defensively, "There is little to be gained from the titles of texts without knowing the translators. Isn't this the purpose of your enterprise here?" He stares at me incredulously. He looks at my scratchings, emits an exasperated sigh, and quickly departs.

This is serious! I am suddenly in a panic. I do not relish another confrontation with that pompous warlord.

I must escape. I look around and spot an opening to the circular staircase. I figure there must be an exit on the ground floor. As I descend the winding stairs I notice, on each floor, a re-enactment of the same frenetic activity. The buzz gets louder as I descend. Each tier appears to be assigned a specific theme. No fewer than four of them are dedicated to ancient Greek and Arabic canons. Three floors are confined to theological texts, four floors to ancient Indian and Chinese sources. An entire tier is devoted to a group of scholars wrestling with the works of Shakespeare and Dante.

As I tiptoe by the floor committed to American literature I stop short. I can hardly believe my eyes. A diatribe has broken out between Mark Twain and a cowed French editor. They are nose to nose arguing over a back translation from the French version of Twain's *The Notorious Jumping Frog of Calaveras County*. The Frenchman is sputtering. "Pardon, Monsieur Clemens. Je vous demande... je suis tres desole... un pauvre traducteur."

But Twain is in no mood for apologies. "Listen to me, you dumb Frenchman. Here is a sample from the story as I wrote it." In a loud sonorous voice Twain reads:

And he ketched Dan'l by the nap of the neck, and hefted him, and says, 'Why blame my cats if he don't weigh five pound!

"Now here is your translation:

Il empoigne Daniel par la peau du coo, le souleve et dit:--Le loup me croque, s'il ne pese pas cinq livres.

Do you have any idea what that says when back translated?" Twain is livid as he glares at the hapless translator. "It says:

He grasped Daniel by the skin of the neck, him lifted and said: 'The wolf me bite if he no weigh not five pounds.

"The wolf me bite!" Twain is apoplectic. Before I could watch the ensuing mayhem, I continue my descent down the vertiginous staircase.

Is there no way out of here? I feel a strange kinship with Dante when he descended the circles of his imaginary hell. Alas, I have no Virgil to guide me. Speaking of Virgil, I pass through an entire tier devoted to the Roman poets — translators working more soundlessly than the turmoil in the upper reaches.

Finally, I reach the ground floor — a wide expanse dotted with relics and steles inscribed with incomprehensible encryptions. I pass a group of solemn scholars hunched over a folio of the Sumerian, *Epic of Gilgamesh*. The floor is strewn with the cuttings of discarded epics. Finally, I spot an unmarked door in the distance. It holds promise of escape. As I make my way towards it I come across a bearded half-naked, half-crazed man imprisoned in a makeshift stockade. He is straightjacketed and watched over by a sleepy guard. When I inquire who he is, I am told he is the man who invented writing.

I quickly head for that unmarked door but the more I approach the further it recedes. The cacophony above me grows louder. When I look back, I see a horde of functionaries leaning over the railing and howling at me — accusatory fingers pointing at me. I am being pursued.

Suddenly, above the din I hear a ringing.

It is my wake-up call. I reach over to the bedside table and shut the alarm. And there on my desk, across the room, lies a solitary sheet of paper. It is blank save for a smudge of indecipherable scribbles.

The Gap: Time: Linear and Otherwise

Time. It keeps passing us by. What to make of it?

As one definition has it, time is an interval along a linear continuum. The emphasis is on interval. What does an interval mean? Well, if our brains are hard-wired in the time domain, then each passing interval is a momentary theft as we drift unsparingly towards a timeless denouement. However, must each interval be the same length? Some jokester defined the briefest interval of time as the gap between the instant a traffic light turns green and the blast of a cabbie's horn at a Manhattan intersection.

Time intervals do have relevance depending how they are construed. Suppose I was to ask you to pick up that chair you are sitting on and move it ten feet across the room. Before you begin, I excuse myself and leave the room for half an hour. When I return, I find you have successfully accomplished the task. However, as far as I can ascertain you may have used the time (that thirty-minute interval) to move the chair a few feet, sit in it for a while as you thumb through your smartphone, get up and move it a few feet, sit down again and so on. In other words, you would have accomplished the 'work' assigned, namely, the force (weight of chair) multiplied by the total distance (ten feet). As a consequence, I will have no way of determining the power or the rate of doing the work. Hence, the interval of time is a vital component of the speed at which anything is executed. It is oblivious of indolence.

Isaac Newton alerted us to acceleration which contains a second derivative of time — the rate of the rate of. Observe a seasoned golfer drive a ball off a tee or a major league baseball player swing a bat. To impart a greater force to the ball the athlete accelerates the club face or bat through the ball. That is to say the time intervals of the swing are decreasing exponentially prior to impact. The force imparted is mass times acceleration. Contrary to sports sabermetrics there is no such statistic as 'exit velocity' but rather exit acceleration. Of course there is the weekend duffer whose high handicap can be attributed to his or her golf club swinging at a constant velocity. Notice, we keep coming back to time intervals.

What about relativistic time? In one of his hyper-imaginative daydreams, Albert Einstein envisioned a space-time continuum wherein time slows down for objects in motion, especially at speeds approaching that of light. One way of recapturing your youth is to hitch a ride on a spaceship, circle our solar system for a number of years and return wrinkle free to the consternation of your peers. As an astronaut in space, you will have noticed your pocket watch ticking away at the same rate as always. But to your companions on earth it was ticking ever so slowly — making you age ever so unhurriedly compared to them.

If this isn't confusing enough, try to imagine time in the frequency domain. You are lying on a beach observing the ocean's tidal waves advancing and receding. It is your impression that they simply appear to come in, roll over and recede. Now watch closely and you may convince yourself of a pattern wherein the crest of each wave moves in synchrony with its corresponding nadir or undertow. That is to say, each wave acts as a component of a continuous distribution — each contributing its own unique power to the overall tide. You are now thinking in the frequency domain. If this isn't baffling enough think of it this way. As you lie on the sand you feel the heat of the sun as a constant sensation. But in reality, that heat is a continual wave function made up of multiple frequencies. One day in the year 1900, the German physicist, Max Planck, felt the heat emanating from a hot iron. Rather than interpret the sensation as a continuous wave he visualized the heat as wavelets composed of different frequencies. He estimated the energy components of each frequency, made some calculations and then startled the world with the theory of quantum mechanics. In the subatomic world, we have come to accept the notion that time is of a completely different order. But, let us not go there.

Instead, let us return to the time interval and consider this physiologic quirk. We appear to think, plan, act and behave as if our brains are hard-wired in the time domain. In other words, we are accustomed to time as the duration of an elapsed interval between two events. And yet most biological processes, not to mention the invisible world of electromagnetic and gravitational waves around us, function in the frequency domain. Frequency is simply the reciprocal of time. Remember in elementary school how you congratulated yourself when you successfully grasped the elements of addition and subtraction? Then all hell broke loose when you had to deal with fractions!

Consider this. Your brain interprets the external world in linear time governed by clocks, sundials and other time pieces. And yet, it is the same organ whose neuronal transmissions are oscillating in frequency mode — independent of time. If you were somehow to slip inside your own brain and listen carefully, you will be bombarded by a cacophony of crosstalk among billions of neurons. Your initial impression will be one of disorganized babble. But listen closely and you will detect a hum oscillating at a frequency of around forty hertz (forty cycles per second). In other words, like an assemblage of crickets or fireflies, our brain is an atonal symphony — entrained to purr more or less at a coordinated frequency.

Paradoxically, the more the staccato of our brain's collective rhythm approaches that of a metronome — a simple harmonic — the more it wobbles unsteadily. This is not an exaggeration. A not infrequent sign of impending doom is the conversion of complex biological signals such as the aperiodic nature of breathing cycles into one that is monotonous and repetitive. And yet our awakened lives are time bound, oblivious of the inexorable age-related shift to periodic oscillations within.

It seems the time-space continuum within the human brain operates on a level distinct from our interpretation of events around us. So, here is a thought. If our waking hours find us wedded to the time domain what about our dreams? Are they in frequency mode, unmindful of time? Wake up a person during REM, or dream mode sleep, and more often than not he or she will estimate their dream lasting much longer than the actual duration of their REM component.

Perhaps it is just as well we live in real or so-called linear time. It saves us the effort of recalibrating time into its frequency components. But more important, it spares us from watching our life slip away as we witness the inevitable swing from healthy chaotic rhythms to a worrisome regularity.

The Fix: Hidden Rhythms Probing the Secrets of our Biological Clocks

Morning Rounds in an Acute Coronary Care Unit
We were about to leave the patient's bedside when I turned to my entourage of junior doctors. "As you all can see, Mr Pascoe appears comfortable. Are there further observations any of you wish to make?" There was a shuffling of feet and a few shrugs.

Mr. Pascoe, a seventy-one-year-old retired electrician, lay motionless in bed. He wore a waxen complexion and had a look of resigned lethargy. But he exhibited no visible signs of distress. Propped up on two pillows he gazed at us with some listlessness. It was day three following his sudden heart attack and, so far, he had survived a worrisome but reversible bout of heart failure. Perhaps his despondency arose from the fact this was his second heart attack within the past eight months.

"I agree with his satisfactory progress," piped Tania, a junior house officer. She flashed an encouraging smile at Mr Pascoe. "As you can see from the bedside monitor, his heart rhythm is stable and regular at seventy beats per minute. His blood pressure, although moderately low at 105 over 80 is within the normal range for someone confined to bed. His lungs are clear and there is no evidence of fluid retention. His blood chemistry results have returned to normal and he is symptom free save for some weakness and fatigue — not unusual during this early phase of recovery. I would say he has a good prognosis." She smiled again at the patient who smiled, weakly, back.

I nodded. We thanked Mr Pascoe for his forbearance and took our leave. As we stepped outside the door I stopped suddenly and directed the group to take one more look at our patient. "Observe carefully," I said. "Anyone wish to comment on his breathing pattern?"

There was a collective gasp as they stared in disbelief. Mr Pascoe had dozed off, wearing an enigmatic expression. Suddenly his breathing stopped! We watched. Gradually his chest moved with slow deliberate heaves — a pattern which intensified with each breath. His chest, like a bellows, surged with each intake. It reached a crescendo only to subside, sputter and stop again. Slow and unrelenting the cycle repeated itself. At first my befuddled acolytes were stunned. Then, almost in unison, they correctly recognised this alternating pattern of periodic breathing as so-called Cheyne-Stokes respiration — an ominous signature of impaired central nervous system control.

"Do any of you wish to revise your prognosis?" I inquired.

Again, silent stares.

A hirsute sceptic, tieless in a rumpled shirt spoke up. "I don't see how this alters his prognosis. Couldn't his breathing pattern simply be a by-product of his medications? Or, how about chronic lung disease? He was, after all, a heavy smoker."

I shook my head. It was time for a lesson in revisionist physiology. "Come along," I said. "I want to introduce you to someone."

A Foetus in Distress

I led the group through a labyrinth of hallways until we reached a side corridor in the obstetrics wing of the hospital. I stopped at one of the doors and poked my head into the cluttered office of Dr George Broseg, an eccentric neonatologist with a flair for bold ideas.

"Good morning, George," I said. "May I introduce you to my young friends here? We have just encountered a fascinating problem in devious harmonics. A patient of ours is displaying the characteristic signs of periodic breathing. Only a self-effacing scholar like you can help us unravel its mystery. Do you still have that tracing?"

Dr Broseg, a tall bespectacled man with a full head of unruly black hair, smiled and welcomed us. He had a disarming effervescence about him. "Yes, I believe I have it stashed away somewhere." Begging our indulgence he scratched his head, as if lost in thought. He began rummaging through his overstuffed desk drawers while we drew up chairs and waited, politely.

After a minute of fruitless fumbling George suddenly stood up, slapped his forehead and, with a sheepish grin, pointed at his desk top. There, exposed for all to see, lay a sheet of paper inscribed with a tachogram of a continuous heart rate record from a foetus in distress.

Here is what it showed:

"What you see here," George explained, "is a continuous tracing of a baby's in utero beat-to-beat heart rate recorded during the hour before death. Observe closely. You see those tiny squiggles. They represent healthy oscillations in the beat-to-beat heart rate rhythm. However, you will notice that well before the terminal fade out, those squiggles abruptly change into a straight line. This means that the interval between each heartbeat is exactly the same. Just like a metronome or the ticking of a grandfather clock. And yet please notice. For at least the next twenty minutes the line does not diverge. There is no change in the average or mean heart rate! Something happened to cause those squiggles, which by the way, represent the normal healthy irregular beat to beat oscillations, to suddenly become perfectly regular. This, as you can see, was a sinister warning of impending doom!"

My innocent charges stared. They were transfixed.

"Reminiscent of Mr Pascoe's periodic breathing don't you think?" I interjected. There was a distinct stirring of unease. Was I suggesting a similar fate for Mr Pascoe?

Sensing their apprehension George intervened. "Obstetricians and neonatologists have long recognised that sudden slowing of a fetal heart rate prior to delivery was a dire distress signal. Alas, having to wait for it often wastes precious time for effective rescue. Here, on the other hand," he pointed to the tachogram, "a light goes on. Note that without any change in the average heart rate — the line does not deviate — those squiggles mysteriously disappear at least a half hour before the terminal deceleration. Those squiggles represent the beat-to-beat variability of a healthy heart rate. The straight line simply means that the baby's heart began tick-tocking like a metronome. You will not have noticed this if you had simply felt the pulse. In other words, you will have missed the transformation because you observe time on a linear continuum." George sat back and grinned.

I jumped in with a standard pedagogical ploy. "Tell us, George. How did this unique observation come about?"

But Tania was more real-world. "Yes, and how does it relate to Mr. Pascoe's peculiar breathing pattern?"

Professor Broseg nodded. "This unique observation was first described by Drs EH Hon, and ST Lee at Loma Linda University in 1963. However, the nature and precise deconvolution of these so-called squiggles would have to wait almost ten years before a bioengineer, Bruce McA Sayers, applied a fast Fourier algorithm to transform heart rate squiggles into its frequency domain." This was met by blank stares. Realizing he had to tread with mathematical care George paused to shake tangles of complex biometrics from his mind and recalibrate his thoughts.

"I apologise. What I will show you is a hidden treasure whereby your perfectly normal heartbeat or pulse contains within it the cross-talk between your brain and your heart. The physiologic significance of these hidden rhythms was first elucidated in 1981 when Richard Cohen and his associates at the Massachusetts Institute of Technology probed the biologic nature of these oscillations. And presto, a whole new world opened up — one that enabled, for the first time, a glimpse into the brain's intricate control of the heart's electrical apparatus. Allow me."

George's cramped office exuded a strange blend of mystique and inscrutability. We settled in and braced ourselves.

A mean looking Mean

George was in his element. He stood up and stared at each of us. "Have any of you ever considered the duplicitous nature of the mathematical mean?" A few raised eyebrows but no takers.

George smiled and went on. "OK. Think of this. Whenever you measure such vital parameters as blood pressure, heart rate, temperature or breathing frequency don't you express them as mean or average values? For example, you report a patient's heart rate to be, let us say, seventy-two beats per minute. What does that measurement truly indicate? In point of fact, it indicates that over the span of one minute the mean or average value of the inverse of those intervals would approximate the number seventy-two. However," George paused and waggled his hands in the air, "from a physiologic perspective, that mean value of seventy-two, by itself, is nothing more than a masquerade — a set point around which beat to beat impulses oscillate."

Again, this was met by knitted brows and helpless shrugs. Fearing he was losing his audience, George regained his composure and continued.

"Forgive me for being obtuse. To put it bluntly, most dynamical control systems in our body act as rheostats. That is to say they oscillate around a so-called mean or optimal value. We have since learned that these integrated systems are governed by an elaborate biophysical balance between forward and negative feedback influences be they neurologic, hormonal, biochemical or whatever." The glazed looks of my charges did not change. Unperturbed, George continued in his customary buoyancy.

"Sad to say, we are habituated to the lure of the mean value. In one sense it is worthless and yet powerfully seductive. Why? Because for any stretch of an oscillating waveform the mean value throughout its time course pops up more frequently and thus overpowers other values in the series. As such, it obscures or dampens the relevant information hidden within. Those tiny squiggles in the tracing I showed you are easily overshadowed by the potency of the mean value in that continuous heart rate series. Don't you see? That is what makes them so tiny and squiggly." The young doctors seemed to give a collective sigh. They were catching on. Satisfied, George continued.

"I submit to you that the mean value is a cover-up, a diversionary tactic to camouflage any underlying process that happens to fluctuate independently. Even clinical epidemiologists and statistical number crunchers, well aware of this seductive mathematical force, caution us with a favourite expression of theirs — 'Beware of regression toward the mean'." Heads nodded knowingly. George had their attention.

"So let us assume that the mean value in any segment of a person's continuous heart rate record is covering up something of value. Why not get rid of it and expose what lies beneath? Let me show you." George pulled out a strip of another tachogram and laid it out on his desk.

"Behold," he bellowed. "Here is a two-minute strip of a continuous heart rate series which, basically, appears to be nothing more than a series of undulations. It squiggles because the inter-beat intervals are not uniform.

"Now try to visualise the mean value as a straight line running through this series. OK? Do you have it in your mind's eye? I will now demonstrate that it is this mean value that stifles the oscillations much like the small squiggles we saw on that fetal heart rate tracing. To rid ourselves of this conspiracy I will use a pair of metaphorical tweezers to remove the mean value and pull — delicately. Just so.

"Eh, voila!

"This is what a 'demeaned' time series looks like." George stood back to let us puzzle over this squawk.

"Please note," he exclaimed. "We are still on a linear timescale. You will now appreciate how utterly grotesque is this oscillatory pattern of your heartbeat stripped of its mean value. It bears little resemblance to a simple sine wave. And yet, rather than discard it into a trash heap, it contains powerful information as long as we stop staring at it in linear time. Indeed, hidden within this wacky hieroglyphic lurks a translatable code for the brain's delicate control of heart rate rhythm."

My young acolytes now sat up, mystified.

Encouraged, George pressed on. "To uncover this secret code, this treasure if you will, we transform this ugly time series into its frequency domain. Our aim is to determine, mathematically, how often a given heartbeat interval repeats itself during the run. We can apply one of several standard deconstruction algorithms. For example, a so-called Fast Fourier analysis if we choose to work our way forwards —

peering into the future as it were. Or backwards, using what is called a regressive algorithm, to see where we have been. Either direction — it doesn't matter. I will spare you the mathematics involved. Trust me." George laughed as he waved a magical wand above his head.

"And now, behold as I transform that unsightly blot from the time domain to the frequency domain."

George paused to let his sleight of hand sink in. "Look — I have nothing up my sleeve," he laughed. "Remarkable, isn't it? From that grotesque time domain tracing on the left we now see it smoothed and double peaked. From a physiologic perspective those two smooth peaks offer a window through which you can visualise the brain's control of your heart rate rhythm."

Did I detect a spark of insight from among the group? Their raised eyebrows expressed more wonder than perplexity. Having aroused our interest, George resumed his wizardry with slow deliberation. He pointed at the figure.

"Let us begin with that second bump herein designated as HF or high frequency. It usually peaks around 0.2 Hertz. Those of you who are mathematically inclined will recognise that a 0.2 Hertz frequency cycles at about twelve to sixteen times per minute. Does this not correspond to your average breathing rate? Now, you may wonder through what nefarious pathway your breathing cycle suddenly appears in your heartbeat rhythm. Well, if I were to inject you with atropine. You all know what atropine is?" A few nods. "Also known as the deadly nightshade? Or belladonna when applied to women who yearn for beautiful dilated irises?" George was enjoying himself.

"By injecting you with atropine I could obliterate that so-called respiratory spike thus confirming that the 0.2 Hertz peak is under the influence of your parasympathetic or vagal nervous system. In fact, if I were to decapitate you and thereby strip your heart rate of all central nervous system control, your heart would naturally start beating at its own intrinsic heart rate — about ninety to one hundred beats per minute. This implies that as long as your heart is connected to the vagal centers in your brain, your resting heart rate will naturally be slowed to sixty to eighty beats per minute and settle under the warm embrace of a protective watchdog. To put it bluntly, the vagal arm of the autonomic nervous system acts as a brake on any unfettered burst of adrenaline from sympathetic nerve centers in the brain. The word sympathetic is a misnomer. Can you imagine what it would be like to be in the constant grip of a flight or fight reaction — our hearts pounding incessantly, our emotions on tenterhooks — and yet feel sympathetic?" George could not contain himself. My young doctors were not amused.

"Excuse me. What does my breathing have to do with my heart rate?" This from the rumpled shirt who seemed to have missed the point.

"It is all interconnected," replied George. "Like a beautiful syncytium. Picture this. All organs in the body possess sensory receptors. When activated, these receptors transmit nerve impulses to the brain. They either beseech the brain's processing centers to react to these sensory inputs or simply remind the brain not to ignore their existence. To answer your question, it was Dr Dwain Eckberg from The Medical College of Virginia who demonstrated that the very act of breathing gates your heart rate rhythm through a major control center in your mid-brain. Whenever you inhale, the sensory receptors in your lung deliver a signal that detours through special receptors located in your neck vessels. A secret transmission code then directs the brain center to disinhibit adrenaline release so that the heart rate can increase during the inspiratory phase of your breathing." George was on a roll. Nothing could stop him.

"When you come to think of it, this curious bond between breathing and heart rate makes eminent sense. As you inhale you are creating a gradient of pressure between your heart and your far-flung peripheral veins in the nether reaches of your body. According to basic hydraulic principles, this gradient serves to suck blood from those lower sites up towards your heart. To aid this pressure differential there is an obligatory increase in your heart rate. How else can you stand or walk erect when your circulating pump is at the wrong end of your body?" A tittering and nods of agreement save from the rumpled sceptic who, with a perplexed frown, remained silent. George smiled and continued.

"Let us now direct our attention to the first spike or bump in that figure. It usually occurs bang on at 0.1 Hertz. This component indicates that every ten seconds there is a distinctive hum in your beat-to-beat heart rate signal. Well, maybe not an auditory hum but you get the metaphor. Its exact physiologic function has been the source of lively debate. Nevertheless, it clearly comprises a major, albeit not exclusive, contribution from the sympathetic nervous system." George paused and was momentarily lost in thought. Or so it seemed. He smiled to himself and continued.

"The late Italian scientist, Alberto Malliani and his colleagues in Milan helped illuminate the physiologic role for these hidden rhythms, especially that elusive 0.1 spike. I could just visualize Alberto — slight of build, delightfully exuberant — posing this question with a twinkle in his eye. 'Whenever you suddenly stand erect from a lying position what prevents you from falling on your face?'

"Before you could respond he would jump-start the answer by pointing to a sharp increase in that 0.1 Hertz peak as a subject stands upright from a supine state — a clear reflex response indicating a correlation between sympathetic nerve activity and this low frequency (LF) component."

Sensing the bewildered stares of my young doctors George pursed his lips and whimpered "Sorry to get carried away. The important lesson here is that your heartbeat is aperiodic — off kilter — a bundle of life affirming frequency modulations. It turns out that the more variable your beat-to-beat sequence the healthier you are. Simply put, your allotted store of potential life energy is expressed, in part, as the degree of irregularity in your beat-to-beat heart rate intervals. Stated in terms of energy equivalence, the more regular your heartbeat, the less the entropy. And you know what that portends? Terminal fatigue. And so, we are made up of a bundle of seemingly deterministic rhythms, well hidden within the deep recesses of our primitive brain."

"Is this what is known as chaos?" inquired one of the students.

"Perhaps," replied George. "One can say with confidence that virtually all biological systems behave as non-linear processes and any drift towards linearity or periodicity is a drift into the tugging arms of lifelessness." George winked at the young doctors. "Although we think and act in the time domain our innards are wired in the frequency domain — a bundle of rhythmic oscillations — interconnected wavelets whose intrinsic power defines our life force. In short, as nature abhors a vacuum so does our complex biological matrices resist any tilt towards numbing regularity." A few puzzled grimaces but no challenges. I sensed my young charges needed a break to digest it all.

"George, could you grant us a reprieve?" I intervened. "May I suggest we regroup tomorrow morning at nine a.m. By then our non-linear brain will be refreshed and ready to explore more hidden treasures." I turned to the young docs. "Would that be convenient?"

With a collective nod we thanked our esteemed professor and left with expectations of mysteries yet to unfold.

In Pursuit of Elusive Signals

The next morning, we assembled once again in George's office. All were present except Tania, the young doctor who offered encouragement to Mr Pascoe. When she wandered in late her shoulders were hunched. She appeared distraught.

"I am sorry to be late," she said with a catch in her voice. "I went to check on Mr Pascoe. It turns out that late last night he had to be transferred to the general ward to make room for an emergency admission." Tania then shook her head in disbelief. "About two hours later he was found dead in bed. Attempts at cardiac resuscitation were unsuccessful."

The others drew in their breath and looked at me with mixed emotions — a blend of awe and consternation. I was at a loss for words. George skillfully intervened to break the mood. "I'm terribly sorry to hear that." A long pause and then he quietly asked, "In light of this tragedy do any of you have any insights regarding yesterday's lesson?"

"Yes," replied the rumpled shirt. "Do any of your fancy mathematics have any clinical significance?"

"Exactly," blurted out an exasperated Tania. "Just as with that fetal heart rate tracing you showed us couldn't we have tracked the time series of Mr Pascoe's heart rate variability and intervened earlier to prevent his sudden cardiac arrest?"

"Good questions," I replied, realising this critical issue was more in my bailiwick. "With all our fancy technology you would think any ominous oscillations in Mr Pascoe's heart rate record could have been detectable. Theoretically, they could be. But how wide does the window of opportunity have to be to enact timely and effective intervention? Sadly, we have yet to bridge that divide. Perhaps, one day Artificial Intelligence with its boundless capacity for data manipulations can help solve the dilemma. It turns out that several so-called markers of impending doom have been proposed but so far, we have had to rely on devices such as intra-cardiac defibrillators as bystanders for patients at risk. However, these devices do not anticipate. They shock after the fact. We desperately need that crazy bearded doomsday freak who is forever crying out 'the end is near' to tell us exactly when that end is near."

I went on hoping to assuage my guilt — as if I felt somehow responsible. "Sadly, as with many prognostic indicators, knowledge of death foretold is an uncomfortable expectancy when there is little that can be done about it. The cutting room floor of medicine is strewn with useless biomarkers that prophesy in vain." I was exhorting one of my pet peeves and about to launch a tirade when, fortunately, I was sidetracked by a question from a solemn looking junior resident — clipboard at the ready. He directed the question at George.

"Sir, can you enlighten us on the biologic basis for these hidden rhythms?"

"Ah yes, the black box," replied George. "We have yet to plummet the inner sanctum of brain-body physiology let alone unravel the intricate mechanisms of most diseases. But this enterprise of non-linear wavelets has opened up a new venture. There are many theories floating about, some of which are eminently testable. Some not. Here is my take and then tell me what you think.

"Engineers are all too familiar with the paradigm of the black box. If you know the nature of the input and output signals then you can surmise whether the black box is a linear or non-linear processor. Consider this analogy. Let us suppose the heart is not just a simple pump but an elaborate sensory organ that constantly sends signals to the brain which, by interpreting these signals, somehow instructs the heart on how best to meet the body's metabolic needs. The sensory signals that the heart is attuned to can be physical, such as muscle fiber stretch, wall tension, spatial distortion or chemical such as hormonal release or nerve stimulation.

Whatever the signal they are ultimately relayed to centers of autonomic regulation in brain.

"Now, let us imagine one of these centers as a black box situated in the lower part of our mid-brain. From a neurophysiologic perspective let us assume those incoming nerve signals enter this box as a tonic waveform. By this I mean a continuous staccato of musical blips that enter the black box, a linear pattern like soldiers marching on parade. If you then sneak around to see what comes out the other side of the box, a totally different configuration of the input signal emerges. Thus, by definition, the box is a non-linear processor, one that integrates numerous inputs from various sources both without and within the brain. Don't even try to fathom the jumble of cross-talk and babble within." George was fired up. His eyes flashed. He spoke rapidly — having already lost most of us.

"Suffice to say, these non-linear outputs serve several homeostatic functions. One of which is to put a brake on nerve discharges from other brain sites — notably those nerves that release adrenaline from overexcited sympathetic nerve centers. Under steady state conditions, there is an orderly march of nerve impulses down both the sympathetic and vagal limbs of the autonomic nervous system to the heart. This is what modulates the heart's unique beat to beat heart rate variability. With age, and certain disease states such as heart failure, the strength of this variability weakens. In other words, the power contained in that doubled peaked spectrum I showed you diminishes."

George looked around to see if he had struck a chord. Silence. I suspected the group was stumped by this time. And so, I tried a pithy explanation.

"Allow me to go out on a limb and offer these speculations. That brake on our over-excitable sympathetic nervous system is what I believe keeps us healthy. To put it bluntly, it is our soothing humming vagal nerve discharges rather than our macho adrenaline, which sustains our vital life force. For many years we believed that to combat poor cardiac performance we needed more oomph — more so-called muscular energy. In fact, it was once considered malpractice to use anti-sympathetic drugs for heart failure. Now everything is topsy-turvy. We have learned to calm the failing, agitated and dispirited heart with so-called restful medications such as beta blockers and ACE inhibitors that keep adrenaline at bay. It may not be a coincidence that these drugs happen to enhance heart rate variability. If you will excuse a bad pun, one can say that the sympathetic nerve, when unrestrained, is not only unsympathetic — it is downright disheartening!"

A few groans from the students. On balance I sensed a mixture of scepticism and acquiescence. George was just getting wound up but the group signalled a silent plea to be dismissed for their next assignment. Permission granted. The junior doctors expressed their appreciation to Professor Broseg. They then, in unison, arose from their chairs and quietly filed out. Much to chew on.

A Sinister Plot
I was also about to leave when George tugged my sleeve. "May I have a word?" he whispered. He seemed excited. There was a conspiratorial gleam in his eyes. His grip on my arm tightened. "I want your opinion on an extraordinary project I and a select cadre of investigators are working on." I sat down, puzzled by the term 'cadre'. George checked the corridor and silently closed the door. He then sat opposite, leaned towards me and launched into a spine-tingling proposition.

"Let us consider your unfortunate patient, Mr Pascoe. I am sure you will agree he was a ticking time bomb. In other words, his heart ticked like a metronome — tick-tock, tick-tock in perfect unison. And then there was silence. Would he have cheated the grim reaper if he had been wired with any of today's electronic surveillance devices? Not likely. Oh sure, there are sophisticated pacing devices that overdrive dangerous rhythms and some that resynchronize the heart's squeeze. But I submit to you, those devices have two major drawbacks. First, they either convert the heart from a highly complex organ to a mere mechanical pump or they impose a brainless periodicity or tick-tocking of their own — emphasis on the brainless."

I was about to interject, when he held up his hand and exclaimed, "Please do not get me started on implanted cardiac defibrillators. Those who truly need it are not infrequently at the mercy of painful repetitive shocks to their chests. A dubious bargain to say the least. Besides, electronic zappers are an affront to nature's delicate balance. There has to be a better option."

George leaned in further. I could feel his fevered breath on my face. He whispered, "I believe I have the answer. Let us suppose that Mr Pascoe's main autonomic processor in his brain was already beyond redemption. After all, judging by his periodic breathing, his brain was sending weak signals to his lungs and heart. In other words, the inter-beat intervals of his heart rate rhythm were already approaching that of a metronome — a doomsday scenario. Now what if we converted those mind-numbing tick-tocking nerve impulses into something more irregular — more phasic so to speak?"

I squirmed uneasily but held my tongue.

George noticed me cringe. "Please bear with me. Given its unassailable complexity, that black box in our brain — the one responsible for sending out those phasic irregular nerve impulses to the heart — is impenetrable. Its internal switches and tangled wires are beyond our ability to engineer it. How can we ever duplicate or supplant the modulatory rhythms that emanate from the box and, more important, how can we ensure preservation of a healthy entropy within the system? Not even Artificial Intelligence could crack that code." The more George's demeanor became aroused the more uncomfortable I became.

Suddenly his eyes widened. He jumped up. "We don't need the black box!" he shouted. "We have already concluded that Mr Pascoe's black box had either stopped receiving healthy signals or somehow had run out of steam. So why bother? But suppose, just suppose, we could deliver healthy phasic nerve signals to the heart *after* it leaves the black box. We bypass the processor. Can't you see it?"

I was dumbstruck. What was he getting at?

"It's simple," he exclaimed. "First, we take a snapshot — a template if you will — of an individual's healthy beat to beat heart rate record when he or she is in the full bloom of life. We file it for future use. Should that individual's heart rate intervals begin to signal unmistakable trends to regularity we implant an electronic device customized to replicate that person's former healthy aperiodic rhythm. We can do this by simply attaching wires to the autonomic nerves directly innervating the heart — leapfrogging the black box. Don't you see? Instead of our current mind-numbing tick-tock pacemakers we can now have, for the first time, a personalized physiologic pacemaker designed to spare the heart from impending doom. A device guaranteed to ensure life sustaining aperiodic complexity!"

I felt a slight churning in the pit of my stomach. "Do you mean creating a surgical surrogate for the brain's natural neural messages?" I asked.

"Why not?" George replied. "I and my colleagues have already confirmed, in anaesthetized dogs, that such a device can deliver signals to the heart without affecting other vital parameters such as blood pressure, heart rate or breathing rate. And so, we can now safely restore life affirming energy to a weakened system. Just think of it." George was now pacing in front of me, gesticulating, eyes ablaze "While others are wasting their time trying to extend life by genetic manipulation of chromosomal telemeres — a surefire way of inducing biological mayhem — our approach is based on sound engineering concepts of restored equilibrium."

He paused to catch his breath but before I could object, he went on. "There is no shortage of technical know-how when it comes to highly developed electronic pacing. I ask you to use your imagination. An implanted aperiodic pacemaker individually customized to guard against the heart's tendency to tick-tock itself to death.

"Are you suggesting a device that confers immortality?" I half-jested.

"Your words, not mine," Borseg replied with a grin eerily reminiscent of Peter Sellers' portrayal of Dr Strangelove. The cramped room suddenly became oppressive. And so, I politely begged to be excused.

"I take it you are not convinced," George cried as I retreated towards the door. "Don't you see? This can be the greatest scientific breakthrough of the century!"

"Maybe so," I said. "But I shudder to visualise our soul trapped inside a crumbled body begging to be free of perpetual life support."

The Gap: Death and Dying

With the advent of antibiotics in the early twentieth century death became less an event and dying more a process. The germ theories of Pasteur and Koch in the late nineteenth century alerted us that human life is at the mercy of interlopers from outside the body. Infectious disease was indiscriminate of age. Aside from the chronicity of tuberculosis, the downhill spiral of deadly diseases such as smallpox, cholera and pneumococcal pneumonia was all too rapid, especially in children. Even in polite societies the bedside vigil was often one of watchful helplessness.

Today, dying is a process oozed out. It primarily affects the elderly, chronically burdened with the debilitations of heart disease, stroke, cancer and dementia. More dis-ease than disease. There is an awareness of turning the corner. The protraction extends the suffering yet offers time to await a restorative panacea while settling one's affairs. Nevertheless, we have yet to come to grips with how best to manage those at the turning point whence dying, the process, is irreversible.

We appear to be the only species on earth unable to confront our mortality without conceiving the inevitable exodus as a theft. So hell-bent are we to defy our natural end we seek to subvert it, either by extending it beyond or shortening it before its allotted time. Nowadays, in modern societies, the majority of death and dying occurs in hospitals. Inordinate sums of money are dispensed to forestall death in our hospitals' intensive care units. Here, a not atypical scenario is seen where a hopeless life, shattered with multi-organ failure, is assaulted by desperate end of life measures. It is as if death, perceived as the enemy, is to be thwarted at all costs. But what, pray tell, could be worse, death or immortality, with its curse of endless tedium?

To be fair not all of us 'rage against the dying of the light'. There are those resigned to a peaceful end while others choose to abbreviate life through well intentioned doctor assisted suicide. Why must a doctor be involved? Let us consider this curious evolution of the doctor's role when having to confront a dying patient. Granted, medical school curricula rarely acknowledge *dying* as a distinctly manageable process. Up to the latter half of the eighteenth century, a physician's primary obligation to the untreatable was to 'comfort' and 'console'. Following the introduction of vaccination, antisepsis and improvements in sanitation the physician's obligation throughout the nineteenth century, was to 'prevent' and, if possible, to 'treat'. Following the advent of antibiotics in the early twentieth century, the expectation was to *cure* and now, in the twenty-first century, there is the added obligation — to 'kill'.

Our human consciousness seems ill-prepared for an amicable departure. Consider the fact that medical science, together with advances in public health, have contributed to a doubling of life expectancy over the past two hundred years. And yet we judge life to be too short no matter how many years are added. This begs an interesting question. If all death is premature, taken before its allotted time, does it follow that something or someone is to blame? Bereavement is not a trait unique to humans. But it is doubtful the elephant, mourning its departed mate, is consumed with a passion to blame another pachyderm for a supposedly premature death.

We are unique among our fellow creatures in devising reverential displays of both death and dying. Inherent in these tombs and totems is a reminder of a life once lived or, at least, the promise of a legacy as a compensation for the drudgery of life on earth. Organised religion offers tropes to flout the finality of death. Whether it is the vision of a heavenly garden beyond St Peter's gates or the greetings of black-eyed virgins or the arrival of a messianic judgement day when the dead are resurrected or a belief in reincarnation, all are efforts to ease that final passage. To be sure, religion offers succor to both the dying and their survivors. Many are those, friends and family alike, who are at a loss for words in the presence of the dying. Relief is afforded by the pastor whose ability to invoke a comforting silence serves as a convenient balm.

And then there is the spiritualist's perspective whence a vaporous and fleshless soul is seen to escape a lifeless body. Elaborate seances offer glimpses into a spectral world in which one can communicate with the dead. The reader will forgive me if I offer this apocryphal yarn of a deathbed scene between two bosom buddies, Lou and Jake. Both have shared a lifetime together playing and loving the game of baseball. Lou is now dying. Jake, standing at the edge of the bed, makes a plea. "Lou, my dearest pal, would you do me a great favor. After you have passed on could you somehow send me a message from the beyond? I have to know if there is baseball in heaven." Lou dies and one night, two weeks later, he appears before Jake in the form of a ghostly image. Jake is overwhelmed by the spectre. However, with great anticipation he calls out. "So tell me Lou. Is there baseball in heaven?"

Lou replies, "Jake, I have good news and bad news for you. The good news is yes, there is baseball in heaven. The bad news is you are pitching this Sunday."

Rather than offer succor the philosopher breaches the emotional divide by expounding on the metaphysical. If death is the ultimate absence of consciousness, or nonexistence, then why are we in fear of it? We are not fearful of sleep without dreams. Nor are we concerned with our non-existence before we were born. The latter, a void also known as 'pre-vital nonexistence', has little meaning to most of us unless we believe in reincarnation or rebirth. Even here, reincarnation is fraught with the inability to recapture a previous consciousness. And yet we are saddled with the fear of a post-vital nonexistence — an unfair swipe at our tumultuous reality. We cannot conceive nor sense nothingness because we lack a reference.

And so, here is something to chew on. Can there ever be harmony with death? An acceptance without rancor? A realisation, whether biological, rational or religious, that the time has come at the proper moment. Surely, it is too great a burden on God to saddle Him with all those 'allotted' times? Perhaps, to achieve equanimity and harmony with death, we need to recognize and accept when the countervailing forces have gained the upper hand.

"Why should we?" you exclaim.

Fair enough. Perhaps the following tale can help realign harmony with death.

The Fix: A Russian Parable

In 1908 the Nobel Prize in Medicine or Physiology was awarded jointly to Elie Metchnikoff and Paul Ehrlich in recognition of their work on immunity. The following year Metchnikoff and his wife, Olga Belokopytova, toured Russia where Elie was regaled a national hero despite his émigré status and Russia's sordid treatment of him in the past. There is no record of Metchnikoff having ever met Leo Tolstoy. But that does not mean it could not have happened, given the similarities in their headstrong refusal to accept society's norms."

On a spring day in 1909, Elie Metchnikoff and his wife, Olga, are cordially received as guests of Count Leo Tolstoy at his estate, Yasnaya Polyana, in Tula, Russia. The literary giant, now an iconic rabble-rouser, is eighty-one years old, physically frail but alert of mind. The three sit in straight-backed upholstered chairs in Tolstoy's study, a somewhat cramped dimly lit room whose walls are covered with large family portraits. Close by is a round table, upon which sits a nickel-plated samovar. Tea is served by a housemaid. Tolstoy's wife, Sophia Andreevna, is intermittently spotted, lurking in the background. Every now and then she appears in the doorway and glares at Olga. But she never enters.

Tolstoy sits unperturbed. His deep-set, grey eyes, still penetrating, are shadowed by a prominent brow. His face is impassive, his demeanor humorless. His forked white beard flows down upon his upper chest, resting on a peasant's blue tunic. His crossed legs are encased in knee length black boots. Olga looks on, silently charmed by the similarity between the dour expressions of Tolstoy and her husband, Elie.

Tolstoy narrows his eyes and barks at Elie, "I am told, Ilya Ilyich, that you have become absorbed in the study of senescence. I do wish you would hurry with a cure. My feeble body is in rapid decline."

Elie frowns. "Like you, Lev Nikolayavich, I am a closet anarchist. I fight a constant battle with those who believe our bodies are comprised of harmonious bits. But how can we be in harmony when we fear death? It is unnatural don't you think?"

"Nonsense," cries Leo. "Granted, my body has parted ways with my mind but I am not in fear of death." Tolstoy shifts his weight and leans toward Elie. "But tell me Illya. There are rumors you have discovered a panacea to immortality. So my friend, before I drift into that eternal unknown, can you share the secret of your life-sustaining potion?"

"Orthobiosis," exclaims Elie, without a hint of flippancy. "It is nothing less than a process that guarantees the ideal way to live one's life both hygienically and morally."

"Spare me the moral humbug," Tolstoy snorts. "I've had my fill of preachers. Now, as a scientist could you describe, in simple words, your hygienic scheme for a long and happy life?"

Elie glances at Olga — silently assuring her that he will avoid a long-winded dissertation. He then addresses Tolstoy who appears attentive albeit somewhat heavy-lidded. "One day, in 1872, I was crossing the Rhone Bridge in Geneva when I was suddenly surrounded by a cloud of winged insects. They were mayflies from the order *Ephemeroptera*. An apt name when you consider that these flying insects have a lifespan of mere minutes to hours. And yet they appear fully formed with short, flexible antennae, large compound eyes and three ocelli."

Elie's eyes widen. He pauses for effect and then tilts toward Tolstoy. "However, they lack functioning mouthparts and their digestive system is filled with air. They do not feed. Can you imagine that?"

Tolstoy grimaces and shakes his head.

Elie continues. "It almost shattered my belief in Darwin's concept of adaptation. I thought to myself, how can the theory of natural selection apply to these insects when they are condemned to a brief life of starvation? It then dawned upon me that perhaps their immature digestive system, while ill adapted for survival, may provide a clue to the genealogy of higher organisms. And so, later that year, when I returned to the University of Odessa, I applied myself wholeheartedly to the study of tiny invertebrates. I focused all my attention on the larvae of the flatworm *geodesmus* which, by the way, also has no gut. I discovered its blastula, the earliest cell stage of embryonic development, while possessing the same triple germ layers found in higher organisms, actually differentiates along a separate path."

Olga heard this remarkable story before but stares transfixed at her excited husband as he unravels the sequence of his famous discovery.

"Unlike the invagination of that innermost so-called endodermal layer which ultimately forms the gut of vertebrates, in such as we humans, there is no such process in these metazoans. Instead, it is their mesodermal or middle layer that contains specialized migratory cells. And it is these cells which go on to fulfil the organism's digestive function. Picture this. Wriggly as an amoeboid, these cells perched on the outer edge of the blastula, lose their flagellum as they migrate from one pole of the blastula towards the center. Here they search for delicacies to sniff and engulf. Think of that! Who needs a digestive tract?

"Even jelly fish and other *hydropolypi* share this form of intercellular digestion during their larval stages. This was a double blessing for me because it allowed me to continue my studies in balmy Messina, off the coast of southern Italy. There, in abundance, were marine fauna at my disposal. One day I stumbled on the observation that certain cells not only have the capacity to digest for nutrition but also to attack and digest intruders."

"Ah yes," Tolstoy interjects. "Phagocytosis! What a clever word. Cells that eat other cells. But what does this have to do with warding off senescence?"

"Ah my dear Lev Nikoleyovich, I hate to disappoint you. It turns out our fear of death is not psychological. We are short changed by a contracted lifespan attributed, in part, to a quirky evolutionary design flaw shared by most mammals, of which you and I are hopeless members. Let me illustrate this by comparing the lifespan of a canary and a mouse. You will agree they are both about the same size. Even their vital parameters such as heart rate, blood pressure and metabolism are similar. And yet the canary enjoys a lifespan more than three times longer than the mouse. Why so? I believe that throughout the animal kingdom the major difference in natural life expectancy lies in the fact that most land-based mammals are afflicted with an atavistic organ — the large intestine."

Tolstoy shudders but says nothing.

Elie notices the rebuff but decides to pour it on. "Yes, we are cheated of a proper lifespan because we are the repositories of putrefied waste. Allow me to explain. Because weight must be minimized in flight, most birds are spared unnecessary baggage such as a large intestine. They discharge their waste spontaneously while we land mammals, when in flight from danger, can ill afford to stop and evacuate on the moment. We carry around this large intestine which happens to contain billions of microorganisms. As we enter so-called senescence, it is these bacteria which eventually transform from consensual to conspiratorial."

Tolstoy makes no response but listens attentively.

Elie shifts his gaze to Olga and then back to Tolstoy. "In old age our detente with these zillions of bacteria comes undone. Instead, sedition slowly develops between our acquired immunity — our army of phagocytic cells — and our intestinal flora. The time dependent wear and tear of our cells and organs render them easy prey. Just look at us, Lev Nikolayavich. Our hair follicles have turned white, our skin is wrinkled, our bones are friable, our breath is short and so on. We are on a fast track to premature senility. We have precious little time to age gracefully. And so, our fear of death is simply a recognition that we have, thanks to overzealous auto-digestion, come to our end prematurely."

"And your cure for this cannibalism?" Tolstoy inquires.

Elie grins. "Sour milk! Think of the Abkhazian people of the Caucasus, of whom you have written so elegantly. They live to an exceedingly old age. Why? Well, it may interest you to know they subsist mainly on sour milk. Our gut organisms thrive in an alkaline media. The sour milk residue, consisting of lactobacilli, will acidify and hence neutralize the gut bacteria. But let me be clear. The intestinal bacteria do not suddenly become the enemy. They are more or less conscripted by our own faltering defense mechanisms. You see, our phagocytes come to visualise our weakened cells as vestigial components that require cleansing. With proper hygienic and moral precepts as guides we can achieve a more natural 'old age' and face death with un-embittered resignation."

Tolstoy turns to Olga, and says, "Do you believe we can ever be in harmony when it comes to dying? I do not want to be unkind but is it not true that my good friend here attempted suicide, not once but twice? How is that harmonious?"

Olga smiles. "Before we married in February 1875, I was warned about Ilya's so-called violent temper and narcissism. Instead, I saw a compassionate, thoughtful and caring man — fiercely dedicated to science."

She turns to Elie. "Dearest Ilya, you have always been thoughtful and compassionate to those you love. When your late departed wife, Ludmilla Federovitch, had to be wheeled like an invalid into the wedding chapel I am told how gentle and caring you were. How you took care of her so lovingly. She had such a short life before she died from consumption. I know, my dear Ilya. The milieu in Odessa was too much for you. The tumultuous battles with your critics served to interfere with your research. Remember, it was shortly after you were appointed docent at the University of Odessa that you took that overdose of opium." Olga reaches over and clutches Elie's arm.

Elie shifts uneasily in his chair. "I don't know what overcame me. I suspect it was a combination of so many unfortunate circumstances. The frustrations engendered by a closed-minded society, the death of Ludmilla, the cold gray weather of Russia — who knows? In any event I took the opium too slowly to have any effect."

Elie suddenly laughs. "Not only did I become too drowsy to continue taking it but its emetic effect forced me to throw up most of the drug."

There follows an awkward silence in the room. Out of the corner of one's eye a glimpse of a black-robed figure vanishes from the doorway.

Elie fumes. "It was a terrible and painful time in my life, interrupted by so many distractions, petty squabbles and internecine warfare. For instance, there was that idiot Wilhelm Kuhne who dared criticise my paper on the vorticella in *Mueller Archives*. My God, he persisted even after I confirmed that the mobile stalk of that ciliated protozoon simulated the muscle activity in higher organisms — clear evidence for a linkage in genealogy."

"Oh Ilya," Olga cries. "That was more than twenty-five years ago. Are you still seething over that trivial insult? Sometimes you are too high strung and impulsive. You could never tolerate criticism. And then, in a fit of exasperation you tried to take your life again. Such unhappiness!"

"My dear Olga," Elie fumbles. "Sometimes I forget my responsibilities to those I love. Yes, that time was particularly upsetting. I was losing my eyesight just as my scientific *raison d'être* was at the mercy of a microscope. But life is full of ironies." He shoots a quick glance at Tolstoy. "In a fit of desperation, I injected myself with a strain of borrelia, the spirochete that causes relapsing fever. Instead of succumbing I relapsed into a healthier state with, would you believe it, a significant improvement in my eyesight. Think of that!" He claps his hand.

Tolstoy roars with laughter and slaps his thigh. "You attempted to cheat a natural death twice and now you lecture me on how to face death harmoniously?"

"Just so," replies Elie. "I admit those acts were foolish, impulsive and precipitous. But let me ask you this, Lev Nikoleyovich. How stark a contrast is my concept of a harmonious modus exodus compared to your horrific portrayal of the dying process?"

Tolstoy raises his eyebrows.

Elie narrows his eyes as he stares at Tolstoy. "Need I remind you of your famous story, *The Death of Ivan Illyich*? What could be so inharmonious? In the story you describe a successful magistrate having to withstand the physical and mental anguish of his own devastating illness. You left little to the imagination as you poured it on, page after page — the agony, the torment and the excruciating conditions that plagued Ivan Ilyich. He is consumed with a loss of dignity. His loneliness is profound, compounded by indifference from his wife and associates. You are uncompromising in your description of Ivan Ilyich's pathetic struggle as he faces imminent death. Quite apart from the physical discomfort, you paint a picture of anger, hopelessness, denial and ultimately profound depression. It is a moribund state you paint — disharmony as opposed to one of concordance."

Elie cocks his head as he glares at Tolstoy. "Don't you see, Lev Nikoleyavich? In the case of your Ivan Ilyich, you have cleaved the body from the mind. You describe opposing forces at odds with each other. In revealing this discordance, this inharmonious separation during the dying process you confirmed my contention that humans, by and large, are incapable of facing death with equanimity and peace."

Curiously, Elie seems more distraught by his outburst than Tolstoy who smiles as he gapes at Elie with a sinister twinkle in his eyes. "My dear friend, I wrote that story, not as a depiction of the dying process, but as a metaphor of a hollow life lived by a man who with all the accoutrements he acquired, could have offered meaning to his existence — but didn't. In other words, his so-called inharmonious dying as you interpret it was a manifestation of a lost opportunity, a transgression. But I dare say, you may have noticed that when death finally came for Ivan Ilyich it was greeted as a 'living light'. Harmony at last!" Tolstoy claps his hand in glee.

Elie's face clouds over. He is about to launch into another defense when Tolstoy waves his hand. "Please forgive me. I must beg your indulgence. I see my Sonia signaling for me to take my afternoon nap. She is so solicitous at times. Besides, fascinating as it may be, I am ill prepared to forsake my troubled soul for your so-called orthobiosis. It smacks of constrained order and I am too much a nihilist to believe in such a harmonious system."

Slowly, and with much effort, Tolstoy rises from his chair. He turns and bows to Olga. He then offers his hand to Elie. They also rise and bow wishing the estimable old man good health.

Postscript

On November 10, 1910, at age eighty-two, Leo Tolstoy died at a remote railway station in the small village of Astapovo. Just a week prior, in the middle of the night, he left his family estate and long-suffering wife, Sonya, in order to spend his last days in peace and solitude. Ironically, his dying was anything but peaceful, let alone harmonious. Word of his impending demise got out and the paparazzi descended in droves. His death became an international media event with hundreds of his followers arriving from all over to join in the vigil. Those in attendance at his bedside were unable to confirm whether the great man experienced a bright light as he entered the void.

On July 16, 1916, at age seventy-one, Elie Metchnikoff died without rancor. As for his concepts on senescence and man's proper readiness for death, it is ironic that on his deathbed Elie said to Olga, "Today I have no death sensation, but I beg you to have no illusions." He then noticed that his watch had stopped at four p.m. He smiled, and with his last gasp, said, "Is it not strange that it should have stopped before I do?"